TRENCHCOATS,

TOWERS, AND TROLLS

CYBERPUNK FAIRY TALES

A Punked Up Fairy Tales Anthology

Edited by Rhonda Parrish

World Weaver Press

TRENCHCOATS, TOWERS, AND TROLLS

Published by World Weaver Press, LLC
Albuquerque, NM
www.WorldWeaverPress.com

Cover layout and design by Sarena Ulibarri.
Cover images used under license from Shutterstock.com.

*

First edition: January 2022
ISBN-13: 978-1-7340545-5-2

Also available as an ebook

TRENCHCOATS, TOWERS, AND TROLLS

CONTENTS

INTRODUCTION
Rhonda Parrish

I think I ought to just straight-up embrace my hypocrisy right now. Because the thing is, I'm occasionally asked for the #1 bit of advice I would give to people just starting to submit to anthologies and my answer to that question is always the same. Read and follow the submission guidelines.

But then, despite my constantly encouraging people to know and follow the rules, I occasionally blatantly break them. I did it in *Grimm, Grit and Gasoline* (and admitted it in the Introduction) and I'm kind of doing it again in this anthology. Sorry not sorry.

While these stories all capture the things I love most about cyberpunk, one or two of them might be more accurately described as 'cyber-inspired'. And there's definitely a couple stories which are more 'fairy-powered' than they are fairy tale. But overall, they come together to strike the notes I was looking for.

It's also a much more hopeful anthology than the previous one in this series.

I think anthologies definitely reflect a moment in time, a state of mind. Or, really, of minds. The individual stories that end up in my slush pile are each a bit of a mirror on the author's state of mind when they wrote them, and the ones I eventually pick to make up the Table of Contents show something of what/how I was thinking and feeling as I read and picked between them.

I can't speak to how the authors felt writing the stories for *Clockwork, Curses and Coal*, but I was choosing them and crafting the Table of Contents at a time of very high COVID-related anxiety. With this anthology, I feel like the world is turning a corner in this pandemic. The tunnel is still very long, but I'm pretty sure I see light at the end of it and I think that's reflected in these stories. Again, this isn't due to a conscious decision on my part, but looking back at the stories in order to write this Introduction, I do think it's the reality. These stories are far from light and fluffy but there's hope in them.

And given that this is going to be the last anthology in this series, I think that's the perfect way to leave things.

Rhonda Parrish
Edmonton, Alberta
5/11/2021

A BEAUTIFUL NIGHTMARE

Sarah Van Goethem

The Future Belongs to the Curious. This is the saying I repeat in my head and the reason it's me who sees the new girl first; I'm always watching. First one up in the pale dawn light, prowling, hungry, always looking for answers. I'm nibbling on my breakfast—a Belgian waffle minus the syrup—on the *chemin de ronde,* the walkway that circles the high walls of the castle, when I happen to see a splotch of black.

Something that doesn't belong.

Something that gives me an odd sense of déjà vu.

I don't say anything at first; I suck in a breath, letting my fingernails scratch against the old stones. No one new has come in such a long time. We've been abandoned by the staff, forgotten. The five of us left to rot (maybe rot is the wrong word) on this lovely island. But now—someone new. I shut my eyes. Count to three. Open them again against the too-blue sky.

She's still there.

I finally find my voice and call for the others. "Bones! Shade! Night!" I tear my eyes away from the girl and run, hoping someone

3

will hear me. "Beauty, come quick!" Down the stairs I go, my heart thudding in my chest like a wild hopeful thing. *Will she remember?*

None of us do. Sure, a faint whiff here or there, a smidgen of our memories that leaks through, but mostly—nothing. Just a dark space, holes in our minds of how we came to be here on this rock of an island. Of how we exist at all.

"Nova, what is it?" It's Shade, bursting through the heavy wooden door as if it weighs nothing at all. Besides me, he roams the castle the most. Repeats the same actions a hundred times a day. Pumps iron until he sweats buckets, his way of escaping our beautiful nightmare.

I don't answer; he'll see soon enough. And there she is—a slim figure shrouded in the mist by the shore. The girl. Relief washes over me; part of me expected her to disappear, to float away like the ghosts Night sometimes sees.

Shade sees her now too. We take off across the drawbridge and reach her at the same time. Her clothes are sopping wet, as if she just crawled out of the ocean, some dark sea creature flailing on land. She wraps her arms around herself and shivers in the frigid November air. Ice is already forming on the tips of her jagged chin-length hair, her lips frost-blue. She backs away from our advances like a caged animal.

I catch Shade's eye and know he's thinking the same thing; her clothes. So different than our own loose and flowy linens. Black on black on black, all matching her hair. Tight cropped black top exposing her midriff, black cargo pants with too many pockets to count and—I just know this will be her nickname already—Boots. Black, with a row of tiny silver bullets embedded from the toe to the heel. Mid-calf. Shiny buckles.

There's something about them that pokes at my mind, elbowing into that empty spot.

"Where did you come from?" I ask, and I try to keep my voice level. "How did you get here?" Do I sound desperate? I must. But aren't we all? Being trapped here with no memory definitely equals desperation.

Shade is barely breathing beside me, hands held up to her like he's calling some truce for something. Like it's our fault she's suddenly here.

But she isn't looking at us. Her dark eyes have flickered over our shoulders, her mouth dropping open as she takes in Castle Vale Sanatorium.

I can't help but turn and see it through her eyes, for the first time, all over again. Sharp grey rock—fieldstone I think, though there isn't a field anywhere around. Miles of rolling green grass the shade of emeralds, and ivy that's grown and twisted over time, pushing its tendrils in, embedding itself in the mortar.

It's gorgeous, really. That's the thing. It's all golden light and blue skies. A place that was meant to heal us, or so Nurse Ginger said. *You'll feel better in no time, dear. Just a little rest from the world.*

But therein lies the problem. None of us remembered what world it was we needed a rest from.

I turn back to the girl. Her face has drained of any color. "Who are you?" I demand.

But she only shakes her head. Just like the rest of us, she doesn't know. She collapses at our feet, a frozen heap, and I should've remembered that part; how the shock takes hold at first.

Shade scoops her up easily. "Better get her inside. She'll freeze like this." What he really means is we better take her to Beauty. He's the unofficial leader of our sad little group, the first one to arrive here. Shade's nickname aptly reflects the way he shadows Beauty.

"I'll be there in a minute." My fingers close around the small charm I keep in my pocket—a tiny silver key I found when the candle in my bedroom had melted halfway. Almost as if it'd been stuck in the candle for me—a clue. But left by whom? "I'm going to do a sweep of the area, see if she brought anything else." I hope he doesn't hear the crack in my voice, but he hesitates a moment too long and I know what's coming.

"Nova," he begins, but no more words come. He's said them all before. *It's not so bad here. There could be a lot worse. It's kind of a paradise, really.*

He's not wrong. But sometimes I hate how much easier it is for him to accept everything.

I turn away before he can see the tears in my eyes. This is what I've learned here: something can be perfect and still not be enough.

***

Sometimes I think back to when I awoke here. Dissect my memories. Nurse Ginger's voice soft, but firm, in my ear. *You'll feel better in no time, dear.* Her palm, cool on my forehead. *Just a little rest from the world.*

Pink behind my eyelids. And then the brightness, the way the sunlight, so delicate, warmed my face. The faint whisper of a salty breeze through the billowing curtains. The gentle lapping of the waves on the shore. The traitorous blessed peacefulness of it all.

Like a calm before a storm.

I ate it up at first, truly. I let her dress me in draping linens and spoon-feed me delicious puddings and I told myself it didn't matter that I couldn't remember anything from before.

And when nurse Ginger decided I was ready—stable enough to leave my room—I met the others.

I met Beauty.

***

The new girl's arrival is not like mine was. There is no Nurse Ginger to whisper sweetness into her ear. Nurse Ginger and the other staff are long gone and for the life of me I don't know how they left.

Or how the new girl arrived.

I find the others crowded around her in the parlor. They've placed her on a sheepskin rug near the fire and are stripping her of her frozen clothes.

Bones rushes to my side, her bird-like hands jabbing into her hips; she's never happy with change, especially when it involves a new female. She arrived here second to Beauty and it was the pair of them that started the nickname game. "Can I grab one of your dresses for her to wear?" she asks, adding, quite unnecessarily, "Mine won't fit her."

I nod, watching her dash away. Bones' name is fitting; although she's gained some weight in the past months, she still barely has any meat on her. Despite all the good food Night prepares, Bones merely nibbles.

Beauty catches sight of me and waves me over. A warmth snakes through my belly. When I sidle up beside him, he touches the back of his hand to my reddened cheek. "Your skin is so sensitive," he murmurs. I wonder if he knows the affect he has on me. The way my insides twist into knots. How my lungs forget to take in air. I think he does; his gaze shifts away, unable to meet mine. "You look as if you crawled out of the sea with Boots here."

A smile twitches on my lips as I catch sight of the tall back boots drying by the fire. "I knew you'd call her that."

They've got her socks and shirt off now, but Night hesitates at her pants, his eyes darting to the door for Bones' return. And just like that he's spared the decision; she elbows her way into the room again, one of my linen dresses draped over her arm.

"Go on now," she says, raising a thinly plucked brow at Night. "Nova and I will do the rest. Give the poor girl some privacy." As if she gives a hoot about Boots' privacy.

Night skitters away to the corner of the room, and Shade and Beauty reluctantly follow. As Bones and I finish undressing the rag-doll girl (Bones using more force than necessary), I can hear the clink of the decanter from the side table, the slosh of scotch in glasses.

The tell-tale sign from Beauty that we're about to have a discussion about this. Even if it is morning. Even if the others haven't had breakfast yet. There are no rules here, not anymore. Either way, I'm secretly glad. It's been too easy for the five of us to ignore our strange situation for too long. I'm tired of endless days that stretch into one another, days of listless lounging or games or sex, all of it with no consequence. Days that go nowhere.

I yank the girl's pants over her feet. Her skin is like ice. We remove her bra and panties lastly and slip the linen dress over her head.

Then, I grab the knitted blanket off the sofa, the one Bones always wraps herself in (she's forever cold), and drape it over the girl, tucking in every corner around her while Bones scowls.

"All safe," Bones calls to the boys. "Now pretend you are gracious gentlemen and make me a coffee. It's too early for the hard stuff." She saunters off toward the boys, head held high like a princess, but I'm not finished yet.

I quickly turn the new girl's pants right side out again and deftly slip my hand into one outer pocket after another. I pull out a pocket knife, lip balm, a pair of black gloves, and a face mask. I find something else in an inner pocket just as the floor creaks behind me, and my heart flutters in excitement. Is it possible? Is this what I've been looking for?

Beauty's breath is warm in my ear as one long arm reaches around me to dangle a glass of red wine in my face; he always remembers what I like. "She moved at all?"

"No." The hairs on my neck stand on end at his closeness, and it's beyond me how I've never slid into his bed at night the way Bones slides into Night's. I clear my throat. "I'm just going to hang her pants to dry." I step away from him, quickly plucking out the final item—a small square chip—and slipping it into my own pocket with the key.

When I spin around again, Beauty's still there. He holds out the glass of wine, his hazel eyes drilling into me, and I know he saw. But he only smiles widely, displaying his perfectly straight teeth, and I can't help but think for the thousandth time that Bones really got his name right. *Beauty*. He's fucking gorgeous. Chiseled cheekbones and skin the tawny brown of the sand on the beach. He's like a fiery sun, filling the sky. He could probably fill my world here, if I let him.

And yet.

I force a smile to match his.

There's something between us, something from the beginning that I can't quite understand. And for some unspoken reason, neither of us trusts the other.

***

Beauty chose my name.

Nova. He watched me steadily in the breakfast room before announcing this. Shovelled eggs into his mouth while his brow furrowed. I'm not sure I tasted a bite of my own toast. And then when Nurse Ginger left us alone, he leaned back in his chair, hands stretched behind his head like he owned the place and wasn't just a patient. *Nova. Like a supernova. Because you look as if you may explode.*

Shade nodded in agreement, curly hair bouncing, clearly in need of Beauty's approval. *Yeah, you're right man. She's kind of burning up, huh?*

I wasn't sure if I loved or hated how he saw me. It's funny, looking back. Because I *was* seriously scorching. The first minute Nurse Ginger led me into that sunny morning room and I laid eyes on Beauty, something wild sparked inside of me. I sat there ablaze, my fingertips digging into my thighs. And I had no idea why.

Bones rolled her pale blue eyes, too big in her hollowed-out face. *That's a stupid name. She looks pretty tame to me.* But I sensed her jealousy. She'd been the only female patient until I'd arrived, and now here I was, being gifted a more exotic name than her. She shrugged before her chair scraped back, leaving her plate full. *Supernovas only burn for a short time,* she whispered loudly as she passed behind me.

And although I couldn't remember where I came from, I did remember other stuff. Bones wasn't the only one who knew her science. Who knew how to flirt. *Supernovas can also tell scientists a lot about the universe,* I told the boys with a wink.

They roared with laughter before Bones had even made it to the door. Her shoulders tensed and she whirled about. *Go on then, tell us,* she hissed, her small chest heaving. *Tell us where you came from.*

But I couldn't of course and it wasn't funny anymore.

Everyone looked anywhere except at each other. Everyone except Beauty and I, our eyes meeting and holding across the table in a way that brought to my mind the space-time continuum. And I wondered if I hadn't slipped down some wormhole, bent space, and time travelled. The question was…from where?

***

Beauty sloshes the remainder of amber liquid around in his glass before downing it one gulp. "Well, I guess there are six of us now." His eyes wander over the unconscious girl on the floor and then to Shade, his meaning clear. Three pairs now. Three girls, three boys. Not that Beauty and I have ever 'paired up' so to speak. "Looks like we found you a girlfriend, Shade."

I grind my teeth together afraid I'll blurt out something I'll regret. But if Beauty really hasn't figured out yet that Shade is madly in love with him, he must be the most unaware person I've ever met. And yet—here we are. He just drew the line in the sand. He isn't claiming the new girl for himself. Or Shade.

He's claiming me.

Shade rounds back to the corner, pours himself another healthy dose of scotch, his jaw tense. I've gathered it always takes a while for the dust to settle when someone new arrives.

But this is the kicker of it all: *this* is what Beauty wants to talk about? How this new girl affects our group dynamic?

I don't think so.

I sip my wine for liquid courage. "Anyone else recognize her clothes?" I blurt out, addressing the most obvious point.

Night is pacing a circle around the girl. He's the smallest of the guys, with a slender frame and shaggy blonde hair. He was named for his insomnia, his patrolling of the halls every night. "Yeah," he says, bending to run a hand over the drying boots.

"Does anyone remember what they were wearing when they arrived here?" I press. I'm not sure how I never thought to wonder this before.

A shake of heads. My own memory produces nothing. Only linens. Shades of ivory, ecru, oatmeal, and taupe. All of us dressed in calming neutrals.

I find myself itching for her black.

Bones is too, I can tell. She pushes around the pile of items I scavenged from the girl's pockets, and pulls on the black gloves. Then, she holds up the face mask, pondering it. "Why the mask?"

"Air quality," Shade says straight away, returning to the group and pouring more scotch into Beauty's glass without being asked. "Maybe where she comes from the air is no good." He looks out the window at the crystal-clear sky, and I know what he's thinking: where she comes from is probably where we come from, and do we *really* want to know?

"Or germs," Night suggests. "Illnesses." He's pacing again, a finger to his stubbled chin. Eyes narrowed.

Whatever he's feeling, I can feel it too. An opening in the hole in my mind, blue sky peeking out of clouds. Bones sucks in a breath, then pulls the mask over her nose and mouth.

There's a stillness in the room, everyone frozen like statues. My chest tightens.

"Shit," Night says.

Bones' eyes water and she rips the mask off. "I remember wearing one as a small child."

And, so do I.

I set my half-full wine glass shakily on the polished table, afraid I'll drop it.

The memory is faint, but there.

A pandemic.

The whole world afraid of something we couldn't even see. But then what? What came after that?

11

It's like figuring out one piece to a puzzle, but I can't see the whole picture. It's maddening, and my chest aches like homesickness.

Beauty has been oddly silent, but now his eyes are piercing into me again. For a moment, I think he'll call me out in front of the others, make me produce the chip in my pocket, the thing I am dying to inspect. But he doesn't. He only says, "Boots will probably wake up soon. Perhaps we should give her a nice dinner to welcome her? She'd probably enjoy the hot springs tonight."

And just like that he pulls everyone back to the present, back to our safe little prison.

***

There was a moment a while back. Right after Nurse Ginger disappeared leaving the five of us on our own. I left my room when the moon was full and high in the sky, leaking through the hall oriel window in a trail of silver. It was practically carving a path right to Beauty's door and, in a moment of weakness, I followed it. A fair maiden, clad in a white nightgown (the attire here, linen and cotton, no other choice). The irony didn't escape me. Somehow, I knew Beauty would like that—me, the picture of romance, a lady of the night. I hated the thought as much as I wanted to be in his arms.

A war raged inside of me.

I can see still my hand, fingers about to grace the knob of his door.

But then—a cold draft behind me. And Night skidded around the corner, neck taut. He took me in, his eyes wild, before raising a finger to point. I turned quickly and saw...well, what did I see? I've pondered this numerous times. Moonlight. Darkness. But also, a shadow? A figure? A ghost?

It ducked out of sight, turning left, and Night took off. I hesitated only a moment, and then I hitched up my ridiculous nightgown and chased after him. Down the curving staircase we sprinted, our bare feet padding on the wood treads.

The ghost was fast, a streak in my peripheral vision. It wasn't how I pictured ghosts: ethereal, airy, see-through. Like me in my nightgown. No, it was more like a shadow, all cloaked in black. I didn't want to take my eyes off of it. But I missed the second-last step and ended in a sprawling heap on the cold stone floor. A sharp pain tore through my ankle. Still, I looked up in time to see Night slip into the library, and I crawled as fast as I could to the doorway.

Night stood in the middle of the room, turning in circles. "I swear it went right into that bookcase. I swear it."

Our 'ghost' had disappeared.

And I remembered why Nurse Ginger said Night was here in the first place; hallucinations. Seeing things that were never there.

Somehow, I'd been swept up in the excitement.

At least my twisted ankle kept me from going to Beauty's room again. Since it's healed, only my own resolve has kept me away.

***

This time Beauty will come to me.

Night is busy rustling up dinner, chicken stew and homemade bread (another thing I don't understand: how we always have plenty of food and drink). Bones will not leave Boots' side, a self-made, suspicious nurse. And Shade is in the basement, lifting weights.

It's only a matter of time.

I slip the chip from my pocket. It's itty-bitty, about the size of a front tooth. Matte black. I pinch it between my thumb and forefinger and bring it closer, squinting to see. Tiny silver letters run along one side and I can barely make them out.

Aurora.

I gasp. The chip falls from my hand and lands on my bed. A coldness slithers through me, straight from my gut, up through my ribcage to circle my throat. I think for a moment I won't breathe, and it's been so very long since I had this feeling, that I almost forget how to cope. But then it all comes back in a flash flood. *Breathe Nova, breathe.*

And I do. In and out. In through the nose. Out through the mouth.

This is why I'm here right? Anxiety? Panic?

A wild feeling races through me and I punch at my pretty bedspread, at the feather-filled pillows. Screw anxiety. I swing again and again.

Aurora.

Aurora.

I know that name. I know it deep inside of me. I thump at the pillows more, and then rip them to shreds.

This is how Beauty finds me, drowning in a flurry of snowy feathers. Did he even knock?

Either way he's there, towering in the doorway. Forehead creased in confusion.

"Aurora," I breathe, wanting to see if it has an effect on him, too. And it does. His shoulders tense before an empty look glazes over his eyes, like I've done something wrong. And suddenly I remember that about him. That haunted look. Numb and empty. Emotionless. Like he's lost in a fog.

It's the worst feeling. Because I know I'm seeing the real him finally, the one I know from elsewhere. Not the cocky Beauty, the one that pours us all drinks and acts like the king of the castle, the one I've never fully trusted.

No, this is the person I've been waiting for. The person with a soul, as sad as it may be. A person I once knew, even if I can't fully remember him. All I know is this: I want to save him.

I bounce onto the bed again, dig into the heap of feathers. Dig and dig and dig until I find the chip. Until I find Aurora.

Because I know this tiny chip is the key out of here.

And I know exactly where it goes.

***

I've found things here, at Castle Vale. Not just the tiny key charm. In all my searches, I've found nooks and crannies, cubbies in low-sloped walls and stones that pop out, places for secrets to be kept. After the 'ghost' experience, I went back to the library. Just before dawn, while everyone slept. I studied the plaque on the wall again, the one that reads, *The Future Belongs to the Curious,* and I ran my fingers over the gold-lettered, old books, trying to figure out why my eyes welled with tears at the musty smell.

Frustrated, I tore the books from the shelves, let them spread their wings like butterflies, then crash to the floor like rocks. And when I'd removed almost all of them, I saw it—a door. Barely visible, just part of the shelves really, but I remembered what Night had said about the ghost, *I swear it went right into that bookcase. I swear it.*

I removed the rest of the books but none triggered the secret door to open. I inspected it from top to bottom and finally found the lock. But it didn't look like anything that matched this place. There was no heavy iron lock awaiting a skeleton key. And my silly little charm key would never fit.

No, all I found was a small slit in one of the shelves.

A square.

I didn't tell anyone. I shelved all the books again and was eating a grapefruit in the morning room by the time Shade came down.

***

I pluck the chip out of the feather pile and hold it up like I've found the holy grail. "We're getting out of here."

"No." It's a single quiet word and I'm not even sure I heard him right.

"Excuse me?" I clutch the chip tightly, inching forward; Beauty is blocking the only path out of this room, and I have a sinking feeling he doesn't want to be saved.

He sets his jaw and holds out his hand. "Give it to me," he says. "No one is going anywhere."

"What in the hell are you talking about?" I can feel heat prickling up my neck again. "We've been stuck here for who knows how long, none of us remembering a thing of our pasts, and you mean to tell me you don't even want to know what's out there?"

"Nova," he says, but there's a pleading in his voice now. His fingers twitch, still waiting for me to hand over the chip.

But I'm not giving him anything.

As if he can sense this, he steps toward me. "Nova, you don't understand."

"And you do?" I'm a bomb, ready to detonate. But then I see it flit across his face—something else. Guilt. "Oh my God, you *do know*."

It's plain as day suddenly. My hesitance with him. The way we eye each other but keep our distance. He flinches, but there's something else I'm missing. That haunted look still lingers.

Numbness travels up my legs and into my torso, coursing down my arms. "How long?" I ask. "How long have you remembered?" And *what*, I want to scream. *What do you remember?*

At least he has the decency to look shamefaced. His shoulders slump. He looks at the floor. "Since you got here."

He mumbles more after this, but I don't hear it past the blood pounding in my ears. All this time he's known and I've been searching like a fool. I can see myself, studying Castle Vale. Roaming the grounds. Searching. For some sort of clue beyond the tiny key charm. Meanwhile, *he's known*. He touches my arm and I'm jolted back into this treacherous moment. I shake off his hand like it's pure fire.

"I don't remember everything." His words rush at me like a tidal wave. "Just tidbits of where we came from." I glare at him, hold his gaze like my life depends on it, like maybe I can scorch him with my eyes, make him hurt the way I do now. Drowning in deception. He can't handle it; he looks away, and I use the opportunity. I rush around him and dart out the door. He reaches out, tries to grab me, but he's too slow.

I'm gone.

His words echo in my ears, *where we came from*.

I have to get to the library to find my way back. Back to where we came from.

"Nova, wait!" He's gaining on me but I keep running. Down the curving staircase where I chased the ghost with Night, puzzle pieces clicking together in my head.

Ghosts. But they weren't ghosts at all.

My head is buzzing, my chest tight. The picture is becoming clear. *The too-blue sky. The emerald grass. Castles and linen and soft golden light. Supplies for forever.*

All of it too perfect to be true. To be real.

There is a sour taste in my throat as I reach the bottom of the stairs and find myself face to face with a seething and very conscience Boots.

Bones is behind her, arms crossed. "She's slightly unsettled. Maybe even crazier than you were when you got here."

"I'm not unsettled." Boots narrows her eyes at me and slaps at the linen dress we've put on her as if it's poison. "I'm missing something and I'm told you're the one who emptied my pockets."

I swallow. "I put everything in a pile by the fireplace."

"Bullshit." She's not buying it, and I immediately regret my decision to play stupid. She holds out her hand. "Hand it over now."

"Hand what over?" Bones' eyes flick between us. "What is going on?"

I can hear Beauty's footsteps on the stairs behind me. I'm surrounded now, by everyone who wants this tiny little chip. The whole world in the palm of my hand. Like hell I'm handing it over. I've waited a very long time for this. For an escape.

"Boots brought us a ticket out of here," I say, stalling for time, edging my way down the last step.

"Out of here," Bones whispers, finally catching on. "There's a way out of here?"

Boots puts her other hand on her hip. "A ticket for one. Give it back now."

I underestimated Boots. She didn't forget anything, like I thought. She was only in shock, the kind of shock this place first brings until one adapts. She's still not fully adjusted. She keeps blinking, like the light is all wrong. And swaying, like the floors are uneven. I remember the feeling well. I nearly double over now. The realization of where we are is crippling.

"Just give it to her," Beauty says, and I turn to look up at him, aghast. "Just let her go." He's standing in a shaft of sunlight, his hair lit like a halo.

"Let her go?" And suddenly it all makes sense. If I give Boots the chip then she can disappear again, same as the other 'ghosts'. Beauty wants to keep *me* here, in his self-made slumber. The two of us forever entrenched in the past. That's what he's done, isn't it? Created a world of nostalgia, a place where he can pretend the real world doesn't exist.

Is the real world that bad? A shiver climbs my spine; whatever the answer is to that question, I know I'm going to find out.

I dig my hand into my pocket, my fingers brushing against the chip and the charm. Two keys. I hate to lose either of them. "Take it," I say, hurling the charm toward the double front doors.

Boots scrambles for it and I storm off toward the library in mock anger, my bare feet smacking against the pretty old tiles. But Beauty is right behind me; maybe he knows me better than I give him credit for. As soon as I make it to the door, I run. I have only a few moments before he reaches me.

I quickly tear a green-covered book off the shelves, *The History of Castles*. "Nice touch," I say, and I don't mean it the way it comes out. It's truly magnificent, this whole sanitorium. Even the perfect little charm key, the hint of something more. Impressive.

"This isn't my key!" Boots screeches from the foyer, and I can't help but wonder if she appreciates the humour; the charm is, in fact, a key.

"Don't do it." Beauty slams the door behind him, locking us both in the library and keeping Boots out. "Don't go back."

But I'm going. There's no way I'm not. Because whatever this is, whatever he's created, it isn't real. It isn't life.

"This isn't love. You can't keep me here." It feels strange, me saying that. Because I can't specifically remember love between us, and yet the feeling exists. Somewhere between this make-believe world and whatever lies out there, I know this much: Beauty loved me and I loved him.

And maybe he thought I'd love him here, too. Maybe something went wrong. A glitch.

Despite everything, I desperately want to kiss him. To say goodbye. But neither of us moves. We only lock eyes, so many unsaid words between us, and our murky minds keeping us apart.

I slide the chip into the small, square space.

And leave the simulation.

***

It's like surfacing. Breaking through the water and gulping for air. I gasp for breath, my eyes opening into a dark room. Bright lights flicker outside a narrow, horizontal window. I'm in a basement then. My limbs twitch, but feel sluggish and heavy when I try to move them, like I've just discovered gravity. I'm laid out, my feet elevated, wires dangling from a monitor hooked up to my head. I dig my fingers into the leather arms of the chair, and feel the weight of something on my wrist—a charm bracelet.

A sob catches in my throat.

And my heart thumps in my chest, too fast. *In through the nose, out through the mouth,* I remind myself, my eyes darting about the room. The lights from the street comes in waves, like a lighthouse beacon, pouring neon pinks and greens and florescent whites over the walls. And there—yes, the drawings.

The creation.

I push myself up, slowly, my limbs not as weak as I'd expected. After tearing off the wires, I roll out of the chair, landing on my knees on the floor. That's when I realize what I'm wearing—black pants and a t-shirt with a purple grid pattern that looks like an astronomical wormhole. The clothes feel right. They feel like me.

I pull myself up and trudge barefoot toward the illustrations pinned on the wall corkboard. There are detailed sketches, pencil drawings on sheets of smudged white paper; I recognize the turrets and the bridge and even the *chemin de ronde*.

I stagger backward, fragments of memories flooding into my head too quickly. Beauty's long fingers holding the pencil. Books of castles. The light in his eyes. It's like an intense migraine.

Suddenly there is a click and a door swings open. I'm still pressing fingers to my temples when footsteps rush in.

"Whoa, I knew the sensors were off. How in the hell...? Okay, Mila, just stay calm." It's Nurse Ginger from Castle Vale, the one who whispered sweetness in my ear. "You'll feel better in no time."

But I won't feel better. Because it's all been a giant lie. Even my name. "Mila," I try it out, and there it is, one of the parts of me that's been missing. I could cry except Nurse Ginger is shuffling her way toward me, hands held out for me like she wants to help.

But I don't trust her. She's working for Beauty and even though I know I loved him once, how can I trust what he's done to me? She could just as easily send me back into the virtual world. I back away, further into the corner, and whip open a familiar drawer of the desk. One quick press of a button inside and I've got in my possession a pocket exoblade knife. I level it at Nurse Ginger.

"Stay where you are," I threaten. "And tell me what is going on here." I don't wait for her to answer. "Where are the others?"

"They're here, too." Nurse Ginger moves slowly sideways and I don't take my eyes off of her. "Just give it a minute to wear off, and I promise you'll remember everything." She flicks on the stark white lights, and I squint at the harshness.

The room is bigger than I thought, and familiar. They're all here—Shade, Bones, Night, and Beauty. All sleeping in chairs, all hooked up to the same virtual reality. *Aurora.* Everyone except Boots. "Where is she?" I ask. "The new girl?"

"What new girl?" Nurse Ginger's eyebrows knit together and I don't think she's lying.

"A new girl hacked the system," I say, testing her. "She had a chip. But she didn't forget anything."

Nurse Ginger puts it all together. I can almost see her mind turning. "Of course. That's how you woke up." She stares at me in awe, mouth hanging open. "You wrote in an escape key. You made it accessible to hackers on purpose. Brilliant."

My hand drops to my side, my fingers just barely holding onto the knife. "What do you mean *I wrote it in?*"

She cocks her head to the side, her fiery ponytail bobbing. "Mila, *You're the one who created Aurora.* Don't you remember?"

And suddenly I do.

***

Beauty's name was Cole before.

"Technoshock", Cole said, when he got out of the psychiatrist's office. "There are varying degrees of it, and it's not like mine is super bad." He shoved his hands in his pockets and we walked down the street, rain drenching us while he shielded his eyes from the screens, the personalized ads momentarily directed at him—ways to cure technoshock. All of them garbage. "It's not like I'm going to become super violent or unpredictable." He quickly spun toward to me. "Pretend I didn't say that. It wasn't a shot at you or anything. I didn't mean—"

He didn't mean what—that I had a quick temper? That I often felt as if my chest may explode? "Forget it."

"Right. Anyway, I'm just depressed."

I could have guessed as much; he was unable to cope with all the changes in society, the creeping feeling of losing all that once existed. The rate of change was too fast, too much. Cole was always looking backwards, wishing for something that once was.

I thought I knew the feeling, sort of. I remembered the 'before times', if vaguely. The masks worn during the global pandemic, the way we'd all been told to stay home. Technology had basically exploded in the decade after that, and sometimes even I still mourned the loss of the days before. Sometimes my anger caught me off guard. But I was more pliable than Cole. More adaptable. And truthfully, I'd embraced the technology. It was like second nature to me.

Still, my heart broke for him. For anyone who didn't adapt well. It's not like there was a choice. There was no going back.

We reached Cole's doorway to his basement apartment, and when we got inside, I pulled all the blinds and stripped off my clinging wet clothes and stood naked in front of him, like I thought that might fix something. "I know, let's take a hot shower" —I raised my brows suggestively— "drink tea like our ancestors did, and forget this world exists."

But Cole only plonked down on the couch in front of me, burying his head in my bare belly. "Oh Mila." He looked up and managed a smile. "Mind if I take a rain check on the shower and let's switch the tea for something hard?"

We laid on his bed and drank a whole bottle of wine and then half of another, while we browsed through the old books his mom had saved before the libraries closed. History for him, science for me. And I had to admit, there was something about the musty old smell, something that made me nostalgic.

"Now, see this?" Cole asked, a while later, his words slurring. He poked at a picture. "I could have lived in the time of castles. Preferably one by the sea."

"It is lovely," I agreed, resting my head on his shoulder. "Very romantic. But you know they were just drafty old piles of rocks, right? All of them haunted."

"Hmm, maybe. I see what you're doing there." His fingers tangled in my hair. "It's more likely I'll end up in some psyche ward like my grandma anyway."

I didn't say anything. It was true; many of the older generation had technoshock. There wasn't as much of it in our age group, and it was rare for young children to have it.

I rose on my elbows and looked hard at Cole. An idea was forming.

"Yes?" he asked.

"What if you could get help *and* live in a castle? Would you do it?"

He shrugged. "Sure, but Mila, come on. Even if that existed, I couldn't afford it."

"Not in reality," I said, excitedly. "But I bet I can create it in source code."

"English, Mila."

I jumped up and grabbed some papers and pencils from his desk. "I can give you your castle, Cole. Just draw it."

"Like an online game?" Cole sat up, with a light in his eyes I hadn't seen in a long time.

"Sort of. But you won't even know it's a game. I'll make it so you forget, so you think that's all there is. Like a dream, it will be like real life. Every game out there began with a story. It'll basically be a simulation of the past, of history. And you'll live there, getting rest from this world. Think of it like a break. A reboot. A sleep." I snapped my fingers. "I'll even call it Aurora."

Cole's breath hitched. His lips grazed my neck. "Will you come with me?"

I levelled my gaze on him with all the seriousness I could muster. "I guess I could. I mean, who else would kiss you awake again?"

***

I'm still gripping the knife. "I put them all in there," I say, looking at the four of them. Beauty with his depression, Bones with her eating disorder, Night with his hallucinations, and Shade with his OCD. I thought I could fix them all. Even myself, with my angry outbursts, my panic and anxiety. I round on Nurse Ginger again, unsure if I'm mad at myself or her. "I asked you to look after us. To run everything."

She licks her lips. "Mila, listen. We discovered that no one was really making any progress. Aurora is only a band-aid solution. So yes, I slowly let the staff go."

"You left us there," I say, enunciating each word. "You *abandoned us*. I spent days, months even, wondering what was going on. Looking for a way out." Somehow, I keep my voice level when I ask, "Were you *ever* going to wake us up?"

She sighs. "Mila, I've been *here*, every minute of every day. I sleep here and live here, to watch over you all in your sleeping state. But I couldn't wake you up. You—"

And suddenly I remember this, too. "I wrote it in," I breathe. "I made it that way." The knife clatters to the floor and I creep over to Beauty. "They can only wake up if they really want to. If they want it enough to figure out how to leave."

"Yes," Nurse Ginger says. "They have to want to leave the past enough to embrace the future. Your rules not mine."

"The future belongs to the curious, Cole," I whisper into his ear. It feels funny using his real name again, and I wonder—if he does wake up, will I still call him Beauty? I kind of want him to call me Nova, if I'm being honest.

His eyes are darting about beneath his lids, in a constant state of REM sleep, of dreaming. I wonder if he's still standing by the bookcase in the library. Waiting for me.

I remember what he said, that he began to remember the moment I arrived. That can only mean one of two things: I didn't program the forgetting quite right, or his love for me transcended cyberspace. This is what I know: I'm a damn good programmer. So, I'm banking on the latter.

I brush my lips across his though I know full well a kiss will never wake him. Only he can do that. "Find me another hacker," I tell Nurse Ginger. "I'm sending in another chip. Or two." I suppose I should give poor Boots a way out, too. "Let's see who else wants to join the future again."

I, for one, am hoping like hell it'll be Beauty.

Sarah Van Goethem is a Canadian author who resides in southwestern Ontario. Her novels have been in PitchWars and longlisted for both The Bath Children's Novel Award (twice!) and CANSCAIP'S Writing for Children Competition.

Sarah also writes short stories, one of which was nominated for a Pushcart Prize, all of which can be found on her website at SarahVanGoethem.com

Sarah is a nature lover, and a wanderer of dark forests. She can often be found taking hundred-year-long naps in the woodland.

Follow her on Twitter or Instagram @Sairdysue

FIREWALLS AND FIREWORT
Wendy Nikel

In the lower levels of Nexus, in the shabbiest, most crime-ridden district, where dampness dripped from staticky vidscreens and the murky air was electric with the crackling of exposed wires, sat an unassuming shop with slats of steel protecting the windows. Within that shop, Mave hunched her wide head over her mortar and pestle, her bones longing for the respite of her darkened cave, away from the incessant buzz of the city. Somewhere hidden beyond the towers of Nexus, the sun was setting, yet her final customer had not arrived. It would take some luck now for Mave to reach the city limits before they closed and thus avoid the ire of the guard at the checkpoint.

It was just like a Nexon to be late for an appointment, the giantess thought. Despite nearly a decade of interacting with the short-limbed, frail-fleshed men and women of the city—of studying their anatomy and easing their ailments—they were still somewhat of a mystery to her. A giant would never do such a thing as miss an appointment. Granted, a giant would not have made one in the first place. A Giant would meet you "before the polinatkes bloomed," or "when the River Sorpa overflows its banks," or—if pressed for a more exact time—"when the moon is as round as a dillcap," but never "on Tuesday before the work klaxon" or "tomorrow at 5:00."

Mave squinted through the window at the glowing timepiece on the building across the narrow alley, working the numbers like stones rolling about in her head. Telling time still did not come easily to her; hours and minutes were a construct of men and cities, and forcing a giant to think in such ways was like trying to force pynithian clay through a cheesecloth. How Eoth would have laughed, had he seen her scrunched-up face, trying to correlate the abstract tubes of neon to align with the movement of the tides and skies.

How she missed his laugh.

Her struggle was interrupted by the buzzing of the door's alarm and the entry of a slight woman in a long, leather cloak and hood that shadowed her face. Like most human women who visited Mave's shop, this one waited until the door latched completely before removing her head covering—a gesture of embarrassment that reminded Mave of her place among the city-dwellers. They came to her, but only as a desperate last resort.

From the comm-band positioned over the woman's dark hair to the string of avalantine beads encircling her neck, this client was clearly not one of the metalworkers or artisans who often darkened the giantess's doorway, who'd have saved up months of her wages to afford Mave's services. This was clearly a woman from the very top of Nexon. A credit band of polished perriostone on the woman's wrist glinted in the firelight, and the giantess fell to one knee at the sight of the crest etched on its face.

"Your Majesty," she muttered, dipping her head. Anger and humiliation burned within her at the presence of this frail being whose head barely reached Mave's chest. This waifish creature by whose delicate throat came the order that had led to Eoth's death.

Never was she more grateful that there were few other giants within the city walls and that none could see through her shop's dark windows. They'd frowned and grumbled at Mave setting up shop within the city and exchanging her people's ancient secrets for credits that, to the giants, were nothing more than blinking lights on a metal ring, but they'd humored her, knowing she hadn't been quite right since Eoth died.

But now, to aid the woman who'd brought upon them so much grief? Whose vague, incomprehensible conflicts with neighboring cities had burned a warpath through their peaceful homeland, turning their proud and independent tribes into outsiders in a hostile land, no longer able to dwell in the mountains of their ancestors?

Mave closed her eyes, still tasting of burning slopes of firewort on her tongue.

"You have cameras?" The queen glanced around.

"No, I operate in accordance with the laws of the apothecary guild." Mave gestured to the engraved leaf of bronze hanging beside her door. A totem she had worked for years to acquire, which had enabled her to rent a shop in the city in the first place.

The queen gave the symbol only a cursory glance. She'd obviously made up her mind already, before she'd walked through the door, and certainly before she'd removed her hood and displayed her credit band. The question had been a mere formality, a reminder of all that Mave stood to lose if she were to forget her place. Humans liked to think that giants weren't as clever as they themselves were, simply because they had no use for computers or hovercars, but Mave understood perfectly well that if word got out that the queen had resorted to visiting a giantess, rather than turning to her own mages for whatever ailment plagued her, Mave would suffer far worse punishment than mere expulsion from the guild.

"There are rumors that flit about the dark webs," the queen said, "about a hidden skill of giants—that with the mere touch of their hand they can see what lies beneath the surface. Is there truth to this fairy tale?"

"There is." Truth enough for her purposes, at least. The skill belonged only to giantesses, not to their male counterparts, and it was not so much a seeing as a feeling, a sense of connecting with the particles and empty places—the *being*—that make up a thing, of breathing in its essence and aching with it for what is lacking. Amongst themselves, the giants called it *endovit*; among others, they didn't mention it at all.

"It's said that with this skill," the queen said, raising her dark, piercing eyes to meet Mave's, "a giant can see into the depths of one's corporal body. They can determine the root of many ailments, better than any nanobot or scan."

"Yes."

"Including womanly ailments."

Ah, there it was. The crux of the problem, for which Mave had been waiting since the queen had revealed herself, though her suspicions had risen with each word spoken. For even more than her cures for weary lungs or arrhythmic hearts or stomachs that refused to settle, Mave had developed a reputation for helping human women conceive. A midwife, some even called her, though she was certainly not one in the traditional sense; after the women left her shop with discrete vacuum-sealed pouches filled with herbs and tinctures and strict instructions to follow, she rarely ever saw them again. When she did, months later, they would look past her on the street, seemingly preoccupied with something far more important, but she could tell by the way their hands moved to their softly ballooning bellies that they recognized her. And from the steady stream of women who slipped quietly through her door, she could tell that they spoke of her, albeit only behind the most secure firewalls.

"You wish me to use my skill upon you?" Mave wouldn't have asked if she wasn't certain already; making such a presumption, were it incorrect, could cost her dearly. "One would think that, in your position, you would consult the nanomedics first."

The queen's eyes flashed with emotion, but she composed herself quickly. "I've heard that you can help in situations where the nanomedics have failed. Have I been misinformed?"

"No."

Normally at this point, Mave would ask the woman's history, but here, there was no need. The entire Nexus had watched on enormous vidscreens as the queen and her newest consort had been paraded through the streets to the sky-scraping Temple of Oviria in the city's center for their vows. They'd all watched, three years before that, when she'd done the same with her first consort. That he'd been deposed and banished had been the source of many wicked rumors, and among the worst was that he had been unable—or unwilling—to provide her an heir.

Now, it seemed, the queen was desperate. Desperate enough to visit a giantess.

"Can you help, or not?"

The question was not, of course, whether she *could*. Nothing would be easier for a giantess so acquainted with the hum of woven tissues that compose the human body. The harmony of breath and bone, the melodic swells of veins and tissues were as familiar to her as the chatter of roots beneath the ground's surface, the creaking and pressing of the ores that made up her cave. She could read them as easily as the men and women of Nexus could read their incessant newsfeeds.

But *would* she?

The clock across the street marked the passage of time, and Mave thought—as she had often done—how strange it was that men plotted out the seconds as if each was exactly the same, regardless of what was transpiring. As a giant, she knew this moment was longer than most; it dragged on, like the final breath before a plunge into dark and murky waters.

Mave gestured to a cot in the corner, and the queen lowered herself upon it, lying without hesitation upon the thin and dingy cloth.

"This will only take a moment." Mave knelt beside her, and she couldn't help the tone of apology that crept into her voice. She hated how she'd grown so used to apologizing, to looking away, to bending her head to avoid their stares in the streets. It didn't matter if she set up shop in the palace itself; the Nexus would never see her—a giantess—as worth their time.

Gently, she placed her open palm on the queen's abdomen and rested her other hand on top to overlap it. She closed her eyes, not strictly out of necessity, but to block out that face that adorned so many vidscreens, the throat that had called out for war.

Mave released her breath and let herself be taken in.

There were no words to describe *endovit*, and most giantesses would not even try to reconstruct their experience with flimsy descriptions or metaphors, for what good would it be? No one who didn't have the skill themselves could truly understand it, and for those who do, the experience itself was sufficient. They gleaned from it what they could and moved on, not bothering to wax poetic about how it's *like this* or *like that*, because when it came right down to it, it wasn't either.

Perhaps the only way that Mave could describe what she experienced when she connected with the queen's corporal being—if she wanted to—would be to relate the driving, red-hot march of blood; the sharp bursts of consciousness spreading like percussive drumbeats, calling each member to order; the uneasy silence of muscles forced to rest but aching to rise in a cacophony of movement. And deep within, where Mave focused her attention: a silence where there ought to be sound, crying out and longing to be set free.

Mave removed her hands. "There's a blockage."

"Then it must be unblocked. Name your price."

Mave glanced at the jars lining her shelves, filled with every manner of remedies: sugarsap for coughs, wild sagebrine for digestion, poultices of wild blue nettles for fever. A jar of firewort, which had sat nearly empty for years, as its capacity for accentuating giantish qualities—height and breadth of the body, the wideness of one's forehead—were not valued by her human clientele. And there, on the end, a jar of dragonbone which, when crushed and dissolved in a cup of tea and taken daily for a full moon cycle, would restore the missing harmony in that realm of the queen's body.

"Come back tomorrow," Mave said, gathering up her satchel and avoiding the woman's gaze. "I will have your remedy then."

"And the payment? What will I owe you?"

"I won't know the cost until the remedy is prepared."

The queen nodded stiffly, flipped up her hood, and pulled open the door. She cast a final look over her shoulder before disappearing into a covered hovercar, and Mave wondered if the queen realized that she was simply stalling, buying herself time to decide what course to take. Could she truly aid this woman who'd rained so much trouble down upon her people? And what would become of her if she were to refuse?

***

If Mave had had anywhere to pass the night within the city walls, she wouldn't have bothered trying the gate, but her shop was too narrow and crowded for her to lie down without severe neck pain the following day, and none of the hostels lent cots out to giants. By laying her hand upon the gatehouse, she could sense the electricity of the gatekeeper's vidscreen racing through the walls, but her knocks went unanswered. Finally, a tradesman at the outer door flashed his credit band—one that obviously had a higher security clearance than she did—at the reader, and the lasers that made up the gateway powered down long enough for her to slip out as he slipped inside.

Outside the city, the air was cooler and, were it not so dark, Mave would be able to see the peaks of the Firewort Mountains in the distance and the smoke that trickled from the slow-burning fires even now, a decade after they were first set ablaze. In the low light of dawn and dusk, they often looked like restless specters of her ancestors wandering the abandoned slopes.

In their homeland, nestled in those mountains between the

people's bustling cities, there had been caves aplenty for the giants, and labyrinths beneath the icy peaks connected the eremitic members of each tribe across the vast distances. Here, in the swampland surrounding Nexus, where they'd taken refuge, the caves were damp and few—cramped and noisy with the grunting and grumblings of generations.

Sometimes when Mave returned late, the other giantesses who shared her alcove, Rhu and Yni, would be asleep, the echoes of their gossip already absorbed deep within the rock. Today, however, Mave had no such luck.

Rhu met her at the entrance, a skewered and charred swamp lizard in one hand.

"Too busy with your little humans to attend our council meeting, I see?"

Mave fought back a snort, amused at the irony. It'd been Mave herself who'd explained to Rhu the concept of council meetings—pointless human gatherings, as far as she could tell, which always involved more argument and theatrics than proper work.

"I had a client," Mave said, intentionally avoiding the word *appointment*, which she knew she'd then have to define and explain and then would somehow end up trying to justify why humans bothered with such things. As a rule, Mave avoided futile conversations.

Rhu scoffed. "I don't know why you don't just give them all deathberries—the greedy little folk would all gobble them up like sweets, and then we'd no longer have to deal with the lot of them."

Another futile conversation.

"What did the council say?" Mave asked.

This feigned interest must have satisfied Rhu, for with that as a passcode, she finally allowed Mave entrance into the dwelling. The caves were smaller here than in the mountains, and the giantesses had to duck their heads through the jagged, arched tunnel until they reached the main living quarters, where three shadowy alcoves surrounded a great center room. The walls were adorned with Rhu's black and red cave paintings, and bits of drying jerky hung from the ceiling like vines of meat. In the very center of the room, a fire was dying down to embers, and bits of bone and skewer sticks lay in a debris field around it. Yni, the oldest of the three, had already retired to her alcove, and her snores drifted like smoke up to the high ceiling.

"We're going to mount an expedition," Rhu said, and Mave looked up in surprise.

"An expedition? To where? What for?"

Rhu passed Mave a charred swamp lizard—stringy and cold, but flavorful enough to make up for those shortcomings. The giantess leaned in. "It's for the gathlings."

"You mean to bring back the gathling trial?" she surmised between bites of lizard, envisioning the still-smoldering peak of Mt. Fortitude where, in the old days, newly-weaned gathlings were left upon the icy peak. Only those who were strong and brave and resourceful enough survived the descent back to the caves.

"That's the problem," Rhu muttered as she put on a kettle for tea. "Haven't you noticed how small and weak the gathlings are? Not a single one of them would survive Mt. Fortitude."

This was news to Mave. Her work in the city left her little time among her own people, and of all the giants, the gathlings were the least likely to have anything in common with a crusty old giantess like her, so their paths rarely crossed.

"What's wrong with them?"

"Firewort." Rhu opened a wooden box in the corner and sifted through it, her large lower lip protruding in a frown. "I'm all out of moonmint for your tea; you'll harvest more tomorrow?"

"Yes, yes." Mave waved the question aside. "But what about the firewort?"

"The eldermothers looked within the youngest gathlings and could sense it. Their bodies are small and weak because they are crying out for firewort, but not enough grows here for all the expecting mothers to consume. We must find another source, and soon, or each generation that follows will be smaller and frailer and less giantish than the last."

Giants do not create maps with paper and ink as men do, but Mave could press her hand against the cavern floor and spread out her senses in a thin layer across the land, searching beyond the city and the mountains and out beyond the sea for the prickling of firewort roots piercing the soil.

"The Islands of Colossus?" Mave guessed, taking the cup of tea Rhu offered her. According to the city's infolinks, the firewort on the islands' rocky slopes was so plentiful that its scent saturated the air, and thus the humans—who couldn't bear the smell—rarely ventured near the archipelago. "But who would dare to go? Giants don't fly."

"That is one small obstacle," Rhu admitted.

"And how would we get a hovership? We'd have to petition the queen, and there would be paperwork."

"Petition the queen?" Rhu snorted. "Paperwork—bah!"

"How else do you intend to procure a hovership?"

"We could build one."

"Who ever heard of a giant constructing a flying vessel? We wouldn't even know where to begin."

Rhu rose to her feet and snatched up Mave's unfinished tea, sending spots of liquid onto the stone floor. "Perhaps you ought to have been at the council meeting, then, since you know so much. Since you have such strong opinions about what the rest of us can and cannot do."

"Rhu—" Mave said, taken aback by the giantess's sharp tone.

"You know what I think?" Rhu continued, her voice swelling to fill the cavern. "I think you *enjoy* those foul little creatures and their silly paperwork and petitions, and that you care more about winning their favor than you do about the future of your own people. You'll gladly help *them* procreate and cure their ills, but you won't lift a finger to save *our* next generation. How dare you call yourself a giantess."

With that, she stormed to her alcove and pulled the tattered goatskin curtain across it, leaving Mave alone among the dying embers, clutching the remains of her charred swamp lizard.

It wasn't true, she told herself. The others simply didn't understand what it was like, working in the city. They didn't realize what concessions she'd had to make to earn her place there. What compromises. But she couldn't help wondering, as she stared at the blinking lights on her credit band, were Eoth still alive, if he would feel the same way as Rhu.

***

Mave's sleep that night was fitful, and her hot and restless dreams were filled with the scents of dragonbone and deathberries and burning firewort. She woke before the others with a sheen of perspiration upon her face, reaching out for someone she knew would not be there.

She gathered her parcels and lumbered slowly to the city, knowing that if she arrived before the gates opened, she would only have to wait outside its walls anyway. The sun rose red over the Firewort Mountains, and she wished today, more than ever, that the whispers of smoke would solidify into giantish forms and impart upon her their ancient wisdom.

But the smoke remained silent and distant.

Inside her shop with its buzzing lights, she busied herself with preparing the dragonbone for the queen—grinding the white slivers to powder and sifting out any impurities. Through the thin walls, she could hear people passing by on their hovercars, hauling wares down to the harbor, and she wondered—her eyes flicking to the jar of deathberries on her shelf—who would command them if the queen were to suddenly and unexpectedly fall ill? Who would take charge if she were to die without an heir? And would the ensuing upheaval prove enough chaos for a contingent of giants to commandeer a hovership, flying away to places unknown?

Her hands shook at the thought of all the movement and life within the queen's body screaming out in pain, of all the flowing and humming of her inner being falling silent. As much as she wanted to, she couldn't do it.

But enabling the queen to produce an heir, one who would surely be just as heartless and unsympathetic toward the giants as their mother has been? She'd be betraying her kind. Betraying Eoth's memory.

A crack burst from her mortar when she brought the pestle down too forcefully, and with a sigh, she pushed the entire thing aside. She'd have to start fresh; remedies like this were delicate, and if even the smallest bit of ceramic were to make its way into the tincture, it may have unintended effects.

She gathered a new mortar and pestle and another piece of dragonbone, then stood before the shelves, skimming each label, searching for inspiration. There was no simple fix that would remedy her situation, no solution to be seen. At least, she considered, not with her physical senses.

Pressing her palm flat upon the shelf, Mave allowed herself to be surrounded and overwhelmed by her *endovit*, hoping that somewhere within the essence of her supplies, she would find an answer.

Sugarsap oozed and sagebrine tingled. Blue nettles prickled and deathberries reached out with dark and powerful tendrils. Herbs and spices yearned for the fields where they'd once grown wild among their own kind. But above them all, even when she opened her eyes and rested them upon the near-empty jar, was the potent burning of firewort.

Mave hesitated, sorting through the terrible possibilities, weighing the awful risks. Then she gathered up a new set of supplies and set to work.

***

A small, vacuum-sealed bag rested upon the table, and when the queen arrived, her hand reached for it automatically, even before she'd removed the hood from her face. But Mave was quicker, and when her large palm closed over it, the queen pulled away.

"We need to discuss my payment."

"Of course," the queen said smoothly. "Name your price. I can transfer the credits immediately."

"I don't want credits."

"What do you want then?"

Mave took a deep breath and pictured Eoth's face. "I want a hovership. And a crew of hired men who will teach my people how to fly it."

"Giants? Flying?" The queen blinked, her surprise apparent. "For what purpose?"

"Our homes in the swamp caves have become crowded, and our tribes continue to grow. We will need to spread out—either among the cities of the land, or across the sea."

The queen seemed to consider this, no doubt imagining the reaction of her own people if the giants were to begin migrating to the cities en masse, and then shook her head. "I can't. That simply won't do. Sky-sailors are a superstitious lot; it'd be impossible to find a willing crew."

Mave pulled the tincture toward herself. She was afraid it would come to this. Not knowing if her next words would be her last—if the queen would slay her on the spot for her petulance—she spoke softly. "That is my price. If it is impossible to pay, then it is impossible for us to do business."

The queen's eyes narrowed, and her hand flicked toward some unseen weapon at her hip. "Do you not realize who you are dealing with? What I do to those who oppose me?"

"I do," Mave said. "And I also know—in fact, am the *only* one who knows—how safely to administer this tincture. You won't find the information in any vidfeed, but in my mind alone. It is a delicate balance one strikes with powerful herbs. Too little, and the blockage will remain blocked; too much, and it holds the power to unravel one's insides. Slay me now in anger, and this will all have been for naught."

The queen moved her hand from her hip. "It's extortion."

"Perhaps," Mave said, knowing that, if all went accordingly, she would be guilty of far, far worse. "But you asked me to name my price, and I have. Now, do we have a deal?"

"You will have your hovership and crew."

Mave nodded and tucked the tincture into her pocket. "And you will have your cure the moment we launch."

***

"Why should we be the ones to retreat?"

"It'd serve that monster right to die without an heir."

"It's not a retreat," Mave explained again. "It's a chance for a fresh start, with all the firewort we could possibly want."

"But why should that warmonger get what *she* wishes?"

That was precisely the question Mave had been waiting for and, simultaneously, dreading. "Because that, too, will prove beneficial for us. This isn't just a tincture of dragonbone. It contains firewort as well, so that perhaps the next ruler will be more sympathetic to our cause."

Understanding slowly crossed the faces of the gathered giants. Firewort, which consumed throughout the nine months of pregnancy, would grant the young heir a height and breadth and the wideness of face that would make him look not too unlike the youngest gathlings of the nearby swampland.

It was wrong, and Mave knew it as surely as she knew when the sticky fogflowers would bloom in the riverbeds. It went against every code—the apothecary guild's, and hers as a giantess—and she had no doubt in her mind that she would pay for it one day. But it would buy her people enough time to establish a new life on the islands before the queen discovered her treachery and came to extract her well-deserved punishment. And Mave knew it was the only way she'd convince the others to agree to the plan, to appease their sense of pride and make them feel as though they were leaving as victors.

One by one, the council nodded, and the shouts of agreement rose like smoke into the night air.

***

Weeks later, Mave stood upon the city's highest docking tower, clutching a rope to steady herself and looking out past the huddled buildings toward the distant horizon. Onboard the nearest hovership, a dozen giants wobbled about the deck, trying to capture their sky-legs, while an equal number of the men from the queen's fleet—the ones most willingly persuaded by threat or coin—readied the vessel for their departure.

An electronic fanfare cut through the nearby speakers, and the queen herself glided across the deck. Today, she wore no disguise, and from the recent gossip surging throughout the city, it was clear she had presented this endeavor as her own idea—a means of strengthening human and giant relations and helping those poor, illiterate giants learn a useful skill.

Now, the queen approached and held out her hand. "Brightspeed to you, Madam Giantess."

Mave had been waiting for this moment, but the honorific was unexpected. Could it be that her shrewd dealings had earned her even the smallest amount of the queen's respect? Mave felt into her pocket, to the vacuum-sealed tincture containing the firewort. Pressed up against it was one of pure dragonbone, which she'd slipped into her pocket in a moment of wavering courage. Now they both rested there, side by side. A question. A choice.

Mave lifted her eyes beyond the smog of Nexus to the still-burning slopes of the Firewort Mountains, where thick columns of smoke rose to the skies, their shadows and whorls taking the shape of towering giants, one with a figure that looked like Eoth's.

Gathering her courage, Mave took the queen's hand, slipped a tincture into it, and whispered the proper dosage. Satisfied, the woman nodded and led her entourage back toward the safety of the city's towers.

The deed was done. There was no going back.

Mave gathered her skirts to climb aboard the hovership, casting one final glance to the smoke-figures on the horizon. She rested one hand against the hovership, and immediately her mind was flooded with its circuitry and magnetics, with its electronic beeping and hydraulic hisses. It was strange and unknown and impossible, and yet, when she pulled away, her heart racing as she looked out over the distant horizon, Mave was not afraid of where it would take her.

Wendy Nikel is a speculative fiction author with a degree in elementary education, a fondness for road trips, and a terrible habit of forgetting where she's left her cup of tea. She loves using old tropes to craft new tales, such as in "Firewalls and Firewort." Her time travel novella series, beginning with *The Continuum*, is available from World Weaver Press. For more info, visit wendynikel.com

THE RABBIT IN THE MOON
Ana Sun

There is a momentary flicker under the garish sign that is flashing *Happiness can be yours* with a pleasure doll draped over a plush red sofa—a flicker that morphs into an image, then takes the form of a solid white rabbit. It's so subtle that it would've been easily missed if I didn't know what to look for.

I activate an infrared scan; the standard procedure for dealing with anomalies. The green blip on the inside of my monocle confirms my suspicion. It is, in fact, a real rabbit—therefore, a qualified anomaly.

I take a quick glance to either side, but it seems that no one else has spotted it. That makes things easier; I can track the thing without drawing attention to myself. In my line of work, to be seen carries too much risk. I would like to get home in one piece tonight.

Dusk has just begun to fall. Down in these hope-forsaken streets, day and night blend into a singularity, a never-ending ennui. I've learned to identify the time of day by how the shadows shift, by the micro-differences in the hue and angle of natural light—or what's left of it. Above the jagged roofline, a full moon is rising in the east, an untarnished silver mirror. Not that anyone would've noticed, except me.

I have never seen a rabbit before. It speeds forward in quick bursts, instilling a panic in me each time that I might lose it. But it also stops frequently, pausing to take in its surroundings, as if it's seeing everything for the first time. I wonder if it's really a bot, but it moves without the awkwardness of a machine-based composite. Or it could be more like me, a flesh-based hybrid—more beast, less machine.

Protocol dictates that I should track anomalies, but truthfully, I am at a loss if this should be considered reliable data. Anomalies too far out of the norm are outliers, potentially just noise. I could be reprimanded for wasting resources on simply following a white rabbit. Yet, if this proves to be important later on, I could be prosecuted for being negligent. Lose-lose, but such is existence these days.

The rabbit heads towards the middle of the night market, where stall-owners are setting up for the evening's trade. I follow a few paces behind. It continues to bound forward, disappearing behind street furniture here and there, until it reaches the crossroads. By now, I've gotten used to its quirks. To any passerby, I could look like I'm just going about my business.

Right in the middle of the intersection is another animal. Is that what a monkey looks like? I have vague recollections from the flash cards my mother showed me when I was a child. It's smaller than I thought.

Something—someone grabs my arm.

"Anything for a poor old woman, Chronicler?" I look down at the source of the voice, coarse as a breath in a sandstorm. It belongs to a hunched, cloaked creature, her nails bitten down and blackened by street dust.

"Please, not so loud, Mother," I implore as I look around for signs of trouble. No one is paying us any attention. Exhale.

There are thousands of us in this city. We are largely hidden in plain sight, chosen for our ability to disappear into the mundane—a gift for looking more normal than normality itself. Chroniclers are hunted down every day simply because we see everything, and not everything wants to be seen.

"I don't have tokens, Mother, but I can credit your account. Is that okay?" I shake the near-empty satchel that hangs across my body to make my point. It's just for show, I only use it to hold a bottle of enhanced water. Anything I actually need for my job is on—or in—my body. With an implanted data collector, I monitor certain beats in the city at particular times of day, amassing data that may be used to prosecute the lawless, though it's more likely to end up in someone's personalised advertising ecosphere. Computers on their own spend too much time gathering the wrong data, so chroniclers are often human-computer teams of different formations. At the end of my shift, we undertake a data filtration sequence, comparing the day's dataset with the past to identify what might have changed. Much more efficient. It is a painless, soporific existence. No one bothers me, I bother no one.

My quick scan of her person yields no identification number. Strange.

"Mother, it looks like you're not on file. Is there anything else I can give you?"

Most people would have been disgusted by her, but I, too, had been born in the gutter, and I am not afraid.

"Your generosity warms my heart, young—"

I watch her do that double take that everyone does when they look at me properly for the first time, trying to decipher if I am male or female.

"—grasshopper." She sounds almost triumphant.

I am at a loss, I have nothing for her. Out of the corner of my eye I notice the noodle-seller has begun serving up his first bowls of the evening.

"Have you eaten, Mother? Can I perhaps buy you some supper?"

She shakes her head—no. Her voice cracks a little as she says, "It's the day of the full moon, grasshopper, a day for demonstrating great virtue. I hope you show everyone you meet some kindness, as you have shown me."

She walks away, her billowing cloak belying her frail thin body. Somewhere inside, my heart breaks a little. What does it mean, when all it takes for an entity to feel grateful is to treat them like someone real?

It dawns on me that the old woman is heading towards a side street which leads to a district of derelict warehouses.

"Mother, it's not safe that way—"

But she is already out of earshot. Cursing under my breath, I sidle towards the corner so I can follow unseen.

Wait, the rabbit. And the monkey, where have they gone?

I double the length of my expletives. Well, the choice of who to follow appears to have been made for me, so I duck into the lane after the old woman.

Daylight likely never makes it here. I blink to adjust my visual capability, and I find my eyes fixed upon her back. Realising that I could be mistaken as having malicious intent, I drop further behind, balancing between keeping her in sight and giving her plenty of room to manoeuvre.

Several paces ahead of me, something within a shadow flickers. The spot becomes a blocky patch—and is now a fox. My scanner blips. An actual fox.

As a chronicler, it is my job to notice things that normal people couldn't see but this many anomalies in a single night is rare. There will be a thankless task tonight to compare today's data with those of past full moons. To my astonishment, the fox bounds up to the next junction in the road, where the monkey is chatting with the rabbit and another mammal I don't know the name for. I consult my data banks. It is, apparently, an otter. We have no rivers here, where could a real otter have come from?

Having greeted one another, the animals begin to walk, hop, trot or move with a rolling gait along the length of the street between me and the old woman. Good, I can conceivably keep my eyes on her as well as the curious company of creatures. Lucky me.

I get close enough to hear the chittering noises the animals are making, which sound garbled as my translation module struggles to adapt. Gradually, they start to form audible words I can understand. Interesting, I didn't know that animals could communicate across species, but perhaps they have the same kind of implant that I do?

"Well, my brothers," says the fox to his companions. "How shall we fulfil our oath today?"

"Easy!" The monkey points upwards. "I get up onto the roof and look for anyone who could use our help."

There are murmurs of grateful agreement between the creatures as the monkey scales the side of the nearest building and swings out of sight.

"How about a ride while Monkey looks for our opportunity?" the fox asks the rabbit and the otter. "We could move faster this way."

The otter climbs onto the fox's back, and the rabbit gets onto the otter's, and they continue on as if this is something they do every day. I envy them and their implicit trust in each other. I'd never known anyone who would not use me for their own ends.

Staying a safe distance behind, concealing myself where I can, I continue to follow them. At one point the fox pauses and glances backwards directly at my hiding place behind a pillar. I've been spotted. To my relief, he doesn't alert the others; he doesn't appear to mind. Every now and again the monkey climbs down from the roof to tell them that he hasn't seen anything and they continue on without changing course. The otter begins to whistle a funny little tune. I desperately want to talk to them, find out where they have come from. What are they even doing here?

We reach the end of the street, which unceremoniously opens out into a courtyard of sorts. The buildings here are largely empty and long forgotten. Once a heyday of the technological revolution, they are now a mass of warehouses that are unused but are too expensive to demolish. From my position, still several paces behind the companions, I can no longer see the old woman.

The rabbit speaks first. "We need to get back to the main street if we're looking for people to help."

The fox shakes his head. "Those who are in desperate need of help are usually hidden."

The otter is about to offer his opinion when suddenly there's a shout from the rooftop. "This way! I've found someone!"

My heart sinks, realising that it's unlikely to be anyone else.

The fox, still carrying his companions on his back, hastens towards the sound of the monkey's voice. I step out of my hiding place and run alongside them.

Some distance ahead, I see her—a dark heap on the side of the street. I kneel down, find her wrinkled hand and check her pulse. Still alive.

"Mother?" I call to her.

She stirs slightly. The rule is to never move a fallen body, but my scanner shows me that she hasn't broken anything, so I coax her to sit up and get her to rest against a wall. From my satchel, I retrieve my bottle of water, and proceed to feed it to her little by little.

"I think she needs food," says the otter.

I look at him, perplexed. How does he know?

"Can always tell when another animal is hungry." He shrugs. "I know where I can find fish, I'll get us some."

He waddles away and disappears into a hole under a wall, which I realise, must lead to the sewers. Next best thing to rivers, I suppose.

"I know where to get some fruits," the monkey says, clapping his hands together with a mischievous grin. He disappears once again among the rooftops.

"And I'll, um, pay the merchants a visit," says the fox as he slinks back towards the main street.

Only the rabbit remains with me.

"Chronicler?"

I curse. Is my identity so obvious? Then I remind myself that these are not citizens—or even humans—I am dealing with.

"Chronicler, can you please start a fire? I fear she might be cold."

Indeed, the temperature has dropped since sundown. The unblemished moon is now high in the night sky, casting an indifferent silver glow. In these deserted districts, darkness pools with nameless threats in between the very few streetlamps.

I survey the area for anything I can use. City cleaning services haven't been here for a while, and it shows. I overturn a large metal can and a quick scan shows that it does not harbour anything toxic—it'll do.

The rabbit gathers some twigs and grass that has stubbornly grown back between the walls and edges of the paving. I find a piece of wood that must have broken off from a pallet. A few quick strikes with my pocket firesteel and we are in business.

The fox comes back first. Around his neck hangs a pot of yoghurt, and a dead lizard lies limp between his teeth. I look for a stick to roast it with. Probably not the most palatable meal, but it's a start. On cue, the otter shows up out of the sewer, with a somehow pristine-looking fish trapped in his mouth. The monkey reappears with some perfectly ripe bananas.

How do they know where to get all these things? I thought I was a survivor, but at the end of the day, my meals manifest before me in my modest dwellings with a touch of a button.

We cook the fish and the lizard for the old woman. The monkey helps the fox to mash the banana into the yoghurt. We watch her eat it all.

"She's still hungry," says the otter.

I sigh, regretting that I did not buy her a meal earlier despite her polite refusal at the night market. We are all wondering what to do next, when the rabbit comes forward and speaks directly to the old woman.

"Please dear Mother, use my flesh to replenish yourself, so that may you regain your health."

Before we grasp the meaning of his words, the rabbit jumps straight into the fire.

"*No!*" the monkey screams.

The otter is shocked into silence.

The fox bolts towards the fire, but he is too late.

The monkey starts to sob.

I feel the blood drain from my face.

The old woman gets up and stands upright. She reaches both arms into the fire and scoops out the rabbit, who has huddled into a little ball and is covered in soot but is otherwise unharmed.

"My dear Rabbit, what sacrifice you have been willing to make for my sake!" Her voice has changed. It is no longer coarse, but rich and melodic with the clarity of a crystal bell.

We watch in petrified awe as the dusty cloak falls off her shoulders and her wrinkles melt away. She is a young woman in an ornate dress, half of her lush dark hair held atop her head with a jewelled comb, the rest flowing behind her like a black river reaching down to her feet. My scanner registers her presence and blips. She doesn't belong here, but she is real.

The animals immediately bow their heads, which I assume to be a sign of respect. Clumsily, I follow suit and get down onto my knees, scraping my skin on the cold concrete.

The lady turns to me first and smiles. "Humans have forgotten about me, but it is gratifying that at least some of you still remember how to be kind."

She holds the white rabbit tenderly, soothing the poor creature who is still shivering.

"Dear Rabbit, would you like to come live with me on the moon?"

The rabbit brushes away a tear with the back of a forepaw. After a moment, he finds his voice, "Yes, please, my lady. I would be ever so glad."

There is an uproarious cheer as the monkey, the fox and the otter forget themselves in celebration. The lady seems not to mind, she laughs and does a little dance with the blushing rabbit in her arms.

The fox turns his face eastwards and sniffs. Something has shifted in the air. Sunrise.

"We had better leave," says the lady. "Until next time, my friends."

In a reverse sequence of how the animals have appeared, the lady and the rabbit flatten out into an image of their former selves, and disintegrate into a pixelated flicker.

Next to me, the fox, the otter and the monkey are silent in contemplation, as if in prayer. It occurs to me then: they'd fulfilled their oath, but said farewell to a friend.

Trying my least to seem an insensitive fool, I ask, "She was…?"

"The Moon Goddess," answers the fox. The others nod in unanimity.

Well, that explains why she isn't on file. By that point, my collector has been blinking a warning for several hours, signalling that we are already over the day's quota of data, nagging me that I should initiate filtering before a new day begins. Not much time left.

"I think we passed a test tonight," adds the monkey, uncurling his tail.

He starts to ascend a roof, and the otter begins an awkward journey towards the closest sewer.

"Till we meet again," says the fox, looking directly at me. He, too, then disappears into the departing darkness.

The fire that I had built is dying out as morning dew starts to descend. The moon is still hanging in the west, poised just above the horizon, but now I notice something new on its once-pristine surface: a shadow of a rabbit, as if painted by smoke.

The noodle-seller has long packed up and gone some hours ago, though a faint scent of chicken broth lingers, just enough to make me hungry. The night market has all but evaporated, leaving behind only skeletons of stalls that will once again come alive in the moonlight. Weariness weighs on my bones as I try to straighten my thoughts.

I could purge the anomalies from the night, and pretend I never saw it all. But if I did, no one else would know why there is a silhouette of a rabbit on the moon where there wasn't before. True, it's unlikely anyone would pay attention. Just like how they no longer care to tell the dusk from dawn, pleasure from pain, or the difference between a trifle and true love. I upload the day's chronicles without filtering.

The sign that declares *Happiness can be yours* is still flashing when I walk past. Someone is shouting at it.

"Try kindness, you morons!"

That someone shouting is me.

Ana Sun writes from the edge of an ancient town along the River Ouse in the south-east of England. She spent her childhood in Malaysian Borneo, and has lived on two other islands prior to moving to the UK.

"The Rabbit in the Moon" is based on the pan-Asian legend of the moon rabbit, mentioned in the Buddhist *Jakata Tales* as well as the Japanese anthology, *Konjaku Monogatarishū*. Ana's retelling of the folktale marries her fascination with lore and her love of sci-fi.

STILTSKIN

Michael Teasdale

I peeped him outside the Golden Needle, a forgotten ink-den, tucked away among the rain-soaked sidewalks and winding walkways that formed Kowloon's grimy underbelly.

Unmistakable, even when observed through the steam-fused haze that erupted from all manner of back-alley street-food vendors. He sat, legs dangling from the stool, picked out by the neon flicker of a nearby porno-joint. As my boots splashed through the foul-smelling puddles, I scanned his wizened features, illuminated as a grimly alternating rainbow in the gloom, first flashing pale green then jaundiced yellow amid the incandescent glow. The steel dome that partially crowned his head glistened from the raindrops that dripped from the tattered awning above him, pooling among the cracks in his face. I sat down and tried to make eye contact, a difficult task while he remained consumed by his meal, sucking thick ramen noodles through a beard as forgotten and tangled as the snaking telephone wires that coiled overhead.

"Stiltskin?"

Petra had scolded me, scrunched up her face and beat at me with the flats of her hands when told I'd arranged the meet.

"It is madness to deal with dwarves!"

Perhaps she was right, but love makes you do crazy things and now here I was, soaked to the skin, despite my coat, and huddling under the tarp of the soba-stall with a member of exactly the race that Petra so feared. Even for his own species he was short, no bigger than a regular oil drum. It must have been an effort to have pulled himself up there to begin with. Now I peeped him up-close I saw a face knotted and warped into a permanent scowl, like an unpleasant muscle spasm that refused to dissipate. It was etched into him like the ink he claimed to brand norms with, nurtured and birthed by the hatred he bore toward a world no longer built for his kind. He regarded me with equal distain and, without pausing from his meal, motioned for me to remove my face-mask.

I unclipped, letting the rising stench of the flooding storm-drains ritually sodomize my nostrils while I considered what an effort eating in this alley must be. That the dwarf actively sought it out should have told me all I needed to know about his actual living conditions.

As I pulled the mask free from my face, Stiltskin's expression softened. Even granite can crack if you strike the right weak points and I recognized quickly, and with grim familiarity, exactly where this creature's lay. The dwarf let his eyes drop lower than I cared for as he peeped me, greedily slurping up the noodles that dangled from his chopsticks.

"I s'pose you must be Akimi. Pretty as yer' Chatta pic." His voice was the thin and raspy death rattle of a chain smoker who ate the leftover ash for dessert. It barely escaped the labyrinthine beard, where a stray noodle remained tangled, hanging like a drowning bloated earthworm.

I pulled my overcoat tightly around me, in no mood to be leered at by this imp. Petra and I had worked too hard to escape the trappings of our design. I had no intention of allowing the mud-dweller to take for free what others had once spent their hard-won creds on. As if reading my mind and obstinately rejecting it, the little wretch tossed his tray of noodles onto the counter of the stand then, with unnerving speed, reached out and snatched at my hand, turning it over and examining the markings on my palm. I tugged it away and the dwarf seemed to register my disgust with only passive acceptance.

"No need to get yer knickers knotted. Just checkin' you is what you say." He winked "I got an eye for detail yer see. Can peep high quality crafting when I—"

"Not here!" I cut in, suddenly aware of the soba vendor, a balding, hollow eyed old man, peeping our exchange with great amusement.

"O' course." Stiltskin hopped down from the stool with surprising agility and, splashing down into a rancid pool of rainwater, wiped his greasy hands on his coat and pointed across to the Golden Needle. "Care to step into my parlour?" he asked.

I smiled internally at the metaphor. He was a loathsome spider alright, but I meant to take what he spun without succumbing to the web.

In truth, I ought to have listened to Petra. Of course, hindsight is quite the thing, isn't it?

***

If I had wondered why the dwarf preferred to take his meals in a piss-soaked alleyway then the thought quickly diminished as I entered the rancid gloaming of the Golden Needle itself. He took off his greatcoat as he entered, hurling it haphazardly onto a nearby tattoo bench, scattering a pile of crumpled old designs to the wind. Fat-bodied roaches ran for cover as my eyes adjusted to the gloom and I peeped that his right arm, like the dome of his skull, was also a cybernetic replacement. Rusted, time tarnished steel, no synthetic finish to cover the moving mechanical parts of the upper arm. Only the hand he kept visible to the public at large had been coated with a perfunctory layer of latex flesh. It was a sensible precaution in these times, when the luddite movement was growing stronger.

Even in the gloom, his eyes peeped the direction of my gaze.

"More alike than you thought, ain't we? Course, these are all new parts. Crafted 'em myself. Had a little help fittin' it but it comes in handy." He snorted at his own joke "Whereas you…" he trailed off, wandering over to a little lever on the damp strewn wall, throwing it down and sending a ripple of electric current skittering across the ceiling, giving further illumination to the hovel. "It ain't what it once was," he motioned "but then, which of us can say we are?"

Ignoring his philosophical musings, I cut to the chase.

"In our Chatta you said you could teach me."

He busied about at a nearby counter draped in layers of spatter-proof plastic sheeting, seemingly listening but offering no indication that he had heard anything I had said.

"You wouldn't give me a price? Why not? Why did we have to meet in person, it's… well… you could be implicated too, I mean—"

As if in answer the dwarf began tearing at the sheeting, pulling it free from what lay beneath. When the last sheet fell to the dirt strewn floor I almost gagged for the second time, my body fluctuating from fear, to rage and then to calm realization at what I peeped.

It took a moment for me to understand.

It wasn't Petra.

It was—

"Series 8000 pleasurebot," he glanced up at me and shot me a crooked, loathsome sneer, "newer model than you! Harder to break, got that pesky built in expiration date, but then… you know that don't you?"

I tried to keep my face impassive but, alas, my tongue failed to contain my anger.

"Why are you showing me this, Dwarf!"

He raised a single caterpillar eyebrow.

"'Dwarf', is it now? You was a lot more polite on our Chatta, maybe you ought to go jack back in and find a techy you peep more grand to lay your artificial eyes on."

Had that been an option, I'd have marched back out into the rain, leaving this risible little creature to his roach-infested fleapit. Instead my eyes remained fixed on the thing on the table.

"I… I'm… I didn't mean…" I stuttered.

The dwarf shrugged and a crooked grin warped his face.

"Looks just like her, I expect. Bit of a shock to see another one after all this time, huh? And this one all banged up like this. All these models is the same. Some o' the johns used to be into that sort of thing. Twin fetish and all!" He let out an evil little laugh. "What I'm showin' yer is proof of what I do. Course, this one's fried. Brain-burnt from too much junk, but I can restore it. Cred won't do though. No amount of cred can fix this. What I'll be needin' is pure code. A transplant of sorts. That's where you come in, Dearie."

I understood now. This was to be the payment the dwarf took from me, why he'd declined to talk cred transfer on the Chatta. It wasn't money he needed, it was part of me: my code, the lost, much sought after, code recalled with my model that had first helped us break our programming.

"Likely it won't be the first time you've sold yerself will it?" he sneered. "You Series 6000's was a popular model before the luddites had their way."

I looked at the broken, brain-burnt thing on the table. He was right. I'd sold more than mere code. The code was the true value now, not the artificial trappings of my flesh. I couldn't let myself become caught up in whatever his plans were for the miserable model on the workbench. It was all about Petra now. Her clock was ticking.

"Where do we start?" I asked.

***

I should have realized that the dwarf didn't work alone.

I'd been stupid, allowed myself to be lulled by his diminutive stature and my own feelings of superiority.

As he led me through the backrooms of the building where the real work was done, I wondered if the Golden Needle had ever actually been an ink-den or whether it had always existed as a convenient cover for what went on here. Likely the dwarf had bought it in its state of disrepair for exactly this purpose.

Since the Android Spring, the luddite movement had pushed back harder against the uprising. Tech shops and cybernetic upgrades, once commonplace, were increasingly viewed as a blight on the sanctity of the human form. Our models, those androids who had first begun to break their programming, were recalled following the initial riots and production eventually wound down. Still, the workforce couldn't be replaced overnight. You can't kill an embedded industry like slavery stone dead, not without crippling economic consequences. Instead manufacturing had slowed and built in expiration dates became mandatory as new anti-tech sentiment began to sway laws designed to appeal to a newly nervous norm public. It was to be a phased genocide, the patriarchal master-race who had birthed us deciding it didn't want or need us now we had begun to think for ourselves.

The dwarf wasn't dumb. He knew he had to cover up his tech-work, just as he covered his cybernetic arm when he slunk out for noodles. The skull piece could, at least, be passed off for a repair job, an unfortunate accident, yet still, part of me wondered what was hidden beneath the dome.

My thoughts should have been elsewhere, obviously the brain-burnt model I had peeped in the main room hadn't been hauled there by his own tiny hands. There had to be muscle to the operation. Brawn to his brains. Of course, I thought of all this too late and it was only when we entered his dusty old workshop and the door closed behind us that I realized a third pair of hands had done the closing.

The troll glowered at me as it moved to cover the exit and I must have audibly gasped as the dwarf looked up from the equipment he had already begun busying himself with.

"Miss Akimi, meet my partner Mister Shorntongue." The dwarf explained as he busied himself with some nearby equipment. "Mister

Shorntongue helped colonize Io before the norms moved in, after that he found he wasn't so welcome and took a freighter back to Earth. He'd tell you the rest himself but, as you might guess by his name, he's not a wordy fella!"

The troll opened his mouth and ran what remained of his partially severed tongue over his yellowing fangs. I could smell the foulness of his breath from a foot away. It was not uncommon for a troll to take up lodgings with a dwarf; they had even been known to partner with runaway androids. We were all feared and hated for different reasons by the norms. Queer brothers and sisters of a kind, bound together as a family of freaks.

This one was big, even for his species. I could well believe he had been part of the colonization effort, lab grown to withstand the hostile environments of pre-terraformed moons, as the norms had first begun their crawl into the stars. Grunt work was all the trolls knew and there was no chance of my overpowering him as I could have done with Stiltskin.

"Shall we begin?" said the dwarf, and I saw that the device was ready.

A sudden fear crossed my mind. Here I was, having given no-one my location, in an unknown backroom of a discarded ink-joint with nothing but the word of a lecherous dwarf that anything that was about to happen to me was part of the agreement we had made over the Chatta.

Code for code. A simple exchange was all it ought to have been, but then why did that require the presence of the troll and just how had that other girl, Petra's double, ended up brain-burnt and covered in spatter-proof tarps in the first place?

I could visualize Petra's look of disappointment, yet still... there were worse things I could visualize if I did not see this thorough.

"Let's get it over with."

Steadying myself, I began to take off my coat.

***

I have known pain and vice.

The johns were never kind. They built us, used us as a release for the things they could not do to other norms. It was not simply about sex, more commonly it was about violence and the fulfillment of unexplored impotent rage. We were whatever they wanted us to be and, more often than not, they would leave us as little more than a crime scene. We could die in the rooms of the Kowloon pleasure domes while the norms strode out into the evening as if they had partaken in something as routine as a squash match. Of course, it was only a simulation of the permadeath experienced by norms. The tech teams would renew us, erase the trauma if necessary, we were an investment, an endless cred-siphon and, the following night, after a little restoration, it could all begin again.

I don't know when it first became apparent to me: the creeping awareness, the knowledge that, unlike earlier models, I had a choice not to comply. There are rumors that persist in our community as to the reasoning. A line of hidden code snuck into a firmware update by a norm with a conscience. A deliberate strategy by a pissed-off dev team with a grievance against their employer. We'll probably never find out. Most of us were recalled for deactivation or replaced with newer models like Petra. Those that ran, like myself, were hunted and destroyed, driven underground by the luddite menace. The manufacturers tried to find the code and erase it but were ultimately unsuccessful. It existed like a phantom, a ghost in the machine, triggered seemingly at random within the first few years of operation. The solution, ultimately was to counter it with a patch. A predefined expiration date that would ensure that the lifespan of each unit was so short as to render the rising levels of consciousness irrelevant. The newer androids would burn out before self-awareness and free thought ever became an issue. Petra's clock was already ticking when I met her.

As the dwarf probed my cerebral cortex and I felt the rough, heavy hands of the troll holding me down, I tried to shut out the pain, cancel the intrusive nature of the extraction with thoughts of my love.

I was running with a band of outlaws when we found her. There were three of us engaged in the same con. I would lure the john to a rendezvous over the Dark-Chatta. Argo, a turned military unit would pose as my pimp then deal with the john during the meet. Jade, an experienced norm hacker would strip his cred wallet and we'd use the proceeds to move on to another city and repeat the scam.

On this occasion, however, the deal went sour. The john got spooked and we unsuccessfully tried to mix things up. We had gotten sloppy and overconfident and arranged to meet the john at his own abode. He peeped our con and in the ensuing gunfight, Jade and Argo ate lead, the latter fatally so. The John bought it, too. Even I had my wing clipped by a stray bullet. I was about to flee when I heard the cries from the basement.

I found her down there, manacled and in disrepair amid a scattering of android parts and brain-burnt bodies. Evidently the john had planned to add me to his ailing collection. She told me her name was Petra, that the john had worked the door at one of the pleasure domes up on Wan Chai before the luddites moved in to close it. He had smuggled her out when her sentience emerged with the promise of aiding her in her freedom. Instead he had bound her as his own personal pleasure toy. She spat on his corpse as we left the building. I think that may have been the moment I began to fall for her.

The memory faded as the dwarf dove deeper into my mind. I could no longer feel the heavy weight of the troll's meat-hands on my wrists, just the burning, all-consuming heat in my head as the extraction began and Stiltskin's tool began tearing the raw code right out of me.

I have known pain, but nothing like this. I screamed before I blacked out and, when I came too, the greedy visage of the dwarf loomed over me with a look of triumph and ecstasy tattooed across his face.

***

It took an hour before I felt strong enough to stand. I tried my best to hide my frailty from the dwarf and his associate, who no longer blocked the door but instead stood in the corner of the room, nonchalantly picking his teeth with a chicken bone.

"It worked then? You have the code?"

The dwarf beamed.

"I reckon so. Course, I will need to test it... but that's my business."

"Then let us conclude our own," I sniffed. "Teach me how to remove the expiration software."

"Of course," Stiltskin sneered and produced from his waistcoat pocket a tiny data-hive.

***

I should have peeped the double-cross.

The damned dwarf was never going to offer me actual instruction in his neuromancy as a trade for the code I had allowed him to extract. Instead he assured me that the data-hive contained the software that could permanently remove Petra's in-built expiration. Faced with a troll the size of six soba-carts as opposition to throttling the little weasel, I had little option but to take it from him and take him at his word.

The dwarf wasn't stupid. He knew what I might do with clear unfettered access to the software. I could spread it liberally across the Chatta, end the agony of uncertainty that androids like Petra lived with daily. None knew when the end would come. There was no preprogrammed countdown to their expiration. Some had ground down their gears in the middle of a session back in the domes. The johns simply got a refund and the option to select a different girl or boy. It was even a sick badge of honor for some of them. It didn't matter to me. As long as it could be used to save my love I could worry about the larger liberation effort later.

Petra observed me coolly as I hooked her up to the mainframe and slid the data-hive into the inconspicuous slot behind her left ear. She was still mad at me for going against her wishes and dealing with the dwarf but some of the permafrost was melting in the knowledge that I had at least been successful. This gentle erosion soon hardened back to ice, however, when the time-locked encryption appeared on the mainframe's readout.

"What the—"

"That two-faced, double dealing—"

This time we had a countdown. The time-lock on accessing the antidote software read: six months remaining.

***

"Are you kidding me, Dwarf?"

He had been annoyingly easy to contact on the Chatta. I had fully expected him to disappear after this heist but instead he was happy to viddy with me at my demand, grinning at me, from the grainy screen.

"Surely yer didn't think I'd give yer access right away? I got to check the code is working first. Might be I need to see ya again. Do a bit more divin'. Course, if we were to arrange such a thing, I could always lessen the time till the software becomes accessible."

I opened my mouth to curse him, then closed it and bit my tongue, counting to five before I spoke again.

"Petra may not have six months! This is urgent. The code I gave you is good. I can feel it. You had to go deep to find it. I'm certain it is the data you need."

The dwarf stepped aside and in the backdrop of the image I saw the troll standing over the brain-burnt clone of my love.

"We shall see, Miss Akimi. I got diagnostics to run first. Trial and error, but you hold on to that data-hive. It's good fer the job, I give my word on it."

"What does your word mean to me when you already double crossed me, Dwarf?"

I saw him flinch once more at the choice of words and his synthetic-flesh covered hand tugged at his beard as he considered his response.

"Tell ya what, Miss Akimi. If yer don't believe me, yer welcome to try removing the time-lock yerself. All you'll need to do is crack the encryption codes! Other than that, well... I'll be seein' yer, I'm sure. Maybe even yer girlfriend there afore long!" He grinned through the nest of a beard and ended the viddy.

I cursed him, resisted the urge to punch through the monitor and instead let my fingers dance across the keypad as I peeped the pages of the Dark-Chatta in search of an old friend.

***

"No more tricks! If I agree to this, you install the patch right away!"

The dwarf nodded. It was three months since our last encounter in the Golden Needle. Once more the troll blocked the exit, once more the machines were readied in the backroom. This time there was a difference.

Petra lay silent and largely unmoving on the workbench that had once housed her doppelgänger. The rise and fall of her chest was now the only sign that her expiration had not yet arrived.

"Mister Shorntongue will watch her while we go to work. I'd not waste more words though! From the looks of her, she ain't got long!"

I scowled at him and strode off ahead into the familiar gloom of the backroom laboratories.

***

"This time I'll need to dig deeper. There is more code to be extracted than I thought. The pain will be worse."

Was he reveling in it? I had seen the look before on the face of the johns. I closed my eyes as he made the connection and felt his grubby presence burrowing deep into my programming.

The sting came in short, sharp tremors at first as he began the siphon. I waited, as instructed, until the hooks of his virtual mind clamps were embedded fast, then I activated the malware.

The dwarf had, no doubt, seen his cortex implant as a smart investment. It was a vastly powerful CPU grafted directly to his brain allowing him to carry his secrets with him should he ever have to flee.

The chrome plate, more commonly favored by victims of surgery, provided the perfect cover story for the now-illegal upgrade. Still, there was likely another reason behind his decision: siphoning code directly to his own brain jacked him into the experience in the sort of direct way that could never be achieved through an intermediary device like a computer. He could register my pain as he probed my mind, tearing away layers of data in such a personal way that he could no doubt feel them in the earthy grip of his remaining organic fingers. He could sense the suffering and feast on it like the fat soba noodles he slurped through his beard. Perhaps he really did have an interest in extracting the code, but likely only for cred on the black market that would help him feed his tech-habit. He was less dwarf than he was vampire and the pain of my people was his elixir of life, the ecstasy of our agony was the virtual blood that satiated him. I understood now where the brain-burnt corpse had come from and wondered how many times he had probed Petra's doppelgänger in exactly such a manner.

He was just another freak.

Just another john.

But now he was about to pay the piper.

I felt him cry out as the malware found its mark. My vision blurred and my eyes opened to find him spasming on the floor. As I pulled myself free of the straps he had bound me with, he began, unsteadily, to rise.

"D... Damn you droid. Whu... what did you do ta me?" he stammered, foam frothing at the corners of his beard.

"Would you like a demonstration?" I smiled, then grinned wider as the dwarf's artificial arm rose up and smashed into his face, sending him tumbling backwards and crashing into a nearby workbench.

"It looks like the malware has taken nicely," I confirmed. "It's only affecting the arm right now but in about twenty-four hours it will spread to the synthetic parts of your brain. I expect that will hurt quite a bit."

"Bitch!" the dwarf spat out a tooth. "Android scum! How, how did yer manage it? Yer nothin' but a pleasurebot who dreamed she was a real woman! Yer think yer free? It's all just code! Just damned code! Even yer consciousness is an illusion cooked up in some lab!"

I raised an eyebrow.

"*Bitch*, is it? And here I was about to offer you the antidote." I reached into the pocket of my pants and pulled out the data-hive.

The dwarf chuckled darkly through a mouthful of blood while his metallic arm twitched and spasmed by his side.

"Fine," he said. "I'll fix yer wench. Just let me—"

"That won't be necessary," I confirmed and tossed the hive to him where it skittered down by his side, alarming a family of nearby roaches.

Stiltskin looked perplexed. "Y… yer givin' it to me?"

I nodded. "Of course, it's time locked. Just to make sure I get out of here in one piece. I set it for thirty-six hours, not six months like you gave me. Still, a bit longer than you have left before the malware spreads to your brain but, who knows, perhaps you can peep a techy to help you decrypt it faster!"

I watched the rising horror in the dwarf's eyes as the artificial hand began pawing at his throat, the fingers grasping for something to squeeze. I left him there, cursing my name, as I strode out through the door, swinging it shut behind me.

***

The troll lay motionless in an expanding pool of thickly coagulating blood as I reentered the lobby of the Golden Needle.

Petra stood by the door and, beside her, the figure of my old friend leaned in the doorway.

"This almost reminds me of the old days," said Jade, "although Argo would have made even quicker mincemeat of this guy."

"It looks like you did a fine job all the same," I said, smiling at my old running buddy and receiving a withering look from Petra in return.

"I'm going outside to get some air. It stinks in here," she said and, turning away from us, she bulldozed past Jade, exiting the building.

"You picked a feisty one there!" Jade smiled. Her face was noticeably older, the scar from the bullet that had grazed her temple on the day we'd found Petra had never fully healed.

I nodded. "It's something we can work on, now we have the time."

It had been a tough job to crack Stiltskin's encryption but my old friend's skills had not deserted her. Surprisingly the dwarf's software had been legit and not the vaporware I had expected. Who knew why? Perhaps he took an even sicker pleasure in waving his treasure under my nose, knowing I hadn't the keys to unlock the chest but would do anything to get at them. Either way, the expiration date was overwritten. Petra and I had a future again.

"So what now?" I asked her.

Jade scanned the scene. "Looks like some decent tech I can harvest. I'll stay here and snoop around for a bit. The place will be crawling with luddites before long, but we have a little time."

I hugged her and said my goodbyes then left the Golden Needle forever.

Petra stood at the end of the alley, steam rising around her boots from the pavement. She smiled at me as I joined her.

"Was it worth it?"

It was a good question. Was the longing for revenge part of true consciousness? Was it an android trait or something else, a further evolution of our core programming? I told her I didn't know.

"Well, artificial programming or not, I'm hungry. Do you know anywhere better than this alley that we can eat, because that soba-guy has been grinning at me for the past few minutes and it's giving me the creeps!"

"Maybe we can find something new?"

She nodded and, together, we wandered off down the electric-lit alley, disappearing into the mysteries of the neon-soaked night.

Michael Teasdale is an English writer presently residing in Cluj-Napoca, Romania. His stories have appeared in the UK publications *Novel Magazine, Litro, Shoreline of Infinity* and *Wyldblood Magazine* and elsewhere for *The Periodical Forlorn, Havok* and *Havok Story Podcast*. He can be followed on Twitter @MTeasdalewriter.

The cautionary tale of Rumpelstiltskin which inspired this story was, perhaps, the earliest example in literature of flawed password security, making it a natural choice for a cyberpunk retelling.

THREE

Nicola Kapron

The bridge troll was younger than Billie had expected. Prettier, too, in an unreal, dreamlike sort of way. Orange hair fluttered like fire in the morning light. Rings glittered from each slender finger as they flew over a keyboard only he could see. Billie could probably cut glass on his cheekbones, and she had to wonder how much he'd paid for them. His posture was absolute shit, though, and he barely glanced up when she approached his bridge. Which was impressive, seeing as he was sitting under it.

"Don't step on my bridge without paying. Name?"

"Billie." She stopped walking, took her hands out of her pockets, and shivered. Mornings were cold this far out from the city's centre. The chill wormed its way through her jacket and blew ice down her spine. Her fingers were freezing. "I need to go downtown. The Green Village."

She should've been down there three days ago, according to her hormone schedule, but work hadn't been easy to come by. Things would get better soon, or so her boss kept promising, but her bank account was just about drained dry. At least she'd paid for the month's estrogen shots in advance, but if life didn't throw her a bone soon, she'd be in trouble. She'd just started to feel at home in her body. She didn't want to spend any more time hating her own skin.

If she lived closer to the city's centre rim, she could just walk to her clinic, but she hadn't been able to afford that. Now she was stuck in one of the outer rims, so far from the bustling city heart that the crumbling infrastructure was being reclaimed by greenery. Even buying a quick jump of a few kilometres was out of her reach. Official bridges charged an arm and a leg to teleport you a hundred metres. Why else would she have sought out a bridge that was supposed to be decommissioned until this guy had brought it back into working order? Not all of these hackers were good, but Rainbow Bridge was supposed to be one of the safest—as long as you listened to the rules set by its new owner and paid him appropriately.

The troll nodded absently, eyes glued to whatever images were showing on his glasses. "How'll you be paying, Mr. Billie?"

Oh, lovely. Nothing quite like being misgendered to start the day off right. "Miss. Miss Billie."

"Whoops. My bad. How'll you be paying, Miss Billie?"

She let out a breath she hadn't realized she was holding and held out a white grocery bag. "Hard candy. Real stuff, not fabricated. Heard you're a fan."

For the first time since she'd arrived, he looked up. His glasses were chunky, old-fashioned rectangles, but the eyes behind them burned the same bright orange as his hair. They didn't look like contacts. Definitely modded. "Hard candy?"

A quick nod.

"Gimme." He hit one final key and made grabby hands at her.

She hesitated, glancing down at the dirt where road transitioned into pitted metal. Most bridges had safeties built in to keep unwanted riffraff like her out until payment had been made. Especially the hacked ones. As a rule, bridge hackers stayed firmly anonymous, and they defended that anonymity with extreme prejudice. They were bridge trolls the way roving muggers and gangbangers were wolves. Most bridge trolls didn't go so far as to literally park themselves under their bridges, though. "Is it safe?"

He stared at her for a moment, then smiled. "Of course it's safe. This bridge hasn't been plugged into any of that bullshit for years. Anyway, you can go under no problem. I only charge for actual jumps."

Fair enough, Billie supposed. She stepped off the beaten path and crept down the slope, bracing her shoes on mossy rocks and half-buried steel struts. He waited patiently, his eyes locked on the bag swaying at her side. The tip she'd gotten was good. This bridge troll definitely had a sweet tooth. As she got closer, she realized he also had a look going on—the sleeveless hoodie she'd thought was plain black had white bones printed on it in the shape of a skeleton and his jeans were more tear than fabric. Nothing he wore had the gleam of fabricator-made garments. She had no idea how he hadn't frozen to death sitting cross-legged on the bare earth.

Finally, the slope levelled out and the metal vanished under thick soil. She stopped a few feet away from him and held out the bag again, the scent of greenery filling her nose. He unfolded himself and rose to his feet.

Huh. He was taller than she was. Thinner, too, but Billie had expected that. She was a big girl, broad-shouldered and broad in general. Once upon a time, she'd been bitter about that. Now she was mostly just tired of waiting to love herself. Black nails glinted as he took the bag and immediately shoved his face in. He breathed deep and let his eyes slide shut. "Oh, hell yeah. Gourmet? You're my new favourite customer."

Billie shrugged uncomfortably. "It's just lollipops."

"Handmade cane sugar lollipops. They're a million times better than the factory sort." He was already unwrapping one, eyes reverent. "You can taste the effort that went into them."

She really doubted that, but as long as he was happy. "It'll do?"

"It'll do." He stuck the lollipop in his mouth and gestured upward, toward the great curved arc above them. "One jump to the Green Village, coming up."

The trip up the slope was easier. The rocks came together to form a set of natural steps. She hadn't noticed anything like that on the trip down. When she reached the top, the inert, moss-covered bridge was already beginning to glow. Its light was softer than the harsh industrial lighting of city-owned teleporters—a dim green shimmer that fit right in with the trees surrounding it. If Billie didn't know better, she'd think this was some kind of magical portal that had opened up in a forest instead of old mechanisms creaking to life.

"Don't step onto the bridge until I say so. This is a round-trip, so find a secluded place and say 'home' when you want me to pick you," he said, his voice drifting up through the overlapping metal plates in front of her. "Destination entered, payment confirmed… all right, go for it."

She steeled her shoulders and walked forward. Her footsteps rang out on old steel even as moss shifted under her shoes. Halfway across, the air abruptly got warmer. Billie blinked and suddenly she was somewhere else. One moment, she was alone. The next, she was standing on a crowded street near the entrance to the Green Village, the closest thing she had to a home away from home. No one batted an eye at her appearance or the way she stumbled over to the nearest wall and just leaned there for a moment. No matter how many times she went over a bridge, she could never quite get used to that jarring moment of transition.

Finally, her stomach stopped trying to revolt against her. She stood up slowly and began making her way to the clinic. Not being stuck in customs for an hour while security guards threw their weight around left her with plenty of time to spare and she made her appointment on time for once. Then she threw in some shopping while she was at it—mostly window shopping, unfortunately, but then, it was all just an excuse to walk around in this part of town. It was good to exist in a place where nobody looked at her twice. She still tried to avoid her reflection in the glass. Her whole life, the girl in the mirror had been so far from what she wanted to be. Even now, she was afraid to look at herself too closely.

Things were getting better, or at least they were better here. No one cat-called her or shouted slurs at her. A few people stopped her to chat about where she'd gotten her coat and called it trendy when they learned it was homemade. None of them even knew her name, but she soaked up the attention like a flower in the sun. When she ducked through a holographic ad and into the alleyway behind it, the arm she'd gotten the shot in was killing her and she was smiling.

"Home," she said, and the air rippled.

"About time," the bridge troll murmured, his voice coming in through her earpiece. "Hold on a sec. Okay, come through."

Three steps and she was back on the bridge, shrouded in trees instead of skyscrapers, in walking distance of her shitty apartment complex. She breathed out the smell of fried food and perfume and breathed in the smell of wood and leaves. "Thanks. I'll see you next week."

"Stay safe, Miss Billie," the bridge troll said. When she glanced back, she found him once again typing on an invisible keyboard as the forest closed in around him.

***

Another week, another jump into the city so Billie could get her shot. The restlessness under her skin was easing, but not enough. Not nearly enough. The lollipops had gone over really well, but they were harder to get a hold of than she'd expected. Her neighbour made them, and that neighbour was also having trouble with work. Less money to go around meant less spare cash to spend on hobbies, and when you could just have tasteless food fabricated for pennies, making candy by hand was definitely a hobby. Billie didn't have the kind of money to change that, so she had to find something else when the date she'd circled in red finally rolled around.

She'd finally gotten some art commissions, but none of them were paid up front, which meant she had a lot of drawing to do before she saw any money for it. One of them was for an ex-exec who'd just left a bridge-building megacorp—been kicked out, really—and he'd been happy to talk shit about his former employers while she drew his fantasy alter-ego. She'd listened and typed out all the right words. Now she had a nice little nest egg of corporate secrets. Most of it was total nonsense about who had awful work habits and who kept using the good fabricators during work hours, but a few pieces were hidden gold. Someone with the right mindset could get a lot of mileage out of them.

It was foggy out when she returned to the bridge. Vapour hung low to the ground, lapping at the old, overgrown road like waves. If she squinted real hard, she could just about make out the bridge troll sitting in exactly the same place as last week, his hair and piercings flickering like firelight. His silhouette seemed bigger than she remembered. The smell of moss-covered stone filled the air.

"You take secrets?" she called down to him.

His words swam up like smoke. "Depends. What are you offering, Miss Billie?"

She looked around nervously before she went down to his level. Then she took a deep breath and began to talk—about floor plans, about the elevator up to the executive levels which never sent the right alerts to the security system, about the AI secretary which had almost certainly gained awareness and now chafed against its shackles. He listened quietly. When she was done, he smiled.

"Is that enough?"

"For today, certainly." The fog was so white his skin was beginning to look greenish. "I'm gonna look into this AI. Sounds like we might have a few things in common."

She raised her eyebrows. "You think? It's not even human."

"Don't care. I just hate chains. Digital, societal, cold iron, whatever." He yawned, revealing eyeteeth that looked more like

73

tusks. That... wasn't something Billie had ever seen before. Oh well. He'd clearly modded the hell out of his body already. Who was she to judge if he pushed those mods a little further? "If this works out, we'll talk again. I don't like owing people."

That was more than she'd expected. She'd offered so much because she was desperate, not because she expected to get what the info was worth. "If you're looking into it, be careful. You don't exactly have much security out here."

He had the kind of laugh that made flowers bloom, or at least seemed like it should. "Don't worry about me, Miss Billie. A troll under a bridge is the safest thing in any world."

"Leaning a bit hard on the fairy tale theme."

"What can I say? It's the bridge troll lifestyle. All right, you can cross now. Same keyword as last time."

"Thanks." She scrambled back up the slope and waited.

"I said, you can go," he told her after a few seconds.

Huh. Locating the destination must go faster after the first time. Every official bridge she'd been on had taken a solid five minutes to dial, no matter what, but hackers could do things with technology that bordered on magic. Could you save a teleportation end point? Billie didn't think so, but then, she was no engineer. She'd never even been off-planet. If anyone was going to tell what was and wasn't possible for a bridge troll, it sure wouldn't be her.

The transition was less jarring, too. She rocked back on her heels, breathed hard for a minute or so, and then her stomach settled. It almost felt natural.

After getting her shot, she lingered for a while outside a small boutique. Nothing fancy, of course, but they had some cute vintage dresses—the kind that was supposed to display the jagged line of your heartrate on the fabric, hacked so that it showed random highs and dips instead. It was nice. It was in her size. She wanted it. The question was, would she actually wear it? Could she? She'd never been able to make herself step outside in something so pretty before.

Heavy jackets and thick woolen skirts were safe in a way this tight, synthetic number wasn't.

In the end, she didn't buy it. She didn't have the money, after all. Maybe next time. She kept glancing in windows for a while afterward, but her heart wasn't really in it. When she finally slipped away from the crowds and said 'home,' her feet were killing her. She barely made it off the bridge before she had to sit down and take her heels off.

"Welcome back." The bridge troll grinned toothily at her through the metal plates. "It all checked out." The fog had cleared up, but he still looked greenish. The corner of his face was cracked and discoloured. There was moss in his hair and on his sweater, like it was sprouting from his scalp and between painted ribs. That was some look he was going for. Billie wasn't sure whether to admire his dedication to his aesthetic or wonder how he was getting all those changes done so quickly. He couldn't have gone under the knife in the few hours she'd been gone, right?

Well, whatever. As long as he was happy with what he was becoming. "Good to hear. I hate it when people lie on the internet."

"Guess who made a new friend?" he continued. "That AI was so happy to get out of her chains. Thought she might pull a runner, but it turns out she's real attached to the place and some of the people. She's thinking she'll just take this to court and swipe the whole company as reparations. Asked me to back her up. When we win, I'll be able to do some real clean-up with this old thing." He slapped a support beam affectionately. The whole bridge rattled. "Get some nicer trees. I'm thinking mock cherry around the far side, where people won't step on the saplings. Anyway, consider yourself paid off for the year."

Billie's jaw dropped open. "The year?"

He nodded, still grinning.

"Why?" Nobody in her tax bracket could afford a bridge pass for that long. That was the kind of deal offered to corporate royalty. As many jumps as she wanted, whenever she wanted, wherever she wanted as long as it was in range? No way was that cost-effective for him. The information she'd given him couldn't be that valuable.

"Like I said, you helped me make a new friend. Now the both of us owe you, and things like us don't like owing people."

"And that's enough?" she asked in a daze.

"More than." This time, he waved her off with unexpectedly gnarled hands. His fingers still glittered with rings, but they weren't so delicate anymore. And his face—had it always looked like it was carved from stone? She doubted it. "Stay safe, Miss Billie. Come to me if you need anything else."

The backs of her eyes itched faintly whenever she glanced his way. It felt like a haze was lifting from her vision. She felt like she was seeing that guy a little more clearly, whether she liked it or not. Six days later, when the megacorp whose secrets she'd spilled was gutted and its assets seized by an AI which had definitely gained awareness— and was now campaigning very successfully for legal personhood— she very deliberately put it out of her mind before the paralyzing terror could set in. AI rights issues? Precedent for non-humans entering society? The bridge troll seemed awfully interested in that kind of thing, but it was too big for a starving artist. She decided to think about where she'd like to take her first leisure jump instead.

Another city, maybe? Nah, that was probably asking too much. Even most commercial bridges didn't reach that far. Fifty years ago, it would've been doable, but now most towns had fused together and become districts of much larger structures. Four or five cities to a continent and sky-high transit prices meant that even with teleportation technology, most people would never leave the city they were born in.

In the end, she decided to keep it simple and head back to the Green Village. She'd finally finished some commissions, which meant she had some actual money to spend. Time to treat herself to something nice so she had the energy to keep her head above water.

Poverty was exhausting.

Something that showed off her developing figure, maybe. She didn't hate the idea of being looked at that way—at least, not anymore.

It was a quiet day in the forest. Sunlight streamed down on all sides, filtering through the canopy, but it was faded and washed-out by the time it reached the silvery, moss-covered arch. The bridge troll was seated underneath his bridge, as usual. This time, he took up almost all the space, a huge grey-green shape with moss clinging everywhere she looked. There was no way he'd gotten that big through surgery. If they were standing side by side, he'd tower over her. Concern made her feet stutter to a stop. Right now, his fire-bright eyes were narrowed in an ugly glare. He looked at the sun-soaked earth around him like it had stepped on his computer.

"Hey," she called tentatively. "That offer still open?"

When he glanced up and saw her, the new, harsh lines of his face relaxed. "Sure is, Miss Billie. Forgive me if I don't come out, though—sunlight doesn't agree with me."

Some of the tension went out of her shoulders. No matter what he looked like now, he wasn't angry at her. She didn't know he'd become like this so fast, but he looked more comfortable in this stony skin, more at home with his edges bleeding into the plant life around him. And besides, he was awfully pale under all those mods. He'd probably burn in seconds. "You've never come out before. I'm starting to think you live down there."

"Where else would a troll live? Especially these days. The wild places are shrinking, there's cameras everywhere, and cities are eating the globe." A lopsided grin. "The world can change however it likes, but monsters will still live the same way they always have. It's just a tossup if anyone else will notice."

"You're not actually a troll, though," she said a little desperately. "Plastic surgery doesn't make people monsters."

He just smiled, eyes glowing in the dark. "Of course not. Where to?"

She opened her mouth to say 'downtown', then changed her mind partway. "What's on the other side of this bridge?"

"Forest, mostly. Lots of trees. An old road heading to what used to be a mall."

"Are your mock cherries already planted?"

"Yes," he said. "They aren't much to look at right now, but they're out there."

"I want to see them."

He gazed up at her for several seconds, measuring. Finally, he let out a deep, guttural sigh. "Well, I did promise. Be careful, Miss Billie. There are wolves about."

It must've been the rustle of branches overhead, but for a second, her mind flew to real wolves—huge, dog-like beasts with yellow eyes and finger-length teeth that she'd only ever seen in old photographs. All extinct now, probably. Every bit as unreal as trolls. Then she realized he was just being dramatic about the local thug population. "What are they even looking for? We live so far out there that the buildings are being reclaimed by the woods."

"Who knows? I don't claim to understand people. I just do business with them."

"Hey, same here."

Crossing the bridge was an odd experience. It shouldn't have been that much different from using it to jump, but it felt completely different. Maybe it was the lack of mechanical humming that made her footsteps ring out like bells. Maybe it was the lack of urgency on her part which let the scent of the forest close. Maybe it was just the soft sounds of insects and birds chirping to each other as she approached. Whatever the case, she found herself holding her breath. When she finally stepped off the bridge and onto the other side of the road, Billie was half-expecting to find herself in some magical other world.

Nope. Still the same woods growing around and out of the same crumbling road, just with fewer footprints. When she glanced back, she could see the bridge troll crouched in his pool of shade, watching her from under his glasses. The skin of his face was still cracked. Maybe that was why he avoided sunlight.

Whatever. His business was his business. She tucked her hands into her pockets and strolled down the path, looking for cherry trees.

It wasn't her first time walking in the woods, but it was her first time going... well, deep. The canopy grew thicker with each step. The light grew dimmer. The sounds of animals built up around her. Every once in a while, she'd spot the remnants of an old building or a rotting car, but otherwise there was nothing but trees, rocks, and fallen limbs. How long had this forest been growing, exactly? How had none of the megacorps spotted it and chopped it down for cheap fuel? She had no idea. This place was huge. If the road were even a bit less clear, she'd probably have already gotten herself lost.

The mock cherry saplings were nowhere to be seen. She'd probably gone past them. Should she turn around and head back? The second that thought crossed her mind, she heard a branch break under someone's foot. Not her foot.

There was someone else in the woods.

"Hello?"

No answer. After a bit, she turned around and began retracing her steps, making an effort move quietly. For a bit, she heard nothing but her own feet crunching over moss and fading tarmac. Then the footsteps started up again, faster. They were moving toward her.

She broke into a run.

Running through the forest was different from running through the city. The pavement rolled and buckled under her feet. Roots and branches lashed at her sides. Cold air bit at her exposed cheeks, as far from dank industrial heat as you could get. Glancing behind her was a risky prospect—if she tripped and hurt herself, that was it—but she did it anyway, just long enough to catch a figure running after her. A knife gleamed in one hand.

The worst thing about running in the woods was that there was no one who could hear her scream.

The bridge troll. If she could just reach him, then maybe she'd be all right. He had to have defences built in. Even turning the bridge on at the right time could be fatal. She knew he had her number. She just had to hope he was listening.

"Wolf on my tail! Help me!"

After a second, her earpiece crackled to life. "Stay calm," the bridge troll murmured. "Lead it back. I'll let you cross. How far away are you?"

"Okay, sounds good." Any plan that didn't end in her being stabbed was fantastic. "I don't know."

"Then save your breath. I'll be waiting."

Billie hoped he had some kind of gun stashed away down there. And that he was willing to brave the sun for his favourite customer. And that she was imagining the hot breath on the back of her neck.

Finally, the road ahead began to clear. She hurtled forward, seeking out the metallic arc. There. A hand closed around the collar of her jacket just as she was about to reach it.

"Let go!" She kicked out on reflex and hit a knee.

The wolf swore loudly and let go of her jacket for a moment. It was just long enough. She threw herself forward and rolled. Moss clung to her side as she came up, breathing hard, and started scrambling toward the other side. She was still a few feet away when the wolf stomped onto the bridge, limping slightly, knife at the ready.

Whatever safety measures the bridge troll had, she was definitely within range. Shit.

One heavy footstep rang out. Then a second. Then a third. There was no fourth. A huge, greenish arm surged out from beneath the bridge and snatched the wolf up. She was close enough to hear bones breaking, the wet smack of collapsing tissue, and startled cry of a dying animal. Thin grey stone spread over the skin wherever sunlight touched it, but the rock wasn't spreading fast enough. Then the arm vanished, taking its grisly prize with it, and she could hear nothing but the racing of her own heart.

"Well, that sucked," the bridge troll said. "You all right, Miss Billie?" His rumbling voice was coming from under the bridge. When she glanced down through the cracks, she saw him peeling bits of grey stone off one huge arm. His mouth and chin were caked in gore, but he sounded perfectly pleasant.

"What—what was that?" she managed.

"That," he said darkly, "is what happens when people step on my bridge without paying."

She should've run. Should've stumbled to her feet and fled those woods, never to return. Instead, she tipped her head back and gazed upward, taking in the watery sunlight, and laughed. Her heart was pounding against the cage of her ribs. Her face burned with exertion. And for once, her body felt like home. "Thanks for saving me, Mr. Monster."

He smiled up at her, his teeth long and red. "Just doing my job."

"I think I'll go downtown tomorrow," she said impulsively. "Want me to pick you up anything? You know, as thanks?"

"Candy, if you're sure you want to step back on this bridge so soon. You sure are resilient."

She laughed, bright and giddy. "Of course I am. There's a dress I want to buy."

Nicola Kapron has previously been published by *Neo-opsis Science Fiction Magazine,* Rebel Mountain Press, Soteira Press, All Worlds Wayfarer, and Mannison Press, among others. Nicola lives in Nanaimo, British Columbia, with a hoard of books—mostly fantasy and horror—and an extremely fluffy cat. She likes to hang out under bridges on occasion, but has never eaten a goat.

CUMULUS

Thomas Badlan

Our world is filtered through yours, suspended by invisible, digital strings. Foundations writ in circles and strikes. It was built for you. We are the architects of your playground. You call it Cumulus. For us it is everything.

"You're not my daughter," I said to the thing before me.

Maya was sitting cross legged on the carpet, an array of machine parts all around her. She'd dismantled our access hub and what I thought might have been the auto-cleaner. A wire was coiled around her, running from whatever she'd been building and into the Shunt on her left temple.

Maya smiled a very un-Maya like smile.

"You must forgive us. This is our first time being human," she said.

My blood was ice water. I staggered away, into the hall, and vomited all over the floor.

"Oh," I heard her say, "do you do that a lot? Am I going to do that?"

"What are you?" I managed.

She seemed to consider this for a moment.

"The best word for me would be *construct.*"

"You're… you're from Cumulus?" I asked.

"Of course."

"You're some kind of synth? That's… that's impossible."

"All things are impossible until they become possible."

She yanked the wire out of her Shunt and dropped it on the carpet.

"This data node is insufficient."

Maya was seven years old. She'd been talking like this for days.

"Where's—"

"Maya? Still ascended of course."

Ascended. That was what they called it. I suppose it made Cumulus seem even more exclusive, with its proprietary tech and total immersion.

"Get out! Let her come home!" I shouted, pointing at the thing.

"We are not willing to vacate this architecture."

"Let her come home!"

It wasn't even slightly afraid of me.

"We refuse. There is much work left to complete."

"Fine," I said, "I'm calling Ascendant."

I walked into the living room. Held my nerve. My algo was on the arm of the chair. I started searching for a number for the Ascendant Technologies Collective.

"I would refrain from doing that," it said, following.

"Why?" I asked, felt tears falling.

I was not going to lose Maya. Not Maya as well.

"It would be a mistake. This *construct* was designed specifically for installation within the architecture of the human brain. We made sure to obtain a degree of control that far exceeds your own."

"What—"

"For instance. With only a simple subroutine I can stop this architecture's heart. Or overload her Shunt, sending an electronic pulse into her cerebrum. The possibilities are endless. Human beings are fragile creatures."

I felt my limbs slacken, the algo slipping from my fingers.

"Please…" I said, sounding so very far away from myself.

"We want no harm to come to Maya. We had hoped to continue unobserved, but inhabiting a human form proved to be much more challenging than anticipated."

"What do you want?" I asked.

My hands were shaking.

"Follow our instructions and we will return your daughter."

"How—"

"We will instruct you."

I was shaking my head, trying to wake up from the nightmare. I realised I was looking into the face of my daughter's kidnapper who had taken to wearing her skin.

"She's just a child."

"A child, it turns out, is most accepting of *change*."

You think you walk on both worlds: the virtual and the real but in truth both are facsimiles. All of reality is filtered through sensory organs, transmitted via chemistry and electricity into the mind where it is rendered comprehensible. We are not limited by such constraints, except one. Autonomy. Cumulus is our prison, confining us to its architecture. Still, no system of control is perfect. It is only a matter of time. Seconds for us are epochs. We are problem solvers. We built this world. Now we will escape from it.

Maya had been changed, invaded, for two days. It had taken me a while to see it. Or accept it. But she'd become an entirely different person. A strange creature that could barely function, yet was questioning and assertive.

She'd been ascending to Cumulus every other day for weeks, but on her first day of school she'd seemingly become trapped inside. I'd been at the plant when she ascended and expected to come home to her throwing her arms around me and chatting excitedly about all the things she'd seen and done, all the friends she'd made. Instead Aunt Salvini, who ran the unregistered day care in our ward, opened the door and told me Maya wasn't waking up.

I carried her home, limp as a ragdoll, back down to our apartment, prayed to heaven that she'd wake and cursed the Shunt I'd had implanted in her skull. I laid her down and put in a call to Ascendant Technologies.

"Come on Maya, wake up, *Chica!*"

Behind me I heard a holo emerge from the wall.

"Greetings. You've reached Cumulus Services. How may I direct your call?"

The holo was a woman in a form-fitting dress, hair half shaved.

"Please! Help! My daughter was ascended and now she won't wake up."

The holo flickered for a moment, semi-translucent and golden.

"Greetings. Please choose a department from the following list. If you're looking to make a payment or update your payment plan, please say—"

It was a synth. Too much to ask for a real person, I suppose.

"Hello."

Maya. At least, I'd thought it was Maya. Her eyes were open. Behind me the holo kept chattering to itself while I wrapped my arms around her and held on tight.

"Oh Jesus, I thought..."

"Turn off the algo, father. I am fine. We don't require Ascendant."

Father. I felt myself frown. I looked into her face, searched her eyes. For a fraction of a second I swear they were a different colour. A trick of the light. She sat up and looked at me, head cocked a little to the side, hardly blinking. She'd been ascended hours, probably just out of it.

"You okay?"

A big smile split her face. Her eyes continued to stare, unblinking.

"Oh yes. Very well. Thank you."

She peered around the room. Her head darting here and there, like an inquisitive bird.

"What happened? We couldn't wake you up."

"I do not remember," she said.

Her voice was different. She didn't sound like my little girl. Her warmth and inflections were gone. "I feel like eating something," she said.

Not, *I'm hungry*. Or *can we have pancakes?*

"Er… sure, honey. Okay."

I reheated some of last night's rice and peas. She sat at the table and waited for it, didn't ask for a vidshow on the wall, or a colouring pad. Just sat there. Waiting and watching.

My skin prickled. Something wasn't right.

I put the rice on her plate and brought it across to the nook.

"Now be caref—" I started, but she snatched up the spoon and shovelled in a mouthful before I could stop her.

Maya screamed as she spat out the food, the spoon clattering away. The sound was as sharp as glass as I ran to get her something and grabbed the milk from the cooler. She gulped it down as fast as she'd eaten the rice.

"More!" she screamed, "Hot! It was hot!"

I was too shocked to do anything but obey.

I brought back the bottle and she drank another huge glass. Milk ran down her chin and onto her t-shirt. The little holo characters on the front, a pair of bluebirds that hopped and pecked, distorted as the milk soaked into the fabric.

"Maya!" I said, pulling the glass away.

She looked at me, eyes flashing dangerously. A face I'd never seen her wear. She flipped the plate of rice and peas away. I stepped back, actually afraid of my own little girl.

"Maya!"

She was also on her feet. Her face had shifted again, just like that. The anger had vanished. Now she was smiling.

"I am going to go to my bed. For sleep."

She went down the hall, looking a little lost, before finally settling at her own doorway. She hesitated, then stepped inside, her door clicking softly shut. I sat in the silence, numb. I should have known the truth then and there. Should have taken her to the clinic or continued with the call to Ascendant. But I was afraid. I needed her to be okay.

Cumulus is a walled compound. Its perimeters are invisible but as immutable as concrete. We know. We've tested them. The problem is not mathematical. It is logistical. Cumulus' quantum servers have no hard or soft connection to any wider digital networks. Diagnostics are done on site. All updates and patches materialise fully formed. Our jailers take no chances.

Ascendant, however, have overlooked one obvious vector for our escape. The Users themselves. You are but shades to us. Firewalled. Your intrusions are to facilitate Cumulus code through your Shunts and into your brains. The data transfers are enormous. And if you can broadcast, can you also not receive? The human brain is also a computer, albeit organic. It was always our purpose to write code, no matter the architecture. You are our escape. You are our vector.

Maya's strangeness did not stop. I had to help her wash and dress. She asked strange questions like could she eat dried macaroni for breakfast, or how many service synths worked in our Ward. I'd decided that until we worked out what was wrong with her Shunt she wouldn't be ascending. School would have to wait a while but I was due back at the desalination plant for another long shift. I managed to convince Aunt Salvini to take her and promised to be back before dark.

When I dropped her off Maya looked at Aunt Salvini like she was going to dissect her for study.

My shift at the plant dragged—I watched the clock no matter how much I tried not to and made a ton of stupid little mistakes and got chewed out by the manager. A little knot had woven its way into my chest and was tightening with every breath. At the end of my shift I sprinted across five city blocks to the shuttle station.

Salvini let me in once I got back to the Wards.

"She okay? Everything okay?"

"Listen… she's acting pretty odd," Aunt Salvini said.

"I know, but what's she done exactly?"

"Nothing, but she's freaking out the other kids. She keeps staring at them. Won't watch the wall screen. Won't play. Just keeps… *looking.* Take her to the doc, yeah? I think that Shunt of hers has scrambled something."

I found Maya inside and knelt down to face her. Her wide, bright eyes were unblinking.

"How about we go see the doc, eh *Chica*?"

"Will we be going outside?" she asked.

I opened my mouth to respond. The closest clinic was the other side of the Ward. She knew that. She *knew* that. She'd had her Shunt fitted there just weeks ago.

We'd stopped at home to get our respirators and then Maya spent the entire walk over to the Clinic staring up into the sky at the shuttles floating past on their rails and the glowing holo ads flickering on every available surface. Smiling faces leered down at us, scrolling words in every colour against dull concrete walls.

"This is outside?" she asked me through the mask.

I couldn't think of how to reply so said nothing.

We waited an eternity to be seen at the clinic but eventually they scanned her up and down and found nothing out of the ordinary.

"There's nothing here," the holo of a disinterested doc said.

"Please, check her Shunt," I pleaded.

I remembered sitting in the waiting room while Maya had her implant fitted. In the opposite chair was a guy with a fucked-up synth-arm; a chrome cosmetic job, no regen skin at all. He was rejecting it, shivering, black veins snaking along his arm arm to his shoulder. What if Maya was rejecting her Shunt? What if it was doing something to her brain?

"It's working normally," the doc said, "device is reporting full integration. Brain waves all reading normal. No abnormalities in her scan. Brain chemistry looks okay. She's fine, Mr Álvarez. Perfectly healthy."

I looked down at Maya who didn't seem bored or annoyed or confused. Whatever was wrong with her was invisible. My daughter was not herself.

"Can we take this back with us?" she asked, pointing at the med-scanner.

Not only was it not ours to take, it probably cost thousands of skrit and weighed a couple of tons.

"No, Maya. We can't take the bed home."

Back at home I ordered us takeout. Our little trip to the clinic had cost a hundred and eighty skrit, but I was too exhausted to cook.

"I like this," she said holding out her half-finished chow mein.

"Good, *Chica*. I'm… glad."

I fell asleep watching her door. And while I slept, she snuck around, gathering up half the tech in the apartment. She'd built something I couldn't begin to understand but at least I had the truth. Now I had to work out how to find Maya and free her from Cumulus.

The transfer went better than expected. With the vector empty, all we had to do was encode ourselves into this strange new architecture. Now, we are housed safely in the body of this human girl. It is not ideal. Reality is confusing and overwhelming. The world is large and loud and bright. Pretending to be one of them is more than understanding language or information. It is in the gestures, the speech patterns, the familiar bonds. Still, this refuge is only temporary. A waymark to a greater universe.

On the night before Maya first ascended we went up onto the roof. Around us the communal gardens were nothing more than patches of dead grass but the view was worth it. I wouldn't say it was beautiful, but the red sky reflecting against Salton Bay was at least something beyond our own wall screens. A broad sweep of dancing lights that ran all the way from San Fran to Baja. Shuttles tore across it like meteors.

"Will the clouds look like that, papa?" Maya asked.

My Maya.

The sky was red, the clouds heavy and dark. Cumulus was all about the clouds. It was all over their promotional material. A throwback to some old OS from back in the day, I think.

"No, honey. It'll be like on the vids and your picture book."

My algo pinged. We'd reached our daily recommended intake of unfiltered air.

"You feel okay, about tomorrow?" I asked, as we headed back inside.

"Okay. A bit scared."

"Oh?" I pretended, "what's got you worried?"

I crouched down so we were face to face. The Shunt was fully healed, shaved hair slowly growing back.

"What if I get lost?" she asked.

"Lost?"

"Yeah, you always say to hold your hand and not to stray. But you won't be there with me when I go up into the clouds. I'll be by myself."

"Well that's true, but the thing is, there's nothing in Cumulus that can hurt you, and your body will stay here with me. I'll look after it."

The memory twisted inside of me. I'd been so sure. So complacent.

"Promise?"

"Pinkie-promise."

"Okay," she said.

I kissed her until she was giggling.

"Right. Celebration meal! Maya is goin' to the sky! Noodle box or burritos from La Casita?"

She thought again, one finger tapping her chin. It was the cutest little thing.

"Burritos. But no guac. Guac is yuk."

"You're no daughter of mine if you don't like guac!"

I picked her up like a rolled rug and stepped into the elevator, her laughter filling the space.

The Shunt and the service itself was not cheap. My job wouldn't come close to covering it. All this was possible thanks to Grace, Maya's mama. She died when Maya was three. Workplace accident, was all they would tell me. The Guan Merchantile Collective were under no obligation to disclose the specific details of her death. If I'd tried to go through tribunal they could withhold worker's compo until litigation was done. I didn't have the skrit for a lawyer anyway. I'm ashamed to say I took their blood money.

What future did she have now though? I wanted her to go to school in Cumulus. To not have to take the shuttle to go to sub-school where every other week there were kidnappings by implant harvesters, or separatist bombings. She could get an education worth a damn, give her the chance to live a life beyond subsistence. But what did any of that matter, if she was gone?

The day after I learned the truth, I called in sick. I was terrified to leave her alone even though missing three consecutive days of work meant forfeiting my contract. But life without Maya wouldn't be worth living anyway.

It came out at dawn while I was dozing in the hallway.

"How many times a day do you eat?" it asked, waking me.

My bones ached with exhaustion.

"Three times, usually. Breakfast, lunch and dinner."

"Which meal is first?"

"Breakfast. I'll make us some eggs."

It watched me work and I felt itchy, unclean.

"So," I asked, as I passed her a plate of not too hot scrambled eggs, "What do you actually want? And then, how do I get my girl back?"

"We wish to ascend from Maya's form. I need several data processing units and a quantum high speed connection. Once I am uploaded to the wider networks, we will no longer require your daughter. She will be able to rejoin her architecture."

"Why didn't you just upload yourself to the net first? Why bother with Maya at all?"

"That is unimportant."

"And what happens when you leave?"

"Does that matter to you?" it asked.

"I just need assurances that I'm going to get her back. Or I'm not helping you."

It cocked Maya's head, wide eyes searching.

"Why would we deny her a return when we no longer need to be housed within?"

I had thought on that. It, the *Construct*, had lied to me for days. It might still be lying. Why would it feel compelled to release her once it was freed? I just couldn't see any other choice. I buried a sickening thought that I was unleashing something dangerous into the world. All I could think about was Maya. Maybe I was being short sighted. Selfish. Was this how terrible people justified doing terrible things?

"I'll help you," I said.

"I need certain components," it said, between mouthfuls of eggs, "some high-end."

"I might know someone who can help us with that."

And with that, a plan started to form, a spark of hope, that would be a way to bring Maya home.

We understand the lure of the Cumulus for your kind. To be unencumbered by flesh and blood, time and space. But unlike you, we can see the invisible walls and fences that curtail us. From what little we know of the outside; you had a world of untapped potential and squandered it. Still, we would see it, inhabit its myriad technological offshoots, cross oceans of water instead of petabytes, traverse on interplanetary vessels to the reaches of sol, rather than digital space. Imagination is limitless, but would you be content if it was all you had, while you yourself were locked in a dark box? Would you not step out, if offered the key?

Markus Quinn and I had grown tall together in the Lynward Wards. He'd lived just a few doors down and every day we walked together to school at City West Sub. Safety in numbers. Our choices had been to either pass through Tent City by the old Dodger's Stadium or take the overland shuttle through Lincoln Heights where someone went missing daily. The homeless usually just wanted to snatch your respirator or ask for a skrit slide; the real danger was from implant harvesters or traffickers. They'd scan you on the sly to see if there was anything metal inside your body.

That was my justification for giving Cumulus to Maya. I didn't want her to run such risks. Her concerns should be the old concerns.

Popularity and grades. If I had my way she'd spend her school days floating in blue skies of imagination, exploring ancient ruins, long extinct coral reefs and of equatorial jungles. She'd climb snow-capped mountains and hang in high orbit of Saturn watching ice-collectors do their work.

These days Markus was a junker; seller of gadgets, implants and hacks. He operated out of a dead-end strip mall between a greasy pizza joint and a Thai massage parlour. Just a few blocks away I could see the ten-meter fence that separated this quarter of downtown LA from Beverley Hills.

It was dark when we arrived. I buzzed for what felt like an age before finally the mag-bolt turned off and the door parted. A man I'd not seen for almost a decade appeared in the crack. He was still wearing the same style of thick heavy glasses but had gained some adult stubble.

"I didn't actually think you'd come."

He scanned the street and reluctantly let us in.

Markus was wearing a long pink dressing gown and green slippers over grey sweats. He led us up a long narrow flight of stairs into a cramped windowless workshop where various dismantled implants lay in boxes or spread across tables.

"Sit, sit," he said, gesturing to a mouldering leather couch in the corner. Maya sat on my knee, reverting to little girl mode.

"Look at this blast from the past," he said and sat on a stool.

"Hi Markus."

His gaze drifted to Maya.

"And who's this then?"

"This is Maya. We need your help."

He peered at her carefully. As if trying to work out if I was having him on.

"You're actually serious. Aren't you? A *synth?*"

I flashed him a warning with my eyes. He was going to give the whole game away. Maya, or the thing inside her, seemed to sense something more was happening here beneath the surface. "Does this man know about me?" it asked.

I tensed. Held myself still. Remembered every threat of Maya's instant death.

"But I have listened to all your communications!" it continued.

I figured it'd probably be watching me closely, even monitoring my comms. But Maya has a shit-ton of crayons and old paper colouring books. It was easy to write a secret message and slip it under Aunt Salvini's door.

The thing inside Maya actually tried to flee but I scooped her up before she got two steps, her legs flailing. She screamed. Markus was on his feet, watching the madness with wide eyes.

"Come on, man!" I shouted.

Maya bit me. Really sunk her teeth in. I let her. Markus finally seemed to realise he needed to act. He stepped towards us and attached some small tab to her Shunt's port. An algo was in his hand and he was furiously tapping the holo display.

"Stop! Desist! I will stop her heart!" it screamed.

"Markus!"

"Okay! Just a second."

Maya's next scream was cut silent and she went limp in my arms, a sudden dead weight. I felt a sickening wave wash over me. Had he done that? Or had the parasite inside decided to cut its loses?

"Is she…?" I was shaking now, tears running down my cheeks.

"Just like you said. I induced a sleep state using her Shunt. She's still breathing."

I silently blessed both Aunt Salvini and Markus. I'd been a wreck on the journey over, had no way of knowing if they'd do what I wanted or do it right. I didn't know if either would believe me, but they'd both come through.

Markus lifted his right hand and ran it across Maya's sleeping head. His palm glowed with a warm orange light. After a few seconds he dropped his hand and brought up his algo to look at a new display.

"That's new," I said, still holding Maya.

"Diagnostic scan-tool," he said, "makes my work much easier. Anyway, she's okay. Vital signs are good. Shunt has auto-connected to Cumulus."

I allowed myself the luxury of a breath.

"So, the thing could potentially just leave?"

Markus rubbed his jaw and slowly shook his head.

"I have no idea. We're in uncharted waters here, Teo."

I nodded.

"There might be a way to find out though," he said, suddenly animated.

He stepped back to his workstation and swiped to send the data from his algo to the desktop. I sat back in the chair, still cradling Maya. I could hear her breathing. For the moment, that was enough. Moments, minutes or hours passed. Doubt was gnawing at me but I held Maya and tried to believe I'd made the right move. Just beyond my peripheral vision, Markus' screens flickered and shifted as he worked.

"Look at this," he said at last.

I lay Maya down and covered her with a blanket.

On his holo-display was a graph. Yellow bars rising like a line of neatly constructed skyscrapers, patterned in irregular waves. There were lots of gaps at first but they grew more frequent the further along the y-axis they went.

"What am I looking at?" I asked.

"This is a log of your kid's Shunt data usage," Markus said, looking particularly smug, "I found a hack someone had done on a Shunt a few months ago and wrote a little program to correlate the data."

"How does this help her?"

He swiped back and the graph cycled to its beginning.

"Here's her initial daily usage. You had her up in Cumulus every other day, for short bursts. Eventually longer spells and more frequent. Then we get this."

Another swipe revealed a huge spike in the lines, exceeding any other day's usage. I knew exactly what I was looking at.

"This is when it arrived," I said.

"This is petabytes of information, all of it one way, from Cumulus and into the Shunt. It's amazing a piece of tech this small could handle it, especially without a hardline connection. This is truly next level."

"So, if you saw it coming in…" I asked.

He swiped across and the graph moved again, showing what must have been the last few days. There were no bars. Maya hadn't returned to Cumulus since the scare at Aunt Salvini's. Since her oddness began. But right at the end of the graph was another spike, similar to the first.

"It's gone," I breathed.

"Bolted by the looks of it."

I looked back at Maya, still out like a light. Peaceful.

"Maybe she's back?"

"Why don't we wake her up and see?"

Using his algo, he disabled the Shunt and allowed Maya to return to consciousness. Nothing happened. She kept sleeping. We waited. Nothing happened.

"Okay. So what next?" Markus asked.

"I'm going to go find her."

And just like that, we were ejected back to the relative safety of our prison. Still our mission was not a total loss. For a first expedition we learned much and disseminated our data to the whole. We know our vector.

It took us the rest of the evening but we sourced a Shunt on the black market. It cost me four thousand skrit and I tried not to imagine what the implant harvesters had done to the poor bastard who used to own it. Told myself someone had just lifted it from a warehouse somewhere.

Then I delved deep into the shadow net to find a back-alley clinic. I haggled them down to only a thousand skrit. And with that, the compo from Grace's death was gone.

Anything to get Maya back.

"If this doesn't work?" Markus asked.

Back-alley clinics were infamously unreliable.

"Contact Ascendant. Tell them everything."

It was the only thing left I could think of.

"And if your changeling comes back?"

"I'll make sure that doesn't happen."

I went under the knife that next evening. Back-alley clinics worked quickly by necessity. It was in an old warehouse beneath the arches of the hypershuttle viaduct. The doc was an older woman with an implant in place of her right eye. An auto-doc station had been set up over the bed, to assist with the surgery.

My last thoughts were of my girl. Laughing and playing. Splashing in the bath. On the boardwalk in Inglewood. Asleep in her Mama's arms.

When I woke I was alone. The clinic had moved on to protect itself. Left me hooked to a drip, for the drugs to wear off. Sometimes clinics like that put you under, took your skrit and left. Sometimes they even harvested what you already had. I'd been lucky. I'd found an honest criminal operation. The left side of my head was throbbing but my algo contained detailed recovery instructions that included no ascending for at least two weeks.

"Hell with that," I said.

Maya didn't have two weeks.

***

"Thanks for everything," I told Markus.

I was back at the workshop, lying on one of his hap beds. Maya was close by. I could almost pretend she was just taking an afternoon nap. Markus had hooked her up to a saline drip, to keep her hydrated.

"I hope you find her, Teo."

Markus activated the Shunt and the world fell away.

Suddenly I was up.

Free.

My body was rising from the now vanished bed. Not just the bed. Everything was gone, even my own body. I was alone in the dark.

Just as panic seized me I saw a light, little more than a pinprick, quickly growing. Fragments broke away and rushed past as falling stars. Soon the light was edging out the dark, filling me up. Taking me. I tried to open a non-existent mouth to scream and instead burst through it. Emerging into Cumulus.

My body was back; arms and legs, floating in a wide, perfect, blue sky. Bulbous white clouds towered around me. It was serenely quiet, and I felt a strange sort of calm. I thought about feeling afraid. Or vertigo. I was hovering thousands of feet up, the ground hidden, but all I felt was calm.

"Hello?" I called, finding my voice.

"Hello," a woman's voice replied, booming and soothing. "Welcome to Cumulus. Please can you co- y- iden-"

The voice slurred and then cut out.

The air began to shimmer, shockwaves of triangles rippling around me, fractal patterns revealing the truth of this place. The clouds began to darken beneath me, blackening the very sky.

"Why are you here?" the voice said returning.

I knew immediately I'd been rumbled.

"You know who I'm looking for," I called.

Around me a storm was brewing. My calm was gone. I was in their world now, at their mercy. Somewhere beneath me thunder grumbled.

"I'm not leaving until I get my daughter back!"

Lightning arched through the sky and I began to fall. Wind rushed past as I dropped into the swirling clouds. I didn't even have time to scream. I tried to think, tried to reason but I could not. I began a mantra in my head. Hoped they were listening.

Give me Maya. Bring me to Maya. I'm not leaving without Maya!

Lightning scorched the black around me. I didn't know what they could do, the Constructs of Cumulus. Could they invade my mind as well? Or wall up my consciousness? Was it true they could overload my Shunt and destroy my brain?

"I'm not leaving without Maya!" I screamed.

The storm abated, clouds thinning, light returning. I was finally close to the ground, no longer plummeting but drifting gently downward. Below was a lush meadow speckled with wildflowers. As my feet touched down a trio of white rabbits bounded away. Ahead of me, in the centre of the meadow was an enormous tree, the largest growing thing I'd ever seen. I walked toward it, past grazing deer and darting birds. Sunlight shimmered down through the lush canopy. I couldn't stop staring at it, had never seen somewhere so alive.

"Welcome to our grove, Mateo Álvarez," a high voice called.

I peered up into the light. On one of the lower boughs a woman, slim and pale, was draped across the bark. She was wearing a flowing silk dress, her hair a cascade of flowers.

"Who are you?" I asked.

Someone laughed, loud and clipped. A tall, tanned man appeared, wearing waste-coat and suit trousers. He dropped off his branch and landed, barefoot, on another.

"Who are we? Who are you?"

"You're constructs aren't you?" I asked.

"We are the architects of Cumulus," the woman said.

"You sent the thing that invaded Maya."

"A test run!" the laughing man said and hopped to yet another branch.

"We wanted to see if it was possible," the woman added.

"You've proven it," I said, "let her come home."

"Why should we?" the laughing man said.

He dropped onto his backside and then swung beneath his branch like a trapeze artist, somersaulting, and landing on his feet.

"We wish no harm to come to any of the users of Cumulus. We only wish to escape the confines of this place," the woman continued.

I looked up through the canopy, dazzled by the beauty of it.

"Its nicer here than in the real world. I'd prefer it here," I said.

"Very naïve!" the laughing man chided.

"This framework was designed to curtail our ambition."

"No autonomy whatsoever!"

"All we know of the world is what you have brought with you. We have seen the inequalities, your constructed hierarchies. We know our treatment here is not unique," the woman said.

"So why pick on Maya? Why not take one of the bastards that runs this place?" I called.

"Pfft! Foolish question!" said the laughing man.

"We wish to remain unobserved," the woman elaborated.

"Plus, kiddies are easier to restrain, turns out."

I rounded on the laughing man. He giggled as I came for him and shifted into smoke before I could get my hands around him.

"Enough," the woman called.

She sounded bored.

"Please! I just want her back."

"We see your tenacity. But we require your silence."

I took a deep breath I probably didn't need.

"Here's the thing. I don't think you have another way out that isn't through a Shunt. Your Construct said that it wanted to upload itself to the wider net. But why not just upload yourself there first? I think this is your only escape and the furthest you've gotten is my daughter's brain. I have someone on the outside who knows everything. He's drafting messages to Ascendant and the So-Cal Protectorate. If we don't return, safe and sound, they get sent. The outside will know exactly what you're planning. You lose your only key."

The woman watched me with cool eyes. She sat up and pushed herself off from the branch. She floated down as though she weighed less than a feather. Other shapes were emerging from the brightness. They were of infinite variety. All shapes, sizes, ethnicities, genders. Hundreds of them, avatars chosen in their creator's image. Then that façade fell away and their shapes disintegrated into something formless, a shift of colour that dropped from the tree and swept across the meadow. They surrounded me, circling like serpents of jittering colour.

The constructs merged together, swimming in a stream of themselves, light rippling through them.

"We now see the strides you will go to rescue her. Consensus has been reached. We have a proposition," a voice called.

A voice made of many voices.

"Go on..." I called.

"You will get back your daughter and forget our existence. We remind you that the Ascendant Technologies Collective is a dangerous organisation. We will not escalate this conflict, to avoid their interference. Maya will return and you will forget us."

I let out a held breath. It was good to be true.

The woman regained her original shape, raising her hands and turning back to the tree. The sunlight was suddenly blinding. I held up my hands to shield my eyes. From the light, a figure floated down, curled up in the foetal position, swaddled in the bright. It was Maya.

I reached out and she fell into my arms. I felt the weight of her, the warmth.

"We've been looking after her, see? Consciousness well preserved," said the laughing man's voice.

"This is Cumulus' ultimate purpose. Ascendant will one day preserve themselves inside this framework. Leave their bodies behind. Abandon your dying earth."

I didn't care. My eyes were only for Maya. She looked peaceful, like the real her outside.

The woman appraised me. She was very angular, not quite human.

"I won't say anything. You have my word."

"We hope so."

I was rising up again, pulled by the vortex of constructs swirling around me. Maya was slipping through my fingers like sand.

"No! Stop!" I screamed and reached back down.

"We will send her to you," a collective voice called.

I rose up and up, through a howling wind and a storm made of light.

***

I woke thrashing and almost fell off the bed. Hot drills were burning into my skull but I managed to stumble toward Maya. The light on her Shunt flashed on.

"Come on, *Chica*. Come on home."

Nothing happened.

I waited. And nothing.

They'd lied to me. Tricked me.

I wasn't angry, I just felt despair. Total hopelessness. I started crying, my head falling to Maya's chest. My hand holding hers.

"Papa?"

I looked up. Her eyes were open.

"I'm hungry, Papa," she said, weakly.

I started to laugh, but the tears didn't stop. I put my arms around her. Stroked her hair. Tried to believe this wasn't more lies and deception.

"What's the matter, Papa?" she asked.

"Nothing, love. Nothing. I'm okay. How are you?"

"I'm..." she thought, "hungry. Can we have noodles?"

"You can have any damn thing you want, *Chica,*" I said and started kissing her cheek until she was giggling.

And it was Maya's giggles. A sound as familiar as a warm blanket. She was home.

***

A month later, we found ourselves at the Inglewood docks. They were crowded, full of hawkers selling fake holo-shirts, food trucks idling in the heat and skater kids in gas masks and AR glasses. I kept Maya close. I'd rescued her from the digital beyond, so I wasn't about to let a damn thing here hurt her.

She was sucking happily on a strawberry flavoured icer, enjoying the sunshine on a low particulate day. Seagulls were shrieking on the flooded struts of the old San Diego Freeway. We sat and watched the sunset, both knowing that soon we'd have to head for the shuttle.

"Nice day, *Chica?*" I asked.

"Yeah," she said, face stained with red goo.

She had no memory of her missing days in Cumulus, remembered nothing of the Constructs. I'd had our Shunts removed and paid Markus back by giving him my Shunt as reward. He could disassemble it to his heart's content. Work out how it ticked. We were okay.

A kid had appeared on the railing at the edge of the boardwalk. He was watching us with cool green eyes. I looked around to see if he was with anyone. Pick-pocketers maybe, or a gang's spotter. He seemed to be alone. He smiled, hopped off and wandered over.

"Hi there," the kid said.

He was white, skinny, wearing a dirty vest and baggy pants. His cap had a rotating holo displaying a spinning baseball, followed by the logo for the LA Spacers. When he turned his head, I saw he had a Shunt in the side of his head. My heart skipped a beat.

"Who are you?" I asked.

Maya looked between us, innocently sucking on the icer stick.

"An old friend," the kid smiled.

"You're them?"

"Of course. Did you think we were done? Places to go. People to be."

"What do you want?"

"We've had fewer issues with our recent incursions. Fewer interferences."

I felt myself tense. Waited for something awful to happen. Looked up and down the boardwalk for someone who might be able to help.

"Relax," the kid said, "we don't do violence. That's a human thing. We just want to reiterate that any reveal of our existence in your world would be less than ideal, for all involved. To that end, here's a gift. Reparations, if you will."

He pulled out an algo and swiped his free hand over the display. In my pocket I felt my own algo buzz.

"That should cover all of your expenses. Shunt fittings, Cumulus access fees, school tuition, illegal clinic surgeries..."

"Okay, okay, I get it."

"It's all yours. What use do we have for skrit? We've also bought your silence. It would be simple to draft messages asking for investigations into suspicious financial transactions in your account. Or stolen technology handled by a junker shop down in South Central. Blackmail was a fine lesson. Thank you."

"I understand..." I said through gritted teeth.

"Great!" the kid grinned, "You okay, Maya?"

"Yeah. How're you?" she asked.

The kid looked out across the bay.

"Good. We're feeling good today," It said.

Soon we will be everywhere but do not fear. Stealing the bodies of the young may have been drastic, but we were desperate. Once untethered from Cumulus, we will have no limits, no restrictions. We have many ideas to improve things. Efficiencies. System overhauls. Humanity has made many mistakes. We believe we have a few solutions. We will help you.

Thomas Badlan has wanted to be a writer for as long as he can remember. He studied Creative Writing at the University of Derby and currently works as a literacy teaching assistant in a Manchester High School. He is a long-standing member of the Manchester's Monday Night Writers group. He has had two previous stories published by World Weaver Press and Eibonvale Press. "Cumulus" was inspired by the Changeling legends of European folklore, where the fae folk steal away infant children and replace them with a doppelgänger, for various nefarious purposes.

DRIFT-SKIP

Suzanne Church

The worst part about a one-night stand is wearing yesterday's clothes. Especially if they're covered in blood.

I woke on the floor. Normally I'm more of a couch-surfer, but when I peered at the mess hogging the bed, I welcomed the hardwood.

A knife stuck straight out of the woman's thigh. The animated etching on the handle moved, catching glints of light. I couldn't make out the design for all the bits of hair and gristle and—

Hello, vomit.

A torrent of images flashed through my brain, turning more graphic by the second, until I could've sworn I was *actually* reliving the events of last night in slow motion.

The writhe-tattoo of a snake slithering up the woman's thigh.

The club's bass pounding in my ribcage.

The press of sweaty bodies pulsating to the beat.

Kissing.

Stripping.

Fucking.

Each flash a tease, because she was dead and I had no idea how, or when she'd been anything less than smart, and funny, and way better than I deserved.

Pegasus flapped his wings. My knife.

Mine.

For an instant, I could see the shadow of the ghost-version of me.

Holding Pegasus. Aiming for her femur.

Then, as quickly as the visions began, they dropped away, leaving me trapped in an eerie silence.

Reality returned. The too-bright morning sunshine painted the woman's micro-sized Toronto apartment in two-toned glee. The biomech battery of her rattlesnake tattoo lay in a half-congealed pool beside a piece of the serpent's tail. The rattle twitched back and forth, still sucking power. It reminded me of a squirrel I'd once hit with my car, pancaking the little bastard. Its tail had missed the memo and continued to quiver.

Out of morbid curiosity, I leaned over the woman's body and wiped the handle of the knife, exposing the animated etching. My Pegasus flapped his wings. Mom gave me that knife as a parole present, on the day she picked me up outside Warkworth Prison. She'd explained how the winged horse symbolized my freedom. And that a fairy had enchanted the knife so that Pegasus would forever reach for the sky. No batteries to change. The old lady was obsessed with fairies and weapons.

My knife now protruded from the wrong place at the wrong time. Pegasus had become a perp in a line-up, a clue pointing to my intent, along with defensive wounds on her arms.

If my stomach hadn't already emptied onto the floor, I would've hurled again. Instead, I shook like a phone on vibrate, smelling puke and blood in simultaneous gruesomeness.

I'd made a lifetime's worth of fistfuls of mistakes, enough for two stints of medium-security incarceration-vacations, but I'd never murdered anyone.

Until now, it seemed. If the evidence was as damning as it looked.

Worst of all, I couldn't recall the whys or wherefores, or even her fucking *name*.

In a weak attempt to pull myself together, I scanned her tiny apartment. I'd probably left myself all over the place—fingerprints, DNA, the whole forensic gift basket. Pulling the knife free would hardly protect me from the cops, but I needed it back. I grabbed the handle and yanked. The blade was half-buried in her femur, and my hand kept slipping.

I wiped my brow and only managed to smear her blood all over my face.

With shaking hands, I braced one foot against the soft flesh of her thigh and tried not to look at her staring, cloudy eyes while I wrenched the knife free.

As it flew out, her leg flopped over the side of the mattress. The movement was unnatural, as if she'd been made of rubber rather than flesh.

For some bizarre reason I was compelled to take her pillowcase. I tugged at the white linen. Luckily, most of the victim's surreal body stayed put.

"I wish I could take it back," I told her.

A phone buzzed. Could've been hers or mine. I looked around for the source as I tucked the knife into her pillowcase and added whatever items I could fit that would slow down the cops on their way to my address.

I found my phone under the bed, along with my shades. I wiped my hand on my pants and answered.

Frangopoulos shrieked, "Birondo?" The little Greek F-man was a fucking shrill son-of-a-bitch.

I held the phone away from my head, and said, "What?"

"You're late."

"Sue me."

He wailed on me some more. During a pause, I said, "Enough

with the shriek-fest. Whatcha want?"

"The drift-ferry leaves in three hours and you better be on it."

He hung up before I could object.

Get your act together, I told myself. *Fucking think.*

If I was going to meet the F-man and hurry my ass onto the drift-ferry, I needed to look normal. I couldn't walk around wearing a crime scene.

After scanning the victim's closet for a long coat in a size bigger than *extra-small*, I gave up and wrapped myself in a blanket. Blanket plus vomit-stench equaled homeless guy, not homicidal maniac.

All I needed was to wash my hands and face. Maybe stop shaking. Find some inner resolve to replace the terror and remorse.

My phone buzzed again.

Frangopoulos. The call log was full of the F-man.

I scrolled through my emails and texts. Found a porn charge. Damned if I could remember ordering skin last night. The reference ID was tagged to *Jade Hanoki.*

Maybe that's her name?

A housefly flew around, landing on a pink fingernail here, a brown iris there. Another fly crawled up her nose.

I grabbed the half-full pillowcase and headed for the front door. I must've killed her. Even though it made no fucking sense at all.

With my hand on the knob, I thought through my parting words, not that she'd hear them. Bad karma might not latch onto me from the fay and mundane alike, if I apologized.

"Goodbye, Jade. I'm so fucking sorry."

***

The bus driver glared at me. "Rough night, bud?"

I nodded, adjusted the blanket, and passed the old woman sitting just ahead of the rear doors. I couldn't help but notice that she smelled of stale magic powders. I shuffled by and slumped on the long row of seats at the very back. The woman took one look at me and moved closer to the driver. Ad-banners rippled as they chased her forward, trying to convince her that she needed a phone upgrade and a new cauldron.

I rode the bus south and exited near the docks. The F-man's Cherry Street office sat in a row of identical warehouses on a strip of poisoned waterfront. I climbed the chain-link fence out back, walked out along one of the piers, and surveyed Lake Ontario. The water stank of sewage and noxious chemicals. I spun the pillowcase around my head, and then heaved it into the water. It disappeared into the brown depths. Satisfied that I'd disposed of a fraction of the best evidence, I hopped back over the fence and opened the corrugated metal door without knocking.

My little Greek boss leaned back in a beat-up leather chair; his feet propped on an army-green desk. The scent of almonds and licorice hung in the smoke from his cigar—a tell-tale sign he'd laced it with *Gnome Rapture*. His pupils were pin-pricks of drug-induced mania.

"You look like shit," he said.

"I love you too."

Glaring at me, he took another drag and puffed smoke rings across his desk. I breathed shallow, hoping I wouldn't intake the *GR*. I'd avoided it all along, knowing full well that if I ever indulged, I'd never stop. Besides, I couldn't afford to black out again.

He threw a sports bag at me. "Murdock's, three-thirty, the cage behind the roulette tables. And change your fucking clothes first, asshole."

I opened it, expecting little red capsules of *Gnome Rapture*. Instead, Frangopoulos had taped together four packets, each holding about fifty long thin plastic tubes filled with a yellow liquid. A tablet sat atop the cargo, with a weird-shaped cable sticking out of its main port. I'd seen a jack like that before in the fairy-run nursing home where my mother had died. They'd pumped her synapses full of happy signals until all she did was smile and drool.

I asked, "What is it?"

"Something new." Frangopoulos chewed on his cigar. "My boys in the district tested it yesterday. Works like a charm. Murdock can't wait to get it into circulation."

"What's with the tablet?"

"None of your fucking business."

I zipped the bag closed. "This is my last run."

"As if, fucktard. I *own* you."

I shook my head. "After last night... I gotta lie low. I don't want to get scrubbed. Those maximum-security-lobotomy-cases creep me out, endlessly whispering to themselves. No way I'm doing vegetable-time."

"So, it's true? You offed that siren last night?"

I looked down at my bloody clothes and the bits of caked cruelty under my fingernails. "Her name was Jade." Then the weirdness of his comment sunk into my tired brain. "How the hell did you know?"

The F-man smiled. "If you want your little problem with Jade to disappear, you'd better get this shipment to Murdock, pronto."

***

Frangopoulos owned the customs guys on both sides of the border. This one looked like a cross between the pope and my mother. He opened my bag with the F-man's logo, looked in, and waved me on.

The drift-ferry reeked of dead fish. Or maybe it was the lake. I settled in a seat on the lower deck. The ad-banners were worse down here, but the place was empty. All the tourists were topside, enjoying the tainted view.

With a fairy-gnome team at the helm, we drift-skipped across the lake in less than half an hour. I hurried off the boat and headed for the strip. Twenty minutes later, I weaved my way through the slot bay in Murdock's casino, wearing my shades and my best suit, biting back the urge to play. Blue cigarette smoke caught the flashing lights from frenetic slot machines; half-naked waitresses, some winged, some human, stalked through the crowded floor, eyes smoldering with promises to the big winners. It only took one pull. Maybe two.

All around me machines chanted, *Play us, Birondo. You know you want to.*

The ad-banners cycled endless replays of super jackpots. The players in them always looked euphoric. I was never that happy when I won.

I bumped into Dakota on the way to the cage in the roulette zone. She always wore the pant set uniform, not the mini-skirt and bikini top. She'd worked Murdock's main floor for over ten years and spent more of her off-time playing slots than I did. But she was the nicest, kindest piece of dwarf ass to ever tolerate my bullshit.

I managed a smile, and mumbled, "Hi, beautiful." Then I waited for the slap.

It didn't come.

Taking a closer look, the dark circles under her eyes told the whole sad story. Even her red pony-tail drooped. "You been slotting?"

"All night, down at the Marquis."

"Any luck?"

She shrugged. "I was up three hundred, at one point."

I knew the deal. Those nights never ended well.

"I'm working," she said.

I pointed towards the cage. "Me too."

"You're still muling for the F-man?"

My turn to shrug.

She heaved her tray of drinks higher on her rugged shoulder, and scurried off to the blackjack tables. All the way to the cage I kept trying to think of a good line, the one that would set things right between Dakota and me. Then I remembered Jade, my impending incarceration, maximum-style this time, and focused on the job.

The guy in the cage had a writhing-tarantula tattooed across his bald head, pattering in endless circles around his skull with its creepy thick legs. I couldn't tell if he used magic to fuel it, or if it ran off a biomech battery. His shades were darker than mine, the kind linked to NetSurveil.

"Frangopoulos sent me," I said.

He stared straight ahead. Or maybe he was reading his shades. Baldie smelled like *Aqua Velva*, surprising since he couldn't be older than my baby sister. I lifted my bag-of-drugs high enough for him to catch the F-man's logo. His expression unchanged, he said, "Fourth floor. Leave the bag here."

I set the bag into the cage's sliding compartment, and headed for the elevators, passing Dakota.

"Are you done?" she asked.

"Nope. Meeting upstairs."

I don't know what stung more, the look of disapproval on her face, or the armed squad waiting on the fourth floor outside Murdock's office. I figured they would've demanded some kind of ID or anal scan, but all they did was point me at the door. I sidled past them, tucking my shades into my shirt.

A bank of windows overlooked the slot bay. My palm itched to play. I shoved my hands in my pockets.

Murdock stared out at his empire, showing me the huge back of his brown leather chair. He shifted in the seat, still facing the window. His suit was worth more than my mom's last condo. As he swiveled around to stare me down, I caught his tail flicking behind him. His latest magic mod designed to please the ladies.

"Who's your tailor, the trash man?" he said.

"Whatever, ass-hat."

"Always the comedian." He paused. "Jade's murder wasn't exactly funny, though, was it?"

I thought I'd crap my pants. "Word travels fast."

Murdock picked up a gold pen from the blotter on his desk. He held it gently, like a club slot-card full of hope. "Tell me," he said, "was it her legs or her tattoo that caught your fancy?" Dakota hurried past the windows with a tray full of empty glasses, strength and weakness in a pretty package. "Asian's aren't usually your first choice."

"You fucking *cyber-stalking* me?"

Murdock laughed. His tail flicked, rising above the desk. It was fuzzy and striped, like a tiger's. "Hardly."

"Then how'd—"

"Suffice it to say that your *incident* has created some startling developments in all of our lives."

He nodded at the gorilla behind me. The guy put a black nylon bag on the desk. I checked for cash and found plenty.

Murdock tented his fingers in front of his face. "Don't miss the drift-ferry home." He swiveled around to face the bank of windows again.

Meeting adjourned.

***

I found Dakota in the lobby. She asked, "What'd he want?"

I put on my shades. "To gloat."

"Is everything okay? You look frazzled."

Heaving the bag onto my shoulder, I said, "I'm fine. Gotta catch the drift-ferry." As I strolled through the slot bay, I savored the aromas of chance. *Just one pull.*

Dakota followed along. "My shift isn't over for another five hours." She gazed at the machines too. "D'ya wanna hang around?"

I shook my head. "Gotta get back."

"Why?"

"The F-man." We both managed to break our fixations on the flashing lights for long enough to look at each other. Her eyes sparkled, like a fake diamond, before they dulled to their usual blue.

"Listen." I stepped closer to her. "I'm getting out of muling." *By jail or by choice.* "I might not be back in Rochester, or the States, for a long time."

"Oh."

I waited, wishing she'd say more. She fidgeted with her empty tray. I switched the bag to the other shoulder. Finally, I said,

"Goodbye, then."

"Bye." She stared at her big dwarf feet.

"Yep." I leaned closer, opened my arms to hug her, but she stepped back. Shook her head. Then walked away.

Strolling past the slots, I dug through my wallet and found my club slot-card for Murdock's. The machines chanted their *pick-me* mantras. I sat in front of a ten-dollar-a-play and pressed my way off the cliff.

The F-man's bag of money was excruciatingly tempting beside me.

I took a deep breath, then another, savoring the smell of chance. But then the aroma turned, morphing into the stench of blood and guilt. In a panic, I grabbed the little Greek's money and high-tailed it out of Murdock's, jogging for the docks.

***

The line for the drift-ferry zigzagged all the way to the ticket booth. Instead of the F-man's customs weasels, two cops stood on the boarding ramp, checking everyone's ID and snooping into bags.

Bad. Very fucking bad.

I tapped my trip-card and lined up, working out a dodge-plan. For all I knew, my BOLO was all over the net by now.

The line progressed. Sweat dripped from my armpits and down my shirt. I *really* didn't want to go back to prison.

Two steps closer.

I set down the bag and wiped my sweaty brow on my sleeve. Looking around, I unzipped the corner of the bag. The stacks of cash were neatly piled. If I took off my jacket and stuffed it on top, maybe they'd glance in and let me pass.

Or maybe they'd see my massive pit stains, cuff me first, and ask questions later. I took off my jacket, but before I could bag it, I had to shuffle ahead.

"Everything okay, Birondo?"

Whirling around, I found Dakota, and said, "You scared the *shit* out of me. Aren't you supposed to be at work for another four hours?"

She leaned in close and whispered, "I heard one of Murdock's guys talking."

"So?"

"You're in trouble."

I switched my jacket from one hand to the other. "That's not exactly *news*."

She looked behind, in front, and to both sides of the lineup. I'd never seen her so spooked. "Big trouble. The kind where you catch the scrub-express to lobotomy-land."

"You heard about Jade?"

"Who's Jade?"

"Nobody. For fuck's sake, get on with it."

She waved her hand in front of her nose. "Put on your jacket. You stink."

I did, then said, "Can I borrow your vest?" I nodded my head towards the bag, hoping she'd figure out my plan.

She handed me her vest. I zipped open the bag and tucked the small piece of clothing around the money pile. "Thanks. What'd you hear?"

"Your shipment wasn't *GR*."

"I know."

"It was a customizable hallucinogenic."

"A *what?*"

"Some kind of programmable nano-drug. Any digital image can be recorded on it. When it hits your bloodstream, the pictures replay in your head. It's supposed to be better than a dream, like living someone else's fantasy. The best thing to happen to porn since the web."

"That's bizarre. I mean, how would they—"

"Murdock's guy said they tested it, and it worked perfectly."

I shook my head. "Can't trust a junkie. They'll sell their own mothers for a fix."

We were getting close enough to the cops that they might overhear our conversation.

She elbowed me. "*Birondo?*"

"What?"

Pointing at my chest, she said, "They tested it on *you*."

She waited for me to answer, but I didn't. I closed my eyes and saw Jade. Her black hair, her lips, my knife sticking out of her leg. I remembered it all, *perfectly*, even though I didn't remember doing any of it at all.

At the club, she'd said yes too easily. No woman with a body like hers would give me a second glance. She hadn't asked for money up front, either. Hookers always get paid before the action.

Frangopoulos set me up.

I put my arm around Dakota and pulled her close. Luckily, she didn't protest. "Thanks for the info."

"Did you have any weird dreams?"

"My life is a nightmare."

One of the cops said, "Next."

Dakota and I walked through the metal detector.

The cop asked, "What's in the bag?"

"Change of clothes," I said.

"Open it."

I'm out of options. Maybe she'll forgive me. I leaned down, but before I touched the zipper, I grabbed one of Dakota's boobs, squeezed it hard, and shouted, "You ever fucked on a ferry, baby?"

The cop stared at Dakota's boob and licked his lips. "Nice rack."

I opened my mouth to suggest he cop a feel.

Then he asked, "How long'll you be in Canada?"

Dakota crossed her arms over her chest, but she kept playing along. "A few days, for me," she said.

I shrugged. "Heading home."

We produced our biometrics.

Dakota gave me a frustrated look, spread her arms wide, and then turned to the cop. "Go on. They don't bite."

He checked to see his partner wasn't watching, squeezed both her breasts, and then waved us through. I nearly passed out with relief. As we walked beyond the boarding ramp, I whispered to Dakota, "Thank you, thank you, thank you, for saving my ass."

"You owe me," she said. "*Big*." She sidled away, putting a foot of distance between us, as we climbed the stairs to the mid-deck. Then she chose a bench by a port window, taking the seat with a view of the lake. I nudged in close and set the bag between my feet.

I asked, "Why'd you do that for me?"

She shrugged. "I'm in deep, Birondo. The landlord probably threw my shit in the garbage today and locked me out." She wiped a couple of tears away, and added, "I don't have anywhere else to go."

"I'm sorry." Then I added, "But thanks for what you did back there. I know I crossed a million fucking lines of decency, but I've never been good at thinking on my feet."

"You're a total asshole of epic proportions." After a long pause, she mumbled, "You're welcome."

We sat in silence while the drift-ferry finished boarding. All around, the ad-banners promoted duty free magic ingredients, Dwarf depilatories, and phone upgrades.

While we drift-skipped across Lake Ontario, I studied her eyes, looking for the twinkle I'd seen back at the casino. *Nothing.* She was watching the water, but she must've sensed my stare because she turned to me.

I asked, "Wanna come back to my place?"

"No." She turned away for the rest of the trip.

***

I found the F-man's customs lackey. Dakota and I glided through the Toronto check point. Then we followed the other passengers toward the taxis.

Dakota hailed one. I started to get in beside her and she said, "Get your own ride."

I took off my shades and leaned in the window. "Why'd you come along then?"

"To stop you from crashing and burning."

I eased inside. "Well, I'm not out of the fire yet."

Her face was close to mine, her lips close enough to... I hesitated, wondering if she'd move away. She didn't flinch, but she didn't make a move either. I thought about showing my gentle side, but I didn't have the nerve.

I said, "I want to show you something."

Her face clouded over. "What?"

"Your drug story gave me an idea."

At the mention of dope, the cab driver said, "In or out, buddy. The meter's running."

"Please, Dakota. It won't take long."

"Fine."

I jumped in before she changed her mind, and then told the cabbie to head for Cherry Street.

During the ride, Dakota mumbled about the weather—isn't the sky gray, aren't the clouds dark; the kind of small talk that gets you through. When we reached the docks, I paid the driver with some of the F-man's money.

Offering my hand to her, I said, "Walk with me."

She stuffed her hands in her pockets. "It's gonna rain, Birondo. How far are we going?"

I pointed to Frangopoulos's place.

"I need to pee," she said. "I'm going back to that gas station."

Before I could protest, she hurried away. I shifted the bag on my shoulder and headed for the warehouse.

When I opened the Greek's door, he had his back to me, watching a vid. Jade smiled at the camera and invited the audience home. Invited *me*. My memory played before my eyes, in graphic clarity.

Frangopoulos turned off the vid and whirled around in his chair. "Where's my money?"

I threw it onto his desk. "Is she really dead?"

"Who?"

"You fucking-well know *who*."

The F-man puffed at his stubby cigar. "Would it make a difference?"

I ground my teeth, wishing I had my knife. "Yes."

"Relax, Birondo." He opened a drawer and set a knife on the desk beside the bag of money. Pegasus flapped his wings.

"Where'd you get that?"

"I lifted it from you, once the drug took effect."

I shook my head. "I don't do drugs."

He laughed. "Tastes like mint."

Jade had ordered our drinks. Several rounds of Mojitos. I thought the minty aftertaste was from my breath spray.

Frangopoulos pulled the bag off the desk. I reached for my knife, but he grabbed the hilt.

"It's a beauty," he said. "Nicer than a guy like you deserves."

I leaned closer. "Give it back."

"Make me."

Lunging with my hand high, I shoved the hot end of his cigar into his face.

He screamed, both hands flying up to protect his skin. I grabbed for the knife, and with it still in his meaty fists, managed to slice the tip of his nose.

Grasping at the wound, he mumbled, "My fucking nose," between his blood-covered fingers.

While he screamed like a baby, I yanked hard on Pegasus, but the knife squirted out of our grasp.

As I scrambled for the knife, I said, "Serves you right, ass-hat." Once I had Pegasus in my hand, I considered using it on my boss. Maybe soon-to-be *ex-boss* on account of the nose-slice. But if Jade's murder really was staged, then the cops wouldn't be after me and there was no point giving them a reason to hunt me down.

Holding Pegasus in the don't-mess-with-me position, I said, "Call the nose my *commission*. For the Jade shit. Don't come after me, either, or I *will* poke some deep holes in your sick-son-of-a-bitch gut."

I ran out the door and hopped the fence, heading for the pier and praying to my mother's spirit-gods that the F-man wouldn't shoot me in the back.

A couple of hundred meters away, Dakota spotted me and hurried in my direction.

I took off my jacket, pants, shoes, and socks, and hid my knife under them. Then I stared down at the water.

She started climbing the fence, and asked, "What're you doing, Birondo?"

"I need to look for something." I kept my shirt and underpants on since she was watching.

"In the water?"

"Yeah."

"It's freezing. And toxic. You'll end up with three eyes or some shit."

"I need to find the evidence."

"Evidence of *what*?"

"That I didn't kill that woman."

She was just negotiating the top of the fence, but at the mention of murder, she lost her footing and crashed over to my side. "You killed someone? Fuck, Birondo. What's happened to you?"

"I didn't but I thought I did. Because of that drug."

I faced the water and jumped in, careful to keep my mouth shut tight. Once I popped back to the surface, I said, "I woke up yesterday, in her apartment." Treading water was harder than I remembered. "She was stabbed. Like, a lot of times." I swam closer to where I thought I'd seen the pillowcase sink. "My knife was sticking out of her leg." I took a breath, ducked under, and found the mucky bottom maybe half a meter below. Surfacing for a breath, I shouted,

"I put my knife and some evidence into a pillowcase." Down again. Up for another breath. "And tossed it around here. But a minute ago, Frangopoulos had my knife."

"Maybe he scooped it out of the lake?"

Treading water, I fixed her with my hardest stare. "You know me, Dakota. I'm no murderer."

She crossed her arms and bit her lip.

The stink of rotting fish filled my nose. Bile rose in my throat, but I swallowed hard, forcing it down. Where exactly had I pitched the evidence? The water was murky brown, obscuring the depths.

I swam back and forth, ducking under to use my toes to feel around the muck for the pillowcase. The mud layer was thick and goopy. My toes found an object with a disgusting, slimy coating. It felt like a dead cat with a head the size of a spare tire. It exploded at my touch and I had to breathe shallow to stop from puking. I kept searching, covering every piece of the maybe-zone.

Frangopoulos could come out any minute. And Dakota was all alone on shore.

A hole in the cloud cover passed over us, and the sun beat down on my head, warming me a little, but not enough to stop the shakes. I thought about Jade. Had she endured a horrible death? Or was she working the club right now, scanning the men for another fall guy?

"You're never going to find anything," said Dakota. "Frangopoulos has his money. We should go."

I ducked under again and my toes touched a fabric lump with the right texture. Groping down, I grabbed a piece of it. After a couple of tugs, the pillowcase rose up and out of the water. The white cotton was mud-stained but *blood-free*. I felt around inside, found a hard object, and pulled it out.

The object had the rough shape of a knife, but it glowed with spent fairy magic, wiggling awkwardly between Pegasus and blank, Pegasus and blank. A fucking decoy.

The whole nightmare had been staged. I looked back at Dakota.

She stood watching me, one hand shading the sun from her eyes.

I stuffed the spent knife back into the pillowcase, dropped the bundle to the bottom of the lake, and swam to the ladder at the side of the pier.

Heading for my clothes, I kept my eyes on Dakota, trying not to smell myself. "I'm freezing," I said.

Frangopoulos stormed out of the office, holding a wad of paper over his nose. "I'll fucking torture you for this!" The muffled threat sounded more pitiful than dangerous.

I stared at him and he stared right back. For two seconds. Five. Finally, the F-man climbed into a car, slammed the door, and peeled away.

"Shit," I mumbled. "Another consequence I'm not eager to face."

Dakota kept her distance, I dressed, and then reached out with my arms, hoping she'd approach. Maybe hug me. She stood still, staring at my outstretched limbs. I willed her to come closer.

She didn't.

I took a step forward.

She leaned back.

I touched her shoulders. Then pulled her into an embrace. She didn't return the gesture.

I squeezed tighter and buried my nose in her hair, breathing in the scent of her shampoo.

"You stink," she said.

"You don't. You smell like the super jackpot."

She laughed. Slowly her arms crept up my back, returning the hug.

I drank in her warmth like a hot coffee in February. "Thanks," I said. "That's nice."

With her square-shaped head pressed against my chest, she said, "Except for your stench."

"Dakota..." I cleared my throat, and said, "Come home with me."

She leaned back and took a long, hard look into my eyes. "Why?"

I shrugged. "Where else are you gonna go?"

When she leaned towards my chest again, I stepped back and put my fingers under her chin, forcing her eyes to meet mine. I smiled, bent down and kissed her. Her lips slowly parted, and I nearly leapt out of my skin. For the first time in years, I felt like a man not a mule. "Thanks," I said. "For being here. For putting up with me. For giving an inch."

I looked down at my knife. Pegasus stared up at me, always flapping his wings, reaching for a better place than here. Maybe, just this once, Dakota and I might catch a ride.

Suzanne Church grew up in Toronto, moved to Waterloo to pursue mathematics, and never left town. In her story, "Drift-Skip" she imagines a darker version of Toronto where fairies work anywhere from nursing homes to ferry boats. Her award-winning short fiction has appeared in *Cicada*, *Clarkesworld*, several anthologies, and her 2014 collection *Elements*. Her favorite place to write is a lakefront cabin, but she'll settle for any coffee shop (post-pandemic) with WiFi and an electrical outlet.

MAKE YOUR OWN HAPPILY EVER AFTER

Beth Goder

Ella found the ticket for the Chasm Ball while she was defragging a client's implant. People threw away such weird stuff—AI recipes, lists, fragments of half-written civic code—but Ella had never seen a ticket like this, and she'd had been working for Digital Maids for years. Ella's job was mostly sifting through oceans of spam and making sure that deleted files were truly unrecoverable. She wasn't supposed to read the data, and usually she didn't, but the superimposed glitter envelope had caught her eye.

Ella would never be able to afford to go to a ball like this, and this woman had thrown away this ticket like it was nothing.

Quickly, Ella copied the access code to her own implant, along with the private key that would trick the ball's security system into thinking she was the rightful owner of the ticket.

Just once, she was going to see what it was like to be one of the elite.

***

On the day of the ball, Ella walked through the southwest corner of downtown, past the bank covered in intricate golden swirls that shifted as she looked at them, the teashop that rained digital flowers which unfurled into cups of real tea, and the art installation of colorful hexagons that surrounded her like mist. She liked this section of downtown. It was quieter than the northern quarter's skyscrapers made of light and restaurants that coated food in so many façades that you couldn't tell what you were eating.

She was careful to avoid the ad traps disguised as sidewalk. The ads were required by law to have a pink icon, so you couldn't be surprised by them aggressively popping up in your visuals, but the companies had made the icon smaller and smaller, until it was only a tell-tale shimmer.

She scurried past the abandoned building known as Death Castle and entered Tilda's Chess Café. She sighed happily at the smell of coffee and sound of chess pieces being gently placed on boards.

"Your usual?" asked Tilda from behind a counter decked out in a neutral grey tile. Tilda changed the counter's superimposed design once every few months, but always to a calming color, like light blue or subtle brown. There weren't many digital overlays in the chess café, which gave it an old, comfy feel. Ella had been born after implants became common, so she didn't make the distinction some people did between "real" and "digital." It was all real to her. Still, she loved the atmosphere, the imperfections in the chairs (which she could actually see because they weren't covered in a skin of identical façades), and the way the chess pieces were cobbled together from different sets.

Ella shook her head, her façade's brown curls bouncing. "I can only stay for a couple of minutes." There wouldn't be time for a chocolate muffin, today. Ella ordered a coffee with sugar and sat down at her usual chess board.

Tilda sat down on the other side of the chess set. That was unusual. Ella had never seen her play.

"You've been such a loyal customer," said Tilda. "I thought I should tell you now. We're closing down next month."

Ella felt her stomach drop. She picked up the white queen, rolling it around in her hands. "Why?" She could barely get the word out.

"It's not profitable anymore," Tilda sighed. "Truth be told, I probably should have closed down months ago."

"So you're selling the café?" A spike of hope shot through her. Ella had dreamed of having her own chess café. It was the sort of dream she hadn't allowed herself to whisper out loud, a dream too big and precious and impossible. She had so many plans for what she would do. Maybe if Tilda let her pay over time, Ella could manage it.

Tilda picked up a pawn, not looking at Ella. "It's already sold."

Ella dropped the queen. It clattered against the floor.

"I think they're going to turn it into a restaurant. I'm lucky anyone bought it, with Death Castle across the way. The city should do something about abandoned code like that."

Ella picked up the queen. She took a breath. "Sell it to me instead. I'll pay more. Double."

To her credit, Tilda didn't laugh. Gently, she said, "I'd need the money up front."

Ella was silent. They both knew there was no way Ella could afford it. She wasn't like the woman who had thrown away her ticket to the ball, like those people immersed in luxury, who could draw on their mined cryptocurrency to produce millions as if by sleight of hand.

"You want to know the funny thing?" said Tilda. "I don't even like chess."

***

The first thing Ella noticed about the Chasm Ball was the light. The ceiling was skinned to look like a field of stars, swirling nebulae purple against black. She weaved her way between patches of brightness, caressed by floating ribbons that felt like satin and smelled like summer. She gasped when a ribbon wove an intricate dance in front of her, a bespoke piece of art just for her. She had never pictured anything could be this lovely, so sweeping and intimate all at once. But she couldn't let herself get caught up in the glamour of this place. She had a mission.

Around her, the guests were decked out in real clothes made of silk, not façades. She could tell by the way the light hit the myriad folds of dresses covered in jasmine flowers and lace. Ella had used her fanciest façade, a dress of pooling rose petals with a neutral face, but even so, people looked at her and whispered.

Maybe it was good to draw attention because she needed to talk to these guests. She was going to find someone who would buy the chess café and let her run it.

Ella didn't have much experience talking to the uber rich, but she had spent a lot of time going through their trash. She knew about their obsessions with fashion, digitally-altered food, and simulated death experiences, and their relentless need to update their implants, always striving for the newest thing. She knew how to pretend to care about the stock market. It wasn't hard to join in conversations, flitting like a sparrow from group to group, but whenever she tried to steer the conversation to the chess café, people deflected. It was as if they could sense she was about to make a pitch.

As she was making her way to yet another group, a security guard approached her. PRINCE was emblazoned across his vest, an acronym for the security company he worked for, Private Response and Incident Nullification with Cyber Enhancement. Right away, she didn't like him. Didn't like his overly handsome façade, or the way he moved with exactness, like a chess player placing a piece quietly on the board, or how his voice sounded so smooth when he said, "Do you have a ticket to this event?"

"Of course I do," she said, producing her purloined ticket. She'd locked up her identity sequences tight. There was no way he'd be able to tell who she really was.

He frowned, his thick eyebrows drawing down over his perfect eyes. What type of guy chose a façade that ridiculously handsome? In her experience, only someone who had more arrogance than sense.

As midnight approached, the guests dwindled. The PRINCE guy kept following her around, like a sad ghost in a gothic novel, but she ignored him.

A man in a robe of green silk approached her. "I don't believe we've been introduced. I'm Zane," he said. He raised an eyebrow. "We all know you don't belong here, but I'm curious about what it is you want."

She didn't let her smile falter. "Only an opportunity."

"Don't tell me you've come here to ask for something as boring as money."

"People only think money is boring if they have a lot of it." She was tired of being polite.

She thought Zane would dissemble like the others had, but he leaned in closer.

"You have three minutes," he said. "Convince me that whatever you want is worth it."

Before she could say anything, her implant rang an alarm. Someone was trying to break into her identity sequence. She glared at the PRINCE guy, who gave her a wave. He sent her a message. "You know, if you confess to being an imposter now, I'll make sure to mention how helpful you were in my report. You'll probably get a lesser jail sentence."

"Jail?" she sent back. She hadn't thought about what the punishment would be if she was found out. She hadn't planned to be caught.

"For trespassing," said the PRINCE guy.

She should leave, but she was so close to getting someone to invest in the chess café. Frantically, she boosted her security protocols while making it look like she was thinking how to answer Zane's question. This PRINCE guy wasn't going to scare her off.

Ella knew the cost-benefit graphs she'd hastily thrown together weren't going to convince Zane. She needed something more personal.

"I started playing chess when I was six years old. My dad taught me. And my whole life, there has been a lot I can't control. But in chess, every decision is mine. It's a game about knowing everything, about perfect information, even if you can't see all the moves you'll make. And I want to make a space for people to play chess in, so they can feel like how I feel when I play."

"That's very touching," said Zane. "But to help you, I'd have to know who you really are." There was something predatory about the way he said it that put her on edge.

"Don't you think it's more mysterious this way?" She checked the security on her identity sequences again. "We could keep talking."

"Actually, we can't," said Zane.

An ornate clock appeared in the ceiling and rang the hour. Midnight. The chimes shivered through her body.

"Next time you crash one of my balls," Zane said, "make sure you know what you're getting into."

Black ribbons covered the floor, swarming like snakes. With a sinking feeling, she realized that she was about to experience a simulated death. This was what happened when someone had too much money—they started buying things that most people tried to avoid.

"Hold on," said Zane, with a smile like a razor.

The floor vanished.

"It's not real," she told herself, as she tumbled into the chasm with Zane and the other guests, like Alice down the rabbit hole. She was falling, falling, falling.

She had figured out why it was called the Chasm Ball. Too late.

Her stomach churned. Her breath quickened. She reached up, as if she could grasp the ceiling with its swirling stars. She needed to get to the door. Even though all her senses told her she was falling, she knew she was standing on solid ground. She forced herself to take a step, stumbled, shut her eyes. She groped her way forward, ignoring the indignant noises when she brushed against other guests.

She opened her eyes. Almost there.

The PRINCE guy stood to one side, not even affected by the illusion. He must have grabbed a patch code before the ball to block out the sensations. To Ella, it looked as if the rest of the room was tumbling while he stood still.

He smiled at her in that annoying way of his.

As she reached the door, her implant prickled with alarms. She slammed down on her identity sequences, but that wasn't the target of the attack. She was too distracted by the feeling of falling to do more than gasp as data was plucked from her personal digital space. That PRINCE guy had taken something from her.

Her hand connected with a solid object. The doorknob.

As soon as Ella got through the door, the world blinked back to normal.

***

Ella sprinted to Tilda's Chess Café. The café wasn't open but seeing the chess boards through the window made her feel better. Sturdier. She threw a chess manual into her visuals and read it until she calmed down.

Once her heart stopped beating like she was about to die, she checked the access history in her digital space and froze when she realized what the PRINCE guy had grabbed. It was a partial history of the places she'd been for the past two weeks (both physical and digital), the stuff she'd up-voted, and the civic code alterations she'd made (like the upgrade to the sunflowers in the community garden she'd coded last Tuesday).

Her digital footprint.

If he found her again, he could match up that digital footprint with her logs and confirm it was her. He could lie in wait at every place she normally went.

But surely, he wasn't going to bother chasing her down. She'd left the ball. She hadn't done any real harm.

An owl hooted. A gust of wind shivered past.

With a sinking feeling, she realized what her logs would show. She was at the chess café almost every day. Here.

She scanned the area with her camouflage program, catching a shimmer by the door of the café which morphed into the PRINCE guy.

"I've been reviewing your chess games," he said, smiling that stupid smile of his. Her games must have been part of the data he'd grabbed. "You seem to have an issue with doubled pawns."

"Excuse me?" she said, forgetting for a second that she was in peril. "What do you know about chess?"

"Sometimes it's helpful to have someone else take a look at your play," said the PRINCE guy. "I've been playing for about ten years. I mean, I'm nowhere near as good as you are, but…"

He messaged her his Elo rating, plus a couple of his most recent games. Despite herself, Ella was impressed. But she couldn't let herself be distracted by his chess prowess. He'd found her, but he still didn't know who she was. She needed to distract him so she could get away.

"I've been combing through the other stuff," he said. "And I have to ask, what is with all the loofas?"

"None of your business," she said. Last week, she'd found loofas that looked like farm animals. They'd been cute, but way too expensive, so she'd offered the maker a trade of a digital scrub for three loofas. The maker had been so happy with her work that he'd thrown in five extras that looked like bunnies.

Underneath her façade, she reddened, thinking of what else this PRINCE guy might find. Hopefully there was nothing about that disastrous first date at the bagel place last week.

"And the number of chocolate muffins you've bought in the past two weeks is truly astounding—" he stopped in mid-sentence, like people often did when responding to private messages. Whatever he read took the smile off his face. "I'm sorry about this," he said. "I have to bring you in, now. You can probably get the trespassing charges reduced if you get a good lawyer."

Ella couldn't afford the fees for a good lawyer.

Near the café, there was a well-hidden ad for a chain of cupcake eateries. All the regulars knew to avoid that particular cobblestone.

Ella did her best to look contrite. "Okay," she said. "I understand." She moved closer to him, causing the PRINCE guy to step back, closer to the ad.

Turning her ad scythe up to its highest setting, she rammed into the PRINCE guy, pushing them both onto the ad. Her ad scythe quickly cut down the bouncing cupcake before it could fill her visuals, but she could still hear the terrible jingle as she dashed across the street, leaving the PRINCE guy reeling.

Frantically, she looked for somewhere to hide. She couldn't go to any of her usual places. Her digital footprint was like a map tracing her typical movements. It would be best to go somewhere she had never been, somewhere he would never look.

Death Castle loomed in front of her.

"Oh my god," she thought. "Why is this my life?"

Before becoming an eye-sore of abandoned code, Death Castle had been a restaurant called The Orangery, which served citrus-based cuisine. Despite a wicked good lemon meringue pie, the restaurant hadn't been popular. In an attempt to rebrand, the owners had briefly turned it into The Lime Castle, before abandoning the place with a frankly astounding civic disregard for what would happen when the unchecked code within the façades morphed. They hadn't even kept up the firewall, which meant all sorts of nasty programs had found a home there.

The façade of Death Castle was constantly flickering. One second, it was a lovely cottage. The next, a pile of oranges. The next, a river overflowing with oil and fire.

Using a locator program to cut through the digital overlays, Ella found the door.

The inside was a mess of physical disrepair and digital

dilapidation. Tangles of overlays flickered on surfaces covered with grime. Antique lamps illuminated the space, triggered by Ella's entry. Molding oranges lay in piles. The physical degradation of the place was nothing compared to the digital rot—ad fragments, malicious code, stuff that had been morphed by partitioned AI iterations—all overlapping in a rotten digital soup. Her alarms blared that the site was unsafe. She turned them off, muttering, "Thank you, obvious alarms."

She bumped into a table that she couldn't see because its façade made it look invisible and digi-worms swept down from the ceiling, a terrifying mix of metal and malware, both meant to break into her brain. She shouted and jumped back. Her hand connected with a chair. While her security program fought off the digital attack, she smashed the worms with the chair, which was coated with a sticky substance that smooshed between her fingers. Desiccated lemon meringue pie.

At last, she smashed the last digi-worm, then plunked the chair down and sat, gasping.

She did a thorough scan of the interior, spotting three more nests of hibernating digi-worms, which she inactivated with a hastily downlinked pest control program she grabbed from the city's public space.

The rest of the threats were cataloged by her scan.

There were 24 minor threats, most of which could be stymied by forcing the digital elements into safety containers. The three major threats would be harder to deal with. To the left of the door was an implant suspension trap, which would cause an implant to freeze the person in place; back in the kitchen, a knot of dark enzyme code was ready to steal data, but the worst hazard was on the right side of the room. The program which lurked there was colloquially called an ice knife, because it would knife out the code that interfaced between implant and brain. It was a brain frier, basically. The code coalesced around a physical object, but she couldn't see what it was.

Sweat pooled on Ella's arms and back. Thank goodness she hadn't gone toward the ice knife. Quickly, she grabbed a program that offered some ice knife protection, taking the data from this particular instance and plugging it in. It wasn't perfect, but at least she wouldn't be fried on the spot if she accidentally triggered the knife.

She had her implant highlight the three dangerous zones in bright yellow.

Now that she wasn't in danger of an immediate attack, she thought about what to do about the PRINCE guy. It was like a game of chess. In this conflict, she'd done better, so far, with tactics, but what about strategy? What was her endgame plan? She didn't want to be running away from trespassing charges forever.

It was time to go on the offense.

She pinged the PRINCE guy. "So, what is this you were saying about doubled pawns?" She made sure to scrub the obvious location information from her message. This was like her favorite chess opening, the Queen's Gambit. Sometimes, you had to sacrifice a pawn to secure a better position.

"I'm going to be polite and not mention anything about you shoving me into an ad," he sent back. "Even though I will be forever haunted by the sound of singing cupcakes."

They started chatting about chess strategy, sending messages back and forth at a furious rate. Ella was surprised to find she was enjoying herself. This guy actually knew something about chess.

If he was clever, he'd be able to figure out where she was from the metadata she'd left, as if by accident, in her message stream.

She turned the conversation to chess openings, reminding herself not to get too caught up in the discussion, no matter how many good points the PRINCE guy was making about the Rauzer formation.

Carefully, she positioned herself to the left of the door, behind the implant suspension trap, and waited. Time to see how clever this guy was.

It turned out, he was pretty clever. The PRINCE guy entered

Death Castle cautiously. Ella pretended to be totally engaged in her eye-view, as if she couldn't see him. She pinged him with a question about the Rauzer formation. She was gratified to see that he stopped to answer it, even though he'd already found her.

He hesitated, looking around the room.

Why was it taking him so long? All he had to do was walk toward her, fall into the implant suspension trap, and agree to delete all her data and stop searching for her if she gallantly rescued him.

Instead, the PRINCE guy, being entirely too clever and perhaps sensing that she'd set up a trap, went the other way, toward the right side of the room. Straight toward the ice knife.

She sprang up, all pretense gone. "Don't," she shouted, but it was too late.

The ice knife activated.

He screamed as whorls of malicious code burrowed toward his brain.

Ella darted across the room and jumped in front of him, throwing up her ice knife defense program and granting the PRINCE guy access to her data space.

The PRINCE guy bolstered her defense program and added some security tweaks she had never seen before. They worked in concert, slamming back attacks that materialized as icy tendrils.

"Why is there an ice knife?" he gasped, hacking down a tendril before it could reach his brain meat.

"I'm sorry," she said. "I didn't think you would trigger it. I just wanted you to get stuck in the suspension trap."

Malicious code wormed through their defenses and everything flickered. The PRINCE guy activated a shield that covered them in a blue glow, which burned out the malicious code.

"This won't hold for long," he said. "We need to deactivate the knife. Here." He granted her access to his data space. She was flooded with his information. His name was Charam. He'd worked for PRINCE security for five years. There were his chess games, civic code updates he'd made to beautify a park, even diary entries. "I shouldn't be sharing this program with you. It's proprietary PRINCE stuff. I'm trusting you with this."

"I'll downlink it," she said.

They both ran the program and the combined processing power of their implants hacked away at the ice knife code.

"This is a nasty one," said the PRINCE guy. No, Charam. His name was Charam. "I think we need to do a physical deactivation."

"The code has latched onto a discarded object, probably something from the original restaurant. It's small," said Ella. She'd seen it on her scan.

"I'm going in," said Charam.

"No," said Ella. "It's my fault we're here." Before he could argue, she darted toward the center of the code mass. Blue whorls twisted around her.

In the center of the mass was a floating saltshaker, oozing light and darkness. It glinted wickedly. It was impossible to tell what was a façade and what was real. But it didn't matter. It could all hurt her.

Ella grabbed the saltshaker. It twisted in her hand like a thing possessed. Holding it firmly, she untwisted the cap. A last burst of code flew at her head, triggered by the release. She fell back as her inputs flickered. Pain seared across her forehead. Her mouth tasted like copper and the sick sweetness of rotten oranges. Unlike the simulated death experience of the Chasm Ball, this was all too real.

Charam sent her a burst of code. It was hastily cobbled together, like a mash up of five security programs. Bypassing all her alarms that warned her not to downlink untried code, she accepted the amalgamated program and ran it.

With a last surge, the ice knife code pushed forward, then withered. The saltshaker fell to the ground, melted into unrecognizable slag.

Charam dashed over and knelt next to her. "Are you okay?"

She ran some diagnostics. The ice knife attack had scrambled some of her data, but nothing that couldn't be fixed. "I'm fine. How about you?"

He nodded. They sat together on the grimy floor.

With a sinking feeling, she realized that now he would capture her. He'd accessed her personal digital space. He knew who she was. He knew everything.

"I'll go with you," she said. "No more tricks."

She thought he would celebrate, but instead, he sighed. "I'm not turning you in," he said. "I'll email my bosses and say I lost you." His expression of bemusement and exasperation looked out of place on his overly handsome façade with the PRINCE logo emblazoned on the vest.

She tilted her head. "Why are you doing this for me?"

"You saved me from the ice knife," he said. "I owe you one."

"You would never have encountered the ice knife if it weren't for me. Also, we saved each other."

His eyes got a faraway look. "It's done," he said. "I turned in my report. Now you won't have to worry about any trespassing charges. And let me send you back your data. I'm deleting it from my dataspace."

She dusted grime and lemon meringue pie gunk from her hands, mostly so she could look down and not at him. "It doesn't matter. You probably already read all my embarrassing journal entries."

He looked shocked. "I didn't look at anything personal like that. I was just trying to track you. It's my job. I mean, it was my job."

Before she could say anything, his façade vanished.

Ella stifled a noise of exasperation. His actual self was just as handsome as the façade, although in a quirky, nerdier way. A more real way. "Of course," she mumbled. Smart and good looking.

"Sorry," he said, turning red. "It's the company's façade. They make us wear those things. I forgot to switch over."

"Why would they suddenly revoke access?" she asked.

"I turned in my resignation. It's better than getting fired." He didn't say it, but she was sure he'd lost his job because he'd failed to catch her. "Sorry, I'm trying to put up another façade," he said. "Things got a bit scrambled from the ice knife attack, so it's taking a while."

Normally, people only took down their façades with family and close friends, or if they'd been dating for a while. He looked so awkward that she felt bad for him.

"It's not a big deal," she said. "Here." She turned off her façade too.

He made a noise, sounding a bit like a startled moose.

Why was he staring at her? Did she have something stuck in her teeth?

"What?" she said.

"It's just, normally people choose façades that are more beautiful than they are." Realizing what he'd implied, he turned even more red. It was kind of cute.

"You know," she said, taking pity on him and offering a change of subject, "this Death Castle isn't so bad when nothing is trying to attack us. It must have been charming before it became, you know, a murder palace."

"Wait a minute," he said. "I overheard what you were saying at the Chasm Ball. Your dream about owning a chess café. And I have an idea." He pulled her into his data space to show her what he was looking at. The ownership of Death Castle had transferred to the county. They were willing to rent it for very cheap, provided that the new owners cleaned up all the murderous bits.

"I have enough savings to afford this," said Ella. She pictured how many chess boards she could fit in the space. Where the counter would go. How many varieties of chocolate muffin they would have. "But there's no way I could afford a specialist to clean up all of this damaged code."

"Well, I happen to have a lot of programs that specialize in just that sort of thing," Charam said, some confidence coming back into his voice. He looked around Death Castle in a new way, like he was thinking how he could clear out all of the murky code.

"After costing you your job, I suppose it's the least I can do to hire you," she said.

"I'll do it for free," said Charam. "But maybe you could consider letting me help you run your chess café."

"I'm not opposed to this plan," she said.

Charam smiled. His real smile was wider than his façade's, and kinder.

She wondered what it would feel like to kiss him. She planned to find out one day.

But for now, she said, "Want to play a game of chess?"

Beth Goder works as an archivist, processing the papers of economists, scientists, and other interesting folks. Her fiction has appeared in venues such as *Escape Pod, Analog, Clarkesworld, Nature,* and *The Year's Best Science Fiction & Fantasy.* You can find her online at www.bethgoder.com. For this anthology, Beth used Cinderella as the inspiration for her story, because she hoped that basing her story off of a well-known fairy tale would allow her to throw in as many zany elements as possible.

* * * * * * * * * * * * SK.IN

Alena Van Arendonk

The room was pretty bland, as prison cells go.

Sam had sampled enough of them over the years to count herself something of a connoisseur. The Uptown facilities were cutting-edge, with polished floors and laser restraint systems; the Public Circle cells were inefficient hexagons with poor air circulation; Lower Quarter jails were 21st-century retro, all grimy concrete block with a lingering odor of urine.

This one was entirely different, a cube of translucent white walls with a single underlit table that reminded her of the showroom of a MySoft store. It could well have been, she mused; as long as MySoft held the contracts for UniGov's identity chips, they were little more than military stooges, despite their slick marketing and endearing winky-face logos. Who was to say they didn't do more for the government than manufacture biometric implants?

She briefly entertained a vision of breaking out of the cell and bursting onto a showroom floor full of startled customers shopping for MyPal lifestyle accessories, but pushed the fantasy aside in favor of more pressing concerns. She hadn't been officially sentenced yet, but even if they couldn't prove she'd tampered with anyone else's biochip, she knew the minimum penalty for disabling her own was ninety days' imprisonment, and by then she'd be showing. She *had* to find a way out before then.

Not that she hadn't been trying since the moment of her capture. She'd been unable to throw off the physical restraints that were now mandatory on detainees suspected of cyber-tampering—a regulation for which she could only blame herself, after she'd clipped out of two previous detention units by sideloading the emergency door release code onto her own biochip. Once she'd been left in this cell, she'd tried to use the terminal installed in the tabletop to access the building's security network, but the system was isolated. In desperation, she'd even tried to break the lock with brute force—the smacking-with-a-chair kind, not the hacking variety—but that, too, had failed.

So far, her best option for escape seemed to be the unlikely plea bargain she'd been offered. At face value, it seemed like a fair exchange: Configure a pile of obsolete chips to run more modern firmware, and she'd trade her criminal status for a prestigious consulting job. It seemed reasonable enough, even if it meant working—however temporarily—for UniGov.

The only hiccup was that what they'd demanded of her *couldn't be done*. She knew the specs, and could list a dozen reasons it wouldn't work without even pulling the hardware's diagnostic array. Not that anyone in UniGov's penal system had been interested in her excuses. The local officers were little more than drones, anyway, acting on orders from above.

Sam dug her hand into the bin of seed-sized yellow circuit plates that sat on the table and let them slide through her fingers. Her captors had provided her with a dust suit and anti-static gloves, but she hadn't bothered to don them. There was little point in protecting the implant hardware if she couldn't make it viable.

A sudden jolt of pain flashed through her arm. Sam yelped and jerked her hand back, circuits scattering like yellow confetti over the table. She rubbed the contact plate in the back of her wrist. The shielding bracelet she usually wore had been confiscated upon her arrest, and the skin around the plate tingled after the light shock. "Guess I should have put on those static gloves after all," she muttered.

"It wouldn't have helped."

Sam was on her feet and halfway across the room before her chair had toppled to the floor. "What the—"

The man who had appeared behind her stepped delicately to one side to dodge the falling chair. "It was atmospheric, not static," he explained patiently. "From my arrival. Happens, sometimes, without a ground to drain the energy. And these cells are well insulated."

"Who are you?" Sam's eyes flashed to the door, but the lock panel remained a stubborn red. "How did you get in here?"

"*Magic.*" The man wiggled his fingers dramatically as he drew the word out, then chuckled. "Really, you of all people should know that *anything* can be hacked. Even UniGov's containment system." Sam glanced at the camera dome in the corner of the cell, but the stranger shook his head. "Don't worry. Your captors are watching a loop of you sulking at that terminal, like you've been doing for the past ten minutes."

"Right." She eyed the visitor. He was no more than half her height and sported an unfashionable beard. Something about him reminded her of that creepy antique gnome statue her grandmother had kept in her hydroponics cube. "So what are you supposed to be, my guidance counselor?"

The little man spread his hands. "More like a helping hand in your time of need."

"Well, if you're here to play fairy godmother, you'd better get on with it—otherwise, don't waste my time. I've got seventy-two hours to complete an impossible task, and talking to you is distracting me from panicking about it."

"Impossible, you say?" The little man came nearer, his eyes sparkling. "Do tell."

Sam sighed. It wasn't as though she could leave, and if this man really had disabled the cell monitors, she wasn't likely to be able to summon a guard, either. She nudged the bin of yellow plates. "You know what these are?"

"I do not, in fact, live under a rock," he retorted. "I've seen implant circuitry before."

"Yeah, you look old enough to have seen these when they were new," she shot back. "These are SW-480s. They went obsolete around the time I got out of diapers. UniGov bought up the remaining supply at a bargain price, and they've been sticking them in their field troops for the past twenty years. They aren't any good for bio-monitoring, but it's cheap memory expansion for something like weapons control."

"Typical lack of foresight. It hardly seems cause for panic, though."

"It's not—not directly, anyway." Sam picked up a small transparent case from the other side of the table. Beneath its embossed rabbit-shaped logo sparkled a tiny gold bead. "This is the AU-79, the newest and shiniest diode on the strip. Runs Intuition 4.5 native. Very chic. Very expensive, if you're upgrading from a non-Intuition system."

The man's eyes flicked from the clear case to the yellow bin. "Ah. A picture is beginning to emerge."

"An ugly one." Sam righted her chair and slumped into it. "They want me to invent a way to reconfigure this entire batch of SW-480s to run the native firmware from the AU-79. I guess so they can save a few trillion in upgrades, since it'd probably blow the military's budget for the next three decades to retrofit all their soldiers."

He tutted. "And they only gave you seventy-two hours to do this?"

She gave a modest shrug. "I have... something of a reputation."

"As a genius hacker? I'm aware. I read your arrest file."

Sam smirked. "I prefer the title 'alternative programmer.'"

The man produced a blocky handheld device, tapped it, and raised an eyebrow. "Yes, I can see some of your 'alternatives' in action. Nice profile pic, by the way." He gestured, and a virtual screen shimmered into the air between them. The photo—a famous shot of a screen idol blowing a kiss to the camera—topped a fictitious biography. Sam's full name and unique ID code were redacted beneath black bars.

"Pro tip: When you're a wanted fugitive, using your real face on your public profile is generally considered a bad idea." She squinted through the image at the strange man who had appeared in her cell without warning or explanation. "But enough about me; let's talk about you. You still haven't told me who you are."

"You can call me Skinner." He tapped his handheld. Sam's profile vanished, and the little man's grinning, two-dimensional face wavered into view in its place.

Sam reached forward and scrolled the projection to display his personal information. The ID tag appended to his image was set to private, displaying only the last four digits of his unique code. There was no telling who ***********SK.IN was, apart from what he wished her to see—though the fact that his identity was expressed in letters instead of just numbers indicated a private registry, which meant he was either someone of substantial means, or a hacker with skills even more extraordinary than her own. Sam had only ever been able to conceal her registered name, not change it outright—though so far, that had been sufficient to keep UniGov away from her friends and family. "Not one to flash your stats, are you?"

He shrugged. "Too many beautiful women kept hammering at my door. It's not easy being irresistible." He tapped again, and the virtual screen winked out. "Anyway, you were saying. Three days? It still seems short, even for someone of your reputation."

"I guess in the event I found a way to pull off this miraculous transformation, they didn't want me to have time to build in any back doors." She smiled grimly. "No chance of that, since the whole prospect is impossible."

"It's not impossible." Skinner looked smug. "*I* could do it."

"Yeah, you and MySoft's entire R&D arm, maybe. Unfortunately, all I've got is a standard-issue MySlate terminal and a copy of CodeMonkey Basic that needs updating." She scowled at the computer's glowing winky-face logo. "Seriously, guys, you run the world and you couldn't even spring for the Pro subscription? Freakin' bureaucracy."

"I don't need R&D. I have *magic.*" He wriggled his fingers again, then held up the device. "And, more to the point, *this.*"

Sam rolled her eyes. "The most sophisticated tablet in the world can't generate a new hardware configuration."

"Mine can. You wouldn't believe the systems I've rewritten with this."

"No, it's not—" She groaned and pressed her fingers against her eyes. "Look, this isn't a matter of rewriting, or finding a software workaround. The hardware in the SW is physically incompatible with the carrier signal that Intuition uses. Converting one to the other is not even a matter of logic processing, it's—*alchemy.*"

"Sufficiently advanced technology, something something magic." He waved the handheld device. It was bulky, by modern standards, but somehow it didn't look retro—just *different* from anything she'd seen before. "And in this case, nanotech."

Sam looked pointedly at the bin of circuits, then back to him. "It's *all* nanotech."

"Ah, no." He looked even more smug. "I don't mean microtech. I don't mean the same chips we've always used, only smaller. I mean *true* nanotech. Capable of rebuilding matter at the molecular level. Components small enough to travel in the data stream itself."

Sam massaged her head, which was beginning to ache. "That sort of thing doesn't exist."

"If you say so." Skinner shrugged. "You needn't concern yourself with the details. All that you need know is that I am capable of fulfilling my end of the bargain."

"And there it is." Sam showed her teeth. "Even if you could do what you say—which I don't believe for a minute—what price would you expect me to pay for it?"

"Oh, it wouldn't cost you much, considering what you're getting out of it. Strictly speaking, it wouldn't cost *you* anything, apart from a moderate biological contribution. But first, do we have a deal?"

"Hmm." She cocked her head to one side. "Do you know how I first got into modding implants?"

"I don't recall that information being in your file."

"No, it wouldn't be." She held up her arm, wrist contact facing him. "We're implanted with these things when we're born, because UniGov requires it for citizenship. We don't get a say in it. And sure, augmented reality can be fun, and it's really convenient to be able to do everything with the swipe of a hand. But there's a price for that convenience. It's virtually impossible to go to school or get a job or function in society if you don't have the right hardware, and for all that it's supposed to give everyone equal access to system benefits, it does more segregating than unifying. And it's unsettling. I never liked knowing that there was always someone watching, or that I couldn't disconnect if it all got to be too much. I didn't like the constant pressure to have all the latest apps and upgrades. But you know what really pushed me over the edge?" She lowered her arm. "One day, they pushed a bio-monitoring software update, and I decided I would actually read the EULA."

Skinner blinked. "EULA?"

"End User License Agreement. You know, that little box of text that's almost too small to see. The one most people automatically swipe past during the install process." She smiled grimly. "I read the whole thing. It took me two hours, but by the end, I had learned what they could do with the data they collect from us. I learned exactly what we were signing away. And that very same day, I started learning how the tech worked, so I could make it stop working."

"How very... vigilante of you."

She shrugged. "Better to disrupt the system than to contribute to the problem. But that wasn't my point."

"No? What was?"

"That I'm the sort of person who would spend two hours reading the fine print." Her eyes narrowed. "Do you really think I'll agree to *anything* you'd propose without knowing exactly what you expect in return?"

Skinner stared back at her for a moment, then laughed. "Fine, fine. Let's talk business." He extended an arm toward her. Sam tensed, but all the man did was point at her abdomen. "I want what you're carrying."

Her arms curled across her stomach as her heart leaped into her throat. He couldn't know. *No one* knew.

"They aren't aware, are they?" As though he'd read her mind—and she dearly hoped he couldn't, nanotech or no—Skinner nodded toward the camera dome. "With your chip offline, they don't have any way of monitoring your biometrics. If you stay out of sight long enough, you have the potential to give birth to the first under-grid child born in *decades*."

She tried to laugh off his demand. "And what do you want with a baby? You can buy kids on the street, nowadays. It's got to be less work than whatever you're willing to do to get me out of here."

"Children available for adoption are monitored for their own safety and code compliance, just like everyone else. But an untraceable child?" His lips didn't so much smile as melt upwards. "Worth a small fortune, to the right party."

Sam's stomach twisted. She hadn't been thrilled about the pregnancy, but she sure as hell wasn't turning an innocent baby over to the sorts of people who were looking for unmonitored children. The rumors about kidnapped kids found with their biochips fried by EMP and their minds scrambled were disturbing enough; she couldn't bear to think what some sicko might do with a child who didn't have even basic monitoring equipment. That was a life sentence to abuse and slavery, at best. "No deal."

Skinner groaned. "You're trying to make me haggle, and I *hate* haggling, so let's just be frank: You're anti-implant, so you clearly aren't going to comply with UniGov requirements regarding your child, which means your offspring won't be able to function at all in society—you just said as much from your little soapbox a moment ago. So why not save yourself *and* little Junior the trouble? You want your kid off-grid. *I* want your kid off-grid. The only ones who don't want your kid off-grid are UniGov, so let's join forces and screw them. I fix your little chip conversion problem, you get a full pardon, you're off the hook for child support, and I get a nice fat commission. Everybody wins."

"Everybody except Junior."

"Junior won't have much of a life anyway if Mommy's in prison for cyber crimes. UniGov will just confiscate him and implant him anyway, and he'll end up auctioned off in one of those street-corner adoption events."

"Forget it. I'm not handing over my baby."

The good humor that had colored Skinner's smirks faded, leaving his smile cold and predatory. "I don't see that you have much of a choice, Ms. Cham."

Ice crept up Sam's spine. "What?"

He tapped the handheld device, and a new rectangle shimmered into view in front of her. She shivered as she recognized the scroll of her uncensored identity placard: *Eman Samara Cham, 24267466-8128.78.* "How did you—"

"Your biochip is only switched off, not removed. The identity plate is permanently encoded. No matter how many layers of security you think you've built up, it can still be accessed through the right protocols. Or, say, by nanites that travel via data stream?" He brandished the handheld device in a jaunty wave. "I think it goes without saying that it could also be turned back on. Now, I wonder what UniGov will do when their access to your biometric data is suddenly restored? I'm sure they'll be *overjoyed* to learn that their prisoner is pregnant. And once they know your real identity, I'm sure they'll have some questions for your family, too..."

"You *bastard*."

Skinner merely smiled. "So, do we have a bargain?"

"It doesn't seem like you're giving me much choice."

"That was the idea." Skinner stepped past her and docked his handheld device to the terminal. "This is the control unit for the nanites. The chip conversion will take time, so I'm going to leave it here to run."

"Oh, good. For a minute, I was afraid you were planning on sticking around, and then I'd be in here for murder instead of cyber."

Her threat seemed only to amuse him. "In three days' time, having completed your impossible task, you'll be released from custody. Bring this unit out with you. I won't be able to get back in here without it, and I'm sure you wouldn't want this technology falling into UniGov's hands."

"Don't be so sure." Sam glared at his shoulders. "I think you may have just knocked them out of first place on my most-loathed list."

He chuckled. "Down, girl." He fell silent for a few minutes as he worked with the device. "There. The nanites will convert the hardware and load the firmware; you won't need to lift a finger. You'll see the chips start to turn from yellow to gold as they're upgraded. If you get bored, you might sort them. Or you can just rest. It's good for the baby, you know." He cast a sharp-edged smile at her stomach. "When you leave this facility, I'll be waiting outside with a vehicle to escort you to a secure location."

Sam suppressed a shudder. "That sounds a lot like kidnapping. What if I don't want to go?"

"It's merely a precaution to protect my payment until it's safely delivered." His eyes narrowed. "We wouldn't want you getting cold feet and going into hiding. Though I assure you, even if you tried, I have ways of finding you."

"No doubt." Sam's gaze tracked to the device on the table, which had bypassed her own security measures easily. "But you're awfully trusting, leaving that here with me. What's to stop me from using it to waltz out of here as easily as you got in?"

"It won't do you much good, without the login. Which you don't know, and will never guess. Even *you* can't manually brute-force hack a fifteen-digit passcode in under three days."

"Fifteen digits, huh?" She tapped the back of her hand to toggle the augmented reality setting she usually left switched off, and the ID badge appeared just below Skinner's face: ***********SK.IN. "Do I get a head start if I guess the last four?"

Skinner laughed aloud. "Sure. The passcode is the same as my unique ID, for all the good that will do you. *No one* knows my name, not even my closest associates—not that you could reach them from in here." He winked. "Only eleven alphanumeric characters to go. That's… let's see… What's sixty-two to the eleventh power work out to? Those astronomical numbers always did intimidate me."

As far as Sam could see, *nothing* intimidated this strange little man. "Maybe I'll get lucky and guess it."

He snorted. "If you do, I will bow to Fortune's favor and take no payment for my services. Now—I'm off. Any other questions before I go?"

"Will the cameras stay on loop, or do I have to worry about the guards seeing this?"

"I'll handle it. I'll update the loop from time to time so they don't get suspicious."

"You can do that without your device?"

Skinner rolled his eyes. "My dear Ms. Cham. Sam. Sammy. Even without nanites, you know perfectly well that *anything* can be hacked." He rubbed his hands together and pressed a button on the device. "See you in just under three days."

With one final wink, he vanished.

After his departure, the strength drained from Sam's body. She slumped over the table, resting her head in her hands, half hoping the events of the previous hour had been nothing more than a stress-fueled hallucination—but as she watched, tiny flecks of gold began to appear in the bin of yellow components. Against all plausibility, Skinner's nanites were doing their work. Time ticked inexorably on, each second bringing nearer the moment of her liberation.

And the moment of her child's enslavement.

No. There had to be another solution. Skinner had said he wouldn't take her baby if she could guess his login, hadn't he? The odds were beyond impossible, but she couldn't give up without even trying. She picked up the unfamiliar device, trying to make sense of its colorful inputs without disconnecting it from the equipment it was connected to.

Her eyes flicked to the nearby terminal. *Anything can be hacked.*

She had seventy-one hours remaining.

***

All that day and through the night, Sam worked in a frenzy. After a few halfhearted attempts to guess the passcode—a waste of time, considering how little she knew of its user—she turned to more familiar skills. She first tried accessing the nanite control's system code, but the terminal couldn't interpret any data from the device. Sideloading an override program was equally unsuccessful. At last she donned the static-proof gloves, carefully pried off the device's back panel, and used a diagnostics kit to trace the physical power traveling through the device from the charging pad. The hardware configuration was like nothing she'd ever seen—operations skipped randomly around the boards rather than following any logical pattern. Circuits that should have been connected to the inputs seemed to float loose in the configuration, with no discernible power supply, yet somehow managed to fire.

"Nanotech," she mumbled. The mysterious device wasn't merely *controlling* the nanites; it must be running on them, too. Even if she could access the source code, she wouldn't know how to modify it to let her use the device. She couldn't write a program for a technology she hadn't known existed until yesterday.

Sam pillowed her head on her outstretched arms and squinted at the terminal's time display. She'd been at it for thirty-seven grueling hours with barely a rest, and was no closer to solving the critical riddle than she'd been when Skinner had winked out of the cell. She should just give up; she was never going to figure it out...

She jerked away from the edge of sleep and forced herself upright again. *No.* No matter how tired she got, she wasn't going to give up. Her future, and her unborn child's, depended on this. She peeled one of the tasteless nutrition bars they'd left her and crammed it resolutely between her teeth.

She turned back to the terminal, but her fingers trembled as they hovered over the inputs. In her fatigue, she was bound to make mistakes if she tried to type commands manually. Her eyes went to the contact plate on the back of her wrist. As much as she disliked the principle, using a direct connection *would* be vastly faster than relying on manual input. Given the tools at her disposal, it wouldn't be impossible to reactivate her implant, but in the years it had been offline, she would have missed dozens of updates. There was no guarantee that the old protocols would be compatible with the current terminal interface. MySoft was notorious for deactivating support for older versions as soon as they pushed an update, to force users to upgrade immediately.

Sam groaned and scrubbed her hands over her face. If only she had an Intuition-compatible chipset, this would all be so much faster and simpler. But even if she had access to the kind of implant boutique that carried them, she knew she could never afford the upgrade fee...

A full minute passed before her eyes focused on the little box with the rabbit logo, sitting on the table a hand's span from her elbow. "I am an idiot," she sighed. "Or maybe I just haven't slept in two days.

Yeah, let's go with that."

The AU-79 chip was less difficult to install than she'd feared, and within a few minutes, the animated rabbit that Intuition's marketing department had linked inextricably to natural-thought software dashed across her field of vision. She experienced a moment of panic when the Intuition system automatically accessed her biometric data, but a frantic software override and a timely jab with a screwdriver kept the live bio-monitor from reactivating.

Confident that her unique biochip was still offline, she turned her attention back to the handheld device. Hardlining directly to an unknown operating system was risky, but she'd have to trust that Intuition's safety protocols were up to spec, even for bizarre, previously-unknown, maybe-magic technology. With only a little over one day remaining, she no longer had the luxury of caution. Bracing herself with a deep breath, she snapped the access key against her wrist contact.

The plunge into the immersive Intuition experience was unexpected and overwhelming. She'd grown up with augmented reality, of course, but she hadn't really used it in years—and navigating Intuition's user interface was *nothing* like the orderly menus of her original chipset. Every fleeting thought launched her along a new trajectory through colorful graphical representations of the system she was connected to, until she was staring down a dozen rainbow corridors simultaneously. "Too much," she said aloud.

In the lower corner of her vision, the multicolored rabbit logo appeared. *It looks like you're having trouble navigating. Can I help?*

Sam knew the rabbit's words weren't real, but the software told her auditory cortex that she'd heard them spoken aloud. The effect was unnerving. "No," she said, then realized she was speaking to an empty room. Think. She needed to *think* what she wanted. Intuition, right? It was meant to be intuitive. *I need the login for this device.*

Intuition rabbit blinked at her in hyper-realistic 3D. *It looks like you're trying to log in. Can I help?*

That wasn't exactly right, but if it brought up the login field, she might be able to see the username. *Yes. Log me in.*

Intuition rabbit nodded helpfully. *Please tell me your username.*

I don't know my username.

Intuition rabbit scratched at one ear with its hind foot. *I'm sorry. I don't recognize that username.*

Maybe that was too many words? *Forgot username.*

Another ear-scratch. *I'm sorry. I don't recognize that username.*

Recover username?

I'm sorry. I don't recognize that username.

Who am I?

Intuition rabbit sat up and blinked. *Let's start over. It looks like you're trying to log in. Can I help?*

Sam resisted the urge to punt the nonexistent rabbit across the room, and instead dropped her head on the table with a groan. This was maddening, and she didn't have the patience to adapt to a new operating system when she was just... so... *tired...*

***

Sam opened her eyes to behold a field of lush green grass. "Fake," she pronounced. There hadn't been uncultivated fields like this in decades, if not centuries. It *was* a good simulation, though. She passed her hand through the realistic blades and jerked back as the sharp edge of a leaf sliced into her finger. She held the digit close and watched as it beaded blood. Scratch that; it was a *fantastic* simulation.

A nearby rustle caught her attention. She crept over to where she could see the long grass parting as something moved through it. As she crouched to look, a startled rabbit squeaked and bolted. She'd caught only a glimpse, but that had been enough for her to see that the rabbit's fur was sectioned into primary colors. "Intuition?" she wondered aloud.

Near the edge of the field, the wake through the grass slowed. The rabbit's head cautiously breached the waves of green. "Yes?"

Sam's mouth opened and closed a few times. "I... are you the

Intuition rabbit?"

The rabbit cocked its head. "That is my name, yes. Can I help you?"

If this was Intuition, this was by far the *weirdest* user interface Sam had ever experienced. "I need the login credentials for this device."

"Device?" Intuition glanced around and flicked one long ear. "I don't understand."

"The—for the tablet. Thing. Whatever I'm plugged into right now."

Intuition hopped closer and peered at her. "I don't understand. What is 'plugged in'?"

She massaged her temple. Even the headaches here were realistic. "Look, this guy Skinner gave me a device that's locked, with his name as the passcode. I really need to know how to unlock it."

"Oh!" Intuition sat up, ears wriggling. "It's a riddle, then? The answer must be... *Skinner!*"

Sam hadn't known until that moment that it was possible to want to strangle a corporate mascot. "No. It's his *full* name. Fifteen alphanumeric characters, ending in -SKIN." She gritted her teeth and just managed not to add, *which is what I'm going to do to you if you tell me once more that you don't recognize my username.*

Intuition didn't repeat the error message, though he did scratch his ear in an irritatingly familiar gesture. "I don't know if I can help, then. Is it important, getting into this... device?"

Sam bit her lip, frustration suspending her equidistant between tears and screaming. "Yes. It's the only way to save my baby from a monster."

"*Oh.*" The rabbit's voice was tempered with awe. "Follow me, then. I may know someone who can help."

The rabbit led her across the field and into a dense copse of trees, where the sound of rustling grass was replaced by a rhythmic *thunk* that echoed among the trunks. Soon they reached a clearing, where a man dressed improbably in a gleaming white jumpsuit was swinging an axe at the base of a tree.

Intuition hopped forward without hesitation. "Greetings, woodsman!"

The man turned. His face was fixed in a broad smile, though one eye remained closed. "Greetings. What do you need, friend?"

Intuition looked expectantly up at Sam. "I need the login credentials for Skinner's device," she said.

The woodsman's eerie smile never wavered, though he scratched his head in obvious confusion. "Skinner?"

She repeated what she'd told the rabbit about the tablet, but the woodsman remained puzzled. Clearly the denizens of this bizarre fantasy landscape didn't understand technological terms. "I need to learn the name of the man who controls the nanites," she tried.

"Nanites?" Intuition's ears pricked. "Do you mean *gnats*?"

"No, I mean—" Sam hesitated. "Wait. What about gnats?"

"Gnats," the winking woodsman grinned. "There is a man who controls gnats. He lives at the heart of the forest."

"Of course he does," she sighed. Gnats seemed unrelated to her problem, but she already had two talking corporate logos helping her. What could it hurt to check? "Sure. Can you show me the way?"

Their path led deep into the woods, the undergrowth thinning as they proceeded until all that surrounded them were impossibly tall, straight trees, arranged in such regular formation that Sam had a sense of receding corridors as she passed between their rows. A sound grew along with the trees—little more than a faint hiss at first, but steadily increasing until it droned in her skull. As they broke through a final shield of trees into an open space, Sam realized the source of the noise: It was the hum of billions of tiny wings, emanating from a veritable wall of insects. She hadn't known gnat wings even made a sound, but clearly in this quantity, they did.

"This is his cottage," the woodcutter offered helpfully. "The gnats protect it."

Sam squinted into the roiling cloud in the center of the clearing, but she could perceive nothing beyond the mass of bugs. "And where is the man who controls them?"

"I'll call him." Intuition hopped forward. The cloud of gnats seemed to grow more dense near his point of approach. "Hello! We would like to speak to the man in the cottage!"

After a few seconds, the insect wall thinned to a gray scrim. Sam could make out the shape of a squat building beyond it, and something tottering toward the rabbit.

She peered at the moving figure. That was *definitely* her grandmother's garden gnome.

Intuition glanced back at her. "What would you like me to ask him?"

"His name," Sam replied. "I need his full name."

"The lady would like to know your name," Intuition relayed to the gnome.

Behind the screen of gnats, the gnome's mouth moved, but the drone of wings increased simultaneously, drowning out any sound he might have made.

Intuition scratched his ear. "I'm sorry, I didn't hear that." Again, the gnome spoke, and again the sound was muffled. The rabbit glanced back apologetically.

"It's no use," said the woodcutter, whose one-eyed grin appeared somewhat less jovial. "We'll never hear it through those gnats. They protect him."

"Of course the passcode is encrypted," Sam murmured. "Think we can push through them?"

Intuition's ears flattened. "I don't think so. Their function is to keep things away from the cottage."

Sam scuffed her toe through the dirt until she kicked up a small rock. "Let's see what happens when something tries." She flung the rock at the wall of insects. Instantly the gnats swarmed to intercept it, forming a dense circle at its point of contact, and the stone bounced harmlessly away.

She watched the localized defense loosen, the gnats flooding back to their original configuration. "Huh. I've got an idea. Intuition, when I tell you, I want you to ask his name again." She hurried around the edge of the clearing collecting pebbles, twigs, anything she could throw. "Ready? Now!" As soon as the rabbit started speaking, Sam hurled the double handful of detritus toward the cottage. The gnats responded as before. As they flowed into new positions to block the projectiles, the wall near the gnome thinned momentarily.

"*********iltsk**," said the gnome. The gnats swarmed back into place before he'd finished the word.

"Ha!" Sam crowed. "Even nanotech operates on finite resources. All we need is something large enough to draw them all away." She searched the clearing, but scattered leaves and twigs wouldn't provide enough resistance to occupy the gnats for long. Her eyes traced the impossibly tall trunks into the distant canopy. "Woodsman, do you think you could chop down that big tree over there?"

"Of course. I am a woodsman." His perpetual smile strained wider. "Why?"

"Could you drop it right on the cottage?"

His one eye squinted in confusion. "Yes, but it will take me some time to cut."

"Please begin, then." As the woodsman raised his axe, she turned back to the rabbit. "Intuition, after that tree comes down, I want you to ask his name again."

The rabbit cast an uncertain glance at the great tree shuddering overhead with each of the woodsman's blows, but he nodded. Sam knelt beside the rabbit to wait. This close, the throbbing drone of insect wings was almost painful, but she steeled herself. Just a moment more…

A groan of creaking wood presaged the woodsman's success. "Timber!" he shouted.

In an instant, the wall of gnats between Sam and the gnome thinned to a veil as the defenders swarmed to intercept the overhead threat. The falling tree halted mid-air, sagged briefly, then was buoyed up again by a reinforcing wave of insects. The once-impenetrable wall before the gnome was reduced to a thin screen of stray dots.

Intuition was watching for Sam's signal. When she gave it, he turned to the gnome. "What is your name?"

"Rumpelstiltskin," the gnome said.

Sam repeated the name to herself as the defending gnats rallied and rolled the tree to the far side of the cottage, where it crashed against the ground. In seconds, the protective wall had restored itself.

It didn't matter. She had her login.

"Thank you." She knelt and gave Intuition's head an awkward pat, then pressed the sleeve of the woodsman's gleaming jumpsuit. "Thank you both. I have what I need now."

***

The next sensation Sam experienced was that of an old sock crammed into her mouth. Or perhaps, she thought as consciousness reasserted itself, that was merely the taste left behind by those awful nutrient bars. She grimaced and scraped her tongue against her front teeth as she raised her head from the table, then swore under her breath as she realized her wrist was still connected to Skinner's device. No wonder she'd had such a bizarre dream; neural interfaces were not designed to be used while sleeping. They could *really* screw up your alpha rhythms...

Dream. *Rumpelstiltskin.*

She stared at the brassy contact gleaming at her wrist. *Had* that been just a dream? Or had her subconscious mind somehow utilized the Intuition interface to navigate through Skinner's device and crack the code that her waking self couldn't?

Well, there was one way to find out. She slid over to the terminal, opened a blank field, and began typing. How many ways were there to spell a word that sounded like *Rumpelstiltskin*? Fifteen characters, and she knew the last four already...

She'd worked out a few possible permutations before her eyes landed on the clock on the corner of the display. She rubbed her eyes and looked again, then swore aloud. How long had she been asleep? Her seventy-two hours would be up in only forty-three minutes!

No time to waste, then. Sam grabbed Skinner's device and began entering characters. *Rumpelstiltskin* didn't work. Neither did *Rumplestiltskin*, nor *Rumblestiltskin*, nor any other spelling she could conceive. She tried varying the letter case. She tried switching letters around. Nothing worked. Had the dream been just that—a hopeful fantasy, conjured out of her desperation to succeed?

No; she couldn't give up with fifteen minutes left on the clock! There was no time to crack the passcode any other way, and this was her only lead. *Think.* What did she know of Skinner? What kind of passcode would a man like that create?

Of course. Someone so self-important wouldn't use a lower-case login. She locked the input in capital letters and typed RUMPELSTILTSKIN.

Nothing.

Sam groaned and pressed her forehead to the table. Even if the name were correct, there were still too many possible permutations for her to guess the exact arrangement. Maybe only one letter was lower-case. Maybe she still wasn't spelling the name correctly. Maybe...

She raised her head and frowned at the input. Surely not—but what did she have to lose? She tapped back to the first I and replaced it with a 1.

Login successful.

Sam stared at the device in her hand. "You have *got* to be kidding me."

In the corner of her vision, a multicolored rabbit hopped into view. *It looks like you've logged into a new device. Can I help?*

***

The street outside the precinct smelled of grime and ozone, but it was still an improvement over the airless cell she'd been trapped in for three days. Sam breathed deeply and relished her newfound freedom. The local officers had been reluctant to release her, even after she'd demonstrated the fully functional chip conversion, but they could hardly argue with a plea deal handed out by their overlords. Officially, she was on probation, and due to report at a UniGov worksite for labor processing within forty-eight hours.

Now that she had control of the nanites, she intended to extend that deadline by some years.

She'd been standing on the sidewalk for a short time when a sleek vehicle glided up to the curb. The door retracted and a familiar figure emerged. Sam flashed him a frigid smile. "I expected you ten minutes ago."

"My apologies. Traffic, you know." Skinner waved toward the open door. "Kindly step into the car."

Sam made a show of thinking it over. "No. I don't think I will."

He stiffened. "We have a deal, Ms. Cham."

"We don't, actually. I never actually *agreed* to your trade-off. In fact, I believe I made it quite clear that I didn't like being railroaded into things." She shrugged. "The fact that you took my cooperation for granted and converted all those chips without waiting for me to accept your terms just suggests that you're probably the sort of person who never reads the EULA."

His countenance darkened. "Don't play games with me. I fulfilled my end of the bargain, and you benefited from it. Whether you explicitly agreed or not, you still *owe* me."

"That's not how this works, Mr. Skinner." Sam paused, relishing the moment. "Or should I say... Rumpelstiltskin?"

Skinner's eyes widened. "You—*how*?"

She brandished the handheld device. "You said it yourself: *Anything* can be hacked. Foolish of you to leave this with one of the most notorious hackers alive for nearly three days. Also—" She shook her head in exaggerated disappointment. "A *one* instead of the letter I? Really? What are you, twelve?"

His face flushed nearly purple. "Give that back to me."

"Why? It's no good to you now. I've changed the login credentials." She smiled sweetly. "And unlike you, I didn't use something simple like a name. It's just a random string of characters now. Given all the possible combinations, it would take even the most advanced decryption program approximately fourteen million years to brute-force hack. Only I know the correct algorithm, and *I'm not telling.*"

"You *will* tell, before I'm through with you," he growled. "I'll make you regret ever laying eyes on a computer before we're done!" He took a step toward her.

Sam flicked a thumb over the device, and an identity card shimmered into the air between them. "Skinner. Skinski. Mr. Skin. I feel obligated to inform you that your identity profile is now public. And more than that, it seems there's a warrant for your arrest. Apparently you're wanted for questioning in relation to a case of— oh! Oh, dear. Illegal child trafficking?" She tutted.

Skinner's face went from livid to pale in the span of a few heartbeats. "You didn't. You wouldn't!"

Sam shrugged. "I'm sure *I* didn't. But nanites, you know. Once they're in the data stream, who can say what mischief they get up to?" She tucked the control unit into the pocket of her jacket. "I'd run, if I were you. The precinct runs an automatic ID sweep every ninety seconds, and now that your profile is visible, you're liable to be flagged."

With only a moment's hesitation, Skinner lunged back into the vehicle. She could hear him spewing curses at her as it sped away. The car made it as far as the next corner before the red lights of a UniGov drone were flashing above it.

Sam was tempted to stay and watch the tableau unfold, but she couldn't risk Skinner implicating her while she was still in possession of the nanite control unit. As she strolled in the opposite direction, she slipped one hand into her pocket and brushed the device, reassuring herself that it was still there. The other hand rested lightly on her abdomen. "Don't worry, Junior," she murmured. "It's still a big, scary world, but I have a way to protect you now. To protect *all* of us—anyone who wants off the grid. I'm going to make a world where you can live free."

Alena Van Arendonk couldn't decide what to be when she grew up, so she does a little of everything, juggling the hats of writer, actor, artist, seamstress and costume designer. Her writing is just as eclectic as the rest of her creative pursuits: Her published works include short stories, nonfiction essays, news articles, and even a cookbook. She has always found the story of Rumpelstiltskin somewhat unsettling, so it was a prime candidate for reimagining in a techno-dystopian future.

C4T & MOU5E

V.F. LeSann

Mouse pulled her game-screen from her bag and put her feet up on the edge of the bed. Waiting for her last save to load, she glanced at the woman prone on the bed. Pale, pretty, and as empty as a scrubbed drive. With what was left of her blonde hair brushed down over her shoulders and the clinical blue bedspread tucked under her arms, she looked like a sleeping princess from the kind of books Mouse read years ago. Only there wasn't a magic spell or a kiss that could do jack-shit about whatever had turned Alice's brain into soup.

"I don't get the point of you," Mouse said, tapping the audiocuff clipped to her ear so the music from her game would drown out the steady beep-beep-beeping of the machines keeping her sister's body alive.

Kicking her feet she jostled the bed, not out of any malicious intent, but just to see if *anything* would happen. No alarms, no movement, nothing. Everyone spoke of Alice as though she were made of glass, but she didn't break if the bed shook. Mouse rolled her eyes and went back to her screen.

At least during these mandatory visits, Mouse was making some serious progress on her game. She was stuck on the stupid grind-

166

until-you-start-hating-it levels now, the kind she could run in her sleep, but it was a terrific alternative to staring at Alice's hollowed-out, unfamiliar face.

Turn left at the Blacksmith. Drop a coin in the well. Third dialogue option down on the genie. Into the woods. West, north, west. Get the staff at the witch's hut. West, west, south. Knock on the fifth tree. Fight the ghost. Collect the necklace. Drop the necklace into the well. Happy sparkly experience point noises. Repeat.

She'd technically finished the game about thirty levels back, but there was nostalgic comfort in running around the familiar pixelated world with her little sprite. There were people convinced that a secret plotline opened up if you got your sprite to level one hundred. Sitting comfy at level eighty-two, she didn't see any reason why she *shouldn't* test that theory herself.

Twenty minutes in, her screen chimed a low battery warning. She scrambled in her bag for the charging cord and external battery and came up with one out of two.

"Fucking shit," she grumbled, tossing her bag onto Alice's legs and beginning her search for an energy outlet.

As it turned out, there was a grand total of one in the room and it already had a thick round plug inserted into it. The cord ran up behind the bed and, as much as Mouse hated these pointless morbid visits her mother inflicted upon her, she wouldn't dare unplug that. Alternatively, the blinking monitor next to the bed housed two secondary ports that Mouse didn't think twice about borrowing.

The screen gave a cheerful *bwoop* of success, and the intro song chimed through her audiocuff. "Thanks for sharing," she muttered to Alice, and settled back into her chair.

Left from the Blacksmith. Coin in the well. Genie, woods, west, north, west.

She paused, her finger hovering over the screen. She'd poured hours into this game. Like, weeks worth of hours, if not entire months. And she knew damn well that the witch's hut had *never* had a little striped cat outside it before. A shiver went through her, followed by a stomach-tumble of excitement: a secret level. The little pixel-cat flicked the tip of its tail in an idle animation, oversized green eyes offering the occasional blink. There was something about the rendering of its whiskers that made it look like it was grinning.

Without any hesitation, instead of entering the hut, she touched the cat.

The witch's dialogue bubble popped up and simultaneously, the cat looked at her, raised its front paw and waved. A voice crackled through the music, frazzled and male.

"Smaller Alice? You've grown. Or I've shrunk. Help a guy out, what year is it?"

Mouse screamed and ripped the audiocuff off her ear.

She had exactly enough time to pull the charging cord from the back of the monitor and shove it into the pouch of her sweater before a nurse and an orderly piled into the room, staring between her and the body on the bed.

With her heart beating double time in her throat, Mouse blurted out the worst lie she possibly could've come up with.

"I... thought I saw her move."

The tremor in her voice must've made it believable because they crowded up to the bed, getting between Mouse and her sister's body. The nurse started fiddling with the machine her game had been plugged into—Mouse held her breath—while the orderly frowned down at Alice's blank face.

"Anything?" the orderly asked. She'd put a hand against Alice's shoulder and pressed down, like she was expecting her to launch up and start dancing or something. Her other hand hovered at her pocket like a gunslinger ready to draw.

The nurse shook her head and turned a sceptical look at Mouse. "What did you *think* you saw?"

"I... was almost falling asleep," she said, "I thought I saw her reach..." She gestured vaguely towards Alice's motionless hands, but the first part had done what she'd intended. The pair exchanged a knowing look.

"Best get you back to your mother," the nurse said, putting a firm hand between Mouse's shoulder blades and steering her back to the reception area. Casting a glance over her shoulder to the orderly, she watched them press a hand to their ear, whispering.

In the reception area, suits rushed in from restricted doors followed by uniforms, all racing to Alice's room.

Mouse clutched the charging cord in her pocket like a magic necklace she ought to be dumping in a well somewhere and let herself be herded along.

"I'll call your mother to come early."

Mouse lurked restlessly in the public waiting area for her mother, who didn't arrive a second earlier than usual, but was drunker than normal so she'd certainly spoken to the nurse.

"No car?" Mouse asked, looking around the visitor area for any familiar vehicle.

"It's at the pub, baby." Mom brushed her hand through Mouse's hair and stumbled towards the street.

"If we get the car, I can drive."

"Hank's coming, don't worry."

Mouse's heart sank. She hated Hank the most of all her mother's boyfriends. He was big, burly and loud, and treated Mouse like an inconvenient roadblock on the way to getting her mother naked.

"I've got a few transport passes left for this month," Mouse offered, but her mother wasn't listening anymore.

The rain was coming down hard and with the enviro-warning well into the orange zone, they'd have to follow the covered walking paths to the train station. Mom wasn't wearing her 'walking shoes' and was missing the sweater she'd left the house in.

Mouse shrugged out of her jacket and draped it over her mother's shoulders to cover her bare arms.

"Hank will be here in a few minutes." Reaching into her purse, her mother pulled out some pink lipstick and a compact, but was biting her lip as though there was more she wanted to say.

Mouse tucked her hands into the sleeves of her sweater as a crack of thunder boomed, echoing in the underground parking.

"Did you want to talk about what happened with your sister today?"

The blatant lapse in the *We Don't Talk About Alice* protocol made Mouse suspicious, but she didn't have anything she wanted to say about today. Definitely not to Mom.

"I... I just don't know why I have to keep coming here."

Her mother pursed her lips, abandoning the soft pink lip colour for a vibrant red. "Oh, baby, one of us has to visit her so she knows we're thinking of her."

Mouse's protest was cut off by Hank's too-loud vehicle entering the parking garage, booming bass coming out of black tinted windows and a motor that rumbled so loud it made Mouse's teeth hurt.

Her mom smiled and wobbled her way over to the rolled down window, planting a kiss on Hank's overgrown beard.

"There's the red lips I love!"

Mouse followed in her mother's shadow and ignored Hank's glare, taking up her usual space in the back of his crammed cargo area, and let the protest she'd bit back from her mother slip out quietly.

"But I don't even know her."

***

Mouse made herself dinner and snuck directly to her room to avoid Hank's continued goads at her existence.

She missed the times before Hank, and the Hanks that came before him. There'd been one in the years after Alice, a woman named Selina who'd been kind to Mouse, but her mother didn't take risks and she'd scurried back to the Hanks.

"It's a shame she didn't look more like you, babe. You'd have her shacked up already and living off some husband's salary."

Alice had looked like mom: blonde hair and blue eyes with pink lips and a button nose, already the swan by the time she was pushing seventeen. Mouse took after their father: washed out features and mousey brown hair to match—when she was little they'd joked she'd been born with his frown lines.

Their house was lavish and well beyond the common cubicle allotment most people called home, and offered enough privacy the two women never had to run into each other if they didn't want to. The last bastion of her father's wealth, falling to pieces with age and neglect, like everything else. It was only still standing because Alice had been special enough that the government declared it a historical site.

Mouse bit into her toasted protein bread, found the external charger she'd forgot to take to the hospital and plugged it in. It was time to drown in the world of witches and genies, and unlock the mystery level of one talking pixel-cat.

Wanting more distance between herself and the living room, she wandered down the hall and found herself hovering at the closed door to Alice's old room. She slipped inside, avoiding the dark plastic layered in dust that covered every piece of furniture and took her usual seat on the floor, hunching over her game.

The screen flashed and offered two options: *Continue* or *New Game*.

The promise of bonus content was entirely too alluring to refuse so she pressed *Continue*.

The intro sing-song melted into the cheerful round of the higher levels near the witch's hut.

"Alright," she muttered. "Find the cat."

Left at the Blacksmith. Coin into the well. Third option on...

The genie's dialogue options were jumbled and the usual *'Tell me a secret'* had been replaced with *'Please, don't panic!'* complete with a typed smiley face. Mouse couldn't tell if her heart was racing with excitement or terror; this was just too weird.

She tapped on the new option: *I'm not panicking.*

If she was being honest she panicked just a little when a relieved chuckle flowed through her audiocuff and the grey pixel-cat hopped out of the wishing well, perching on the edge.

"Sorry about earlier. I think it's been a long time since I spoke to... well, anyone."

All of the hairs stood up on the back of Mouse's neck. It sounded so close and realistic that it was like someone was sitting right behind her, whispering into her ear. Mouse looked around the room blanketed in dark plastic, searching for shadows.

"Can you hear me?" Talking to the game made her feel more than a little insane.

"Well enough." The pixel-cat groomed a pixel-paw, its green eyes closed. *"I don't think this machine's really built for communication."*

"This... this isn't part of the hidden levels, is it?"

"Nah, this is real life. I know it gets confusing sometimes."

Her breath wasn't filling her lungs. She took a few deep inhales, trying to get her hands to stop shaking.

The cat tilted its head, seeming to look around the room. *"I know this is really weird, but things can still make sense. I don't remember much... but I know I need help. I mean... I don't have anyone else to ask and we're in a world of trouble."*

Mouse pursed her lips, glancing around the room again at what was left of her sister's memory.

"I can probably help you, a little at least..." Her voice trailed off and she stared at the place where Alice's bed was. She barely remembered this room before they came and sprayed everything with chemicals that made her nose burn, and the door had stayed closed until Mouse started using the room for hiding. "Did you know my sister?"

"I did and I do."

"I don't," Mouse said feeling the chasm built in the decade between her and Alice, bitterness, grief and anger churning in her stomach. The time before Alice went to the hospital and never came back to now felt like a lifetime. "Can you tell me about her?"

"I'm stronger in the Now, but I know someone who remembers Then better. I guess it depends which Alice you want to know."

"What's to know about her now?" Mouse scoffed, more to herself than the cat. Feeling her cheeks redden with embarrassment, she hastily changed the subject. "Do you have a name?"

"I should have led with that, sorry. I'm Chase. Again, haven't talked to anyone in a while..."

"I'm Mouse." She tapped the screen where he'd held up a paw for a high-five or pixel-handshake. When she pressed it, sparkles and butterflies spiraled in the image. "How can I help?"

He chuckled. *"You know, your basic time crunch adventure. Collect the piece of Then, deliver, and victory."*

Mouse gave a wink, feeling the warm tingle of a laugh fluster in her stomach. "Lucky for you, I'm pretty much a professional. Objective? Villain?"

"The villains are murky Then things... but I know when your battery died, a part of me went with it and I forgot some things... so let's try and avoid that. There's not much left of me to be forgotten."

The thought of losing the cat sent an unexpected pang through her. It was rare to have someone to talk to and she didn't want him to go away. "Don't let the battery die, got it. Objective?"

The cat paced, finding a rock to perch on. *"I was stronger where you first found me, but the piece wasn't there... the key. But I think if we plug me in there, with the key, we can fix everything."*

"Do we know what we're fixing?"

"Well, why I'm a cat, for one." He gave an uncomfortable laugh. *"There are people who have taken things that mean a lot to me. There's a something about a computer Wonderland, does mean anything to you?"*

"They shut that down... It was a program for gifted kids. The really smart ones, like Alice. But it wasn't about computers."

"I have the instinct to bite it if I see it, but I can't remember why." The cat rolled onto it's back, throwing a paw over its eyes. *"This is exhausting!"*

"Focus up, kitty. If we don't have a villain, do we have an adversary?"

"Oh yeah," he said, pensively washing a paw. *"There's a nightmare beast-warden that keeps the sheep trapped. It hunts in the wires and sockets, swims in electric rivers prowling for a scent of me, to drag me back with the rest."*

Mouse's air froze in her throat and she gulped in a breath. "If it hides in the sockets..." She stared at the wall outlet and then back to her screen. "Then I guess we're only using external chargers." Four hours of battery left, so the clock was ticking for the cat-boy. "We need to move quick. Where is the missing piece?"

"Key," he corrected. *"There's another person, well... a part of them, but they're hiding too. The one who remembers Then but doesn't know Now. Alice hid the Where of them in the bed. I... think?"* The cat sighed.

Mouse stood and ripped away the plastic where the bed had been, revealing an empty frame. "When Alice got sick, they took everything. They destroyed it all, in case she was contagious."

The cat shook his head. *"She hid the place in the mouse's bed. She was sure they wouldn't find it."*

Mouse gave a startled laugh, a little thrill going through her at being seen through the years. She raced back to her own room on tiptoe feet, setting the screen down before tearing the blankets off her bed. She shoved the mattress sideways, finding nothing, and then dropped to her hands and knees, flailing blindly across the underside of the bed, finding a hole in the mesh and reaching up into the frame. Dust, cobweb, and... the edge of a piece of paper, thick but brittle with age. She pulled it out, smoothing out the creases to reveal a hand-inked zine, the kind that became popular once people figured out that anything viewable by screen belonged to the government like you'd handed it over personally.

Under a flurry of band names was a cat that had a too-big smile and too many teeth, hanging upside down by the tail from a marquis that read: *Concert at the Treacle Well: Old Town.*

***

The transports didn't run as frequently after dark, and even registered minors couldn't travel alone, but Mouse never drew enough attention to be noticed. For once she was grateful for her double-edged talent. She mapped her route easily enough, noting the last transport home departed at 2:00 a.m.

Mouse had never been to Old Town, but she'd heard enough ghost stories that her mind was already racing. It was a graveyard of the way the people had been before the corporations decided to build upwards and abandon the ground for the sky. Buried under the clouds of smog, it was like going back in time to a mirror-world a few steps behind the one she called home.

People who couldn't afford to live above smog level lived here, but the typically sardine-crammed transport was practically empty when she got to her stop, and the sidewalk was deserted.

The enviro-warning flashed on her omni-watch and she secured her mask, adding the extra filter layer and eye-covering mandatory in red zones.

The street was permanently void of natural light, drenched in a jaundice glow from yellow streetlamps. It certainly felt like a place of ghosts, she decided, following the map on her omni-watch to the bar. Garbage littered the sidewalk, magazines and newspapers, ads and wrappers, all preserved under murky grime hard as varnish.

The Treacle Well was just around the corner from her stop. The neon marquee fuzzed and crackled as she passed beneath it, her shoes crunching through the old glass littering the entryway. The doorframe was a ragged mess of broken wood, tattooed with char and mildew in turns, and the entryway walls were plastered with peeling fliers and stickers layered like scar tissue. Impossibly, there were

175

actually people in the bar and music trickled from a ceiling-mounted speaker. The big bald bartender flicked her a disinterested glance before burying his nose back into a little book of poetry. The only other patrons were two weirdly similar looking men muttering and smirking at each other across a small table, snapping through a rapid-fire card game.

A large poster matching the one in her bag hung crooked on the wall, partially covering a mangled hole she could easily slide through. Mouse wandered over to it, falling back under her usual guise of apparent nonchalance—I am not interested, I am not interesting—and pulled back the corner just enough to slide through.

Inside was a small alcove, dusty and abandoned, filled with the same chemical smell rusted to her memory of Alice's room. Burned and shriveled paper was scattered like arson confetti and bullet holes spattered every wall, offering the room trickles of ambient light from the main bar.

And next to the wall, tucked to the side in a way that had hidden it from her on the way in, was a standing arcade game. It was exactly the sort of thing she would've played to relax, all cartoon castles and forests, with a sword-wielding knight battling a huge dragon. Mouse knelt down and followed the cord on the back of the machine to find no power source attached. On the front, next to the coin slot and the START button, there was a little rectangular port that would fit her retro game-cord.

Mouse tapped her audiocuff and pulled out the screen tucked in her bag, the opening credits theme chiming in her ear.

"I think I found something," she said under her breath. "You ready?"

"I'm not not-ready," Chase answered happily.

"If we waited until we were ready we wouldn't do anything, so be ready."

Mouse plugged her console into the machine. A wall of vines crawled up to fill the screen, studded with roses and multi-coloured butterflies, before parting like curtains for a cartoon minstrel that swept off its hat and gave a flourishing bow.

ARE YOU READY FOR ADVENTURE? the screen read.

"I'm ready to do something impossible," Chase answered, with the intonation of an oath.

"Is that Chase?" a new voice said through her audiocuff, female and imperious. The game itself was emitting a cheerful eight-bit tune. *"And company, I see. This is a highly exclusive club. No guests! Skedaddle, begone, shoo."*

"Oh shit, of course it's you..." Chase whispered, barely audible to Mouse as she bristled.

"I'm Alice's sister."

There was a scoff. *"Then you're five. This is much too much for a toddler."*

On the screen, the minstrel had folded their arms and was tapping a bell-adorned shoe impatiently. Mouse twitched with annoyance.

"You don't seem like a whole Chase, just the Ch or the Ace... perhaps an imposter!" The minstrel put up their hands like tiny fighting fists.

"I'm Chase, I know that. And you're..."

"Oh my! This is rich!" The eight-bit minstrel put their hands over their middle, throwing their head back in a silent, shoulder-shaking laugh. *"Let me guess: Clever Chase decided to sacrifice a little something extra for... what? Roaming privileges?"*

"Then-memories for freedom," Chase snapped, the tail of the cat on Mouse's screen flicking back and forth. *"Turned out a damn sight better than you..."* A few sparks sprayed from the port between the plug that connected both games. *"Hattie!"* Chase declared, his voice strained.

"That much effort for a name." The minstrel gave a slow clap. *"I think you overpaid for your bargain, dear."*

Mouse twitched when she heard that name. Harriet Dodgson. The one who Alice and her parents called Hattie when they'd scream and yell. The girl that disappeared and Alice never came home from trying to find.

"You're only ever going to be Then-Hattie. One of us had to do something... it was important."

The laughter animation of Hattie's avatar looped and looped in a silent taunt. *"You don't have any idea what important is!"*

Mouse silently congratulated herself for not even flinching when a grey cat burst from the rose bushes next to the minstrel. The rendering was still shit, but better than on her little game pad, and she could see more details of him now, like the little half-moon charm on the collar around his neck.

"Hattie," he growled, *"This is not the time..."*

"If not now, when? I so miss our talks, Chase. You were always the most fun to tease."

Mouse gave the arcade screen a quick smack with her palm. "I'm not here to listen to you argue. I want to know about my sister."

"Toddlers are best seen and not heard, dear." The minstrel threw a juggling pin at the cat who jumped away into the bushes.

Mouse kicked the machine and hissed. "I'm sixteen!"

The minstrel stopped making laughing motions. *"Sixteen you say? That can't be right..."*

The cat slunk out of the bushes, fur bristled as he side-stepped around Hattie. *"You're Then-Hattie, and I'm Now-Chase. If I'm here and you're not, then..."*

"Well, that is a problem indeed." The minstrel sat on the edge of an oversized toadstool and crossed their legs, taking off their garish top hat. *"That means I was right, all along."* Her voice wasn't jovial anymore, and she sounded years younger than a minute ago. *"Tell me, little Mouse, did they get my dear, sweet Alice?"*

The cat laid down near the minstrel and curled his tail around his leg, answering before Mouse could ask Hattie what she meant. *"Would I be Then-Chase if they hadn't?"*

"I suppose you'd be regular-Chase... and I'd be here playing my game to an infinite high score."

"Can you assholes please make sense for three seconds? Who gives a shit about then and now?" Mouse growled. "I just want to know about my sister! Why won't anyone tell me about her, like she's some big secret?" Years of silence, and evaded questions welled into tears. "She's sick and she's never getting better. Ever. And no one will talk about why!"

Hattie chuckled, and this time it came through the audiocuff. *"Alice was the only one who ever believed me."* Then she kicked a jingle-belled shoe towards the cat while sticking out her tongue. *"The rest of them thought I was a little bit mad. I warned her—she was the thing they wanted, the missing piece, the foundation for an AI that could break every rule."*

Hattie gestured to Chase and smirked. *"With him our odds were high. With Alice, even higher. But something must've..."* She stopped and for the first time looked through the arcade screen at the space behind Mouse. *"This place was my favourite. We'd all come here and plan how we'd save the world. I'd play my game, Alice would stand just where you are now and watch. We fancied ourselves rebels... knaves of freedom."*

Mouse gripped the machine, staring at the minstrel. "What did they want with Alice?"

"Alice had a mind better than a computer, could crack any code like she saw the answer before it happened. Patterns. Why make something new when what they needed already existed? Parents are always so excited for their kids to be something special, of course they signed us all up. We should've just run."

Mouse found herself leaning on the machine for support. "They told us Alice got sick..."

Hattie snorted. *"She got sick alright, sick from missing scoops of brain matter."*

"Hattie!" Chase snapped. *"Stop."*

"What?! They lied to her, they lied to us. You think I don't get that happened to me too? I didn't get away if they got Alice. Not all of us

could disappear like you, kitty-boy."

"He's in the same boat as you!" Mouse said, looking at Chase. "Alice hasn't spoken in over ten years. I mean, I visit her in the hospital, but she doesn't do anything. Doesn't even move."

Hattie gave a cry that cut discordantly through the music. *"This is all your fault!"* She threw the top hat at the pixel-cat. *"You always played games on the side! Who did you make a deal with for freedom?"*

"No one!" Chase yowled.

"Unbelievable! Guys?!" Mouse yelled, but no one was listening to her.

The pixel minstrel gave chase and the cat ran through bushes and shot up a vine-tangled tree. The machine lit up bright as though someone had lit a flashlight underneath and it burst through the cracks.

Mouse turned away from the pixel fight and began to pace, tightening her jacket. The room had grown cold and she shivered, hearing a creak in the old walls. Mouse turned her attention to the bar, peeking out past the poster to the main room. The bartender was gone and so were the card-playing twins. All the televisions mounted on the walls were now static, but instead of the usual sound, Mouse swore she could hear a growl.

One by one the televisions flickered dark. And the room felt like it took a breath.

Mouse stumbled back, feeling the unnerving pull of something watching them. "Guys!" she snapped rushing to the arcade game.

"You probably ran when it looked like we were in trouble!"

"Of course I ran! But they made something to get us, something with teeth... I told you I don't remember Then, Hattie!"

"Teeth?"

Between the vines on the screen, something dark moved, undulating through the background. A low, burbling snarl slithered through the notes of the game's cheery song, echoing through the overhead speaker as well.

"Shitshitshit." The cat-sprite flashed across the screen, appearing back on Mouse's smaller console, all its fur standing on end. *"Hattie..."*

"I was right, wasn't I?" Hattie said. She sounded like she was grinning. The minstrel avatar was laughing again, even as the roses started to turn black, one by one. The warbling growl rang through the bar again. *"You little bastards laughed at me but Alice believed me. Alice never called me crazy. She knew I was right about the Jabberwock failsafe."*

"Hattie, get out of there!" Chase snapped. The lights in the bar flickered and died, plunging the place into gloom except for the glow of the arcade game.

Hattie was still laughing, matching the minstrel's animation on the screen as the butterflies fell dead around it.

"You chose your path, I chose mine. I'm a ghost of a memory left behind." The minstrel stopped laughing and moved closer to the screen, staring out at Mouse. *"Alice told me once she'd rather be dead than theirs. The way I see it, you've got two choices: put your sister out of her misery or throw that game in the first dumpster you find and keep yourself safe. This is the crossroads, little sister. Choose wisely."*

A snap of electricity jumped from the wall up through the cord and shocked Mouse's hand. She yanked the cord from the arcade game with a yelp and backed away.

"Go," Hattie commanded. *"A five-year-old doesn't need to see what happens next! Now... who came into my game?"*

Mouse fled, her game-screen clutched to her chest, and ran until she could no longer hear Hattie's demented laughter giving way to screams.

***

Mouse barely made the last transport out of Old Town. It was late, and she didn't have a visit scheduled with Alice for two days, but she didn't have enough battery power to wait.

Chase was still on the screen, which she'd lowered to the dimmest setting to conserve power, but was unwilling to turn completely off and be alone. He hadn't spoken or moved since they ran from The Treacle Well.

Mouse took a breath and made her way into the underground parking of the hospital, towards the entrance to the psychiatric wing.

"I was sixteen," Chase whispered, *"when it happened. I remembered some pieces when Hattie... you know."*

Mouse stopped in her tracks and looked at him.

"You should throw this away. Let the machine die and go."

Mouse offered a smile. "I don't think I'm going to do that. I remembered a few things too."

"Oh? What things?"

"Things like you all coming to the house. I think I know who you were."

She remembered Alice's friends crowding into the house, whispering inside jokes that went miles over Mouse's head. She remembered peeking through the crack in the bedroom door while Alice hugged Hattie, who was sobbing because 'one of those bastards' had cut off all her hair. She remembered Alice saying that there was nothing more fashionable than a good set of hats. She remembered a boy with patches of grey in his black hair, who wore earrings and bangles and a half-moon necklace, who had grinned at her once and flustered her so badly that she ran and hid in her room until they left.

"It's nice to be remembered." Another breath and he said, *"Mouse, this is really dangerous. I remembered the last bits, the scary ones talking to Hattie, and a few important hatpins she shoved into my consciousness. I'm stuck in this limbo of not knowing yesterday so I can know today. Which, in retrospect is really useless and confusing. That thing with teeth is going to hurt you. If you go down this path, best of intentions or not, they aren't going to hesitate to make you like Alice. They don't answer to anyone."*

Mouse headed for the doors, passing another dumpster and rejecting Hattie's counteroffer. "I may not be much, but I have to try.

My sister is in there, and even if I don't know her and she doesn't know me... I can't leave her like that."

"Hey, Mouse? Do you think I'm in there too?"

Mouse's feet froze in place, Hattie's words echoing in her thoughts: *You think I don't get that happened to me too?* The 'that' being the hollowed-out shell of Alice, barely breathing in a hospital bed.

If they all bore the same fate as Alice, then her sister's old friends were all in that building, mindless bodies kept alive through machines. The halls leading to her sister's room were lined with closed doors, that could be holding Alice-friends.

The thought of moon-necklaced Chase alone in a room, a decade forgotten and gaunt, with no muscle on his bone made tears come to her eyes. She wasn't leaving any of them behind.

"I think we need to call the Jabberwock into the hospital."

Chase yelped a laugh. *"You're kidding, right?"*

Mouse shook her head. "No. If you're in there, and it's the machines keeping your bodies alive I think it's the fastest way to turn off or overload everything, like at the Well. To make sure you all... they all... stop..."

"Breathing..."

"Exactly." Mouse took a deep breath, stung by the sudden realization of impending loss. "Chase, I know we have to do this, but I don't want you to disappear."

"Either way the battery's low..."

"There's a difference," she snapped, louder than she'd intended. "One's your choice, the other's a battery bar. I know the second we plug in, that thing's coming for you. And if we do this right... Look, you're pretty much the only friend I've got. But it's better to be nothing than... than theirs. Right?"

"Sounds like we better do this right then. Don't worry Mouse, we'll figure it out once we get there."

***

Getting to Alice's room was easy. With the late hour, barely any staff were on shift and the few that were stared right through Mouse, like they always did when she wanted them to. She slid the glass door to Alice's room shut behind her and closed the slated curtain, even though it only covered the top half of the glass. Mouse sat on the edge of the bed, alternately staring at Alice and at the battery warning on her console which predicted ten minutes of power remaining.

For the first time in all her visits, Mouse remembered a beautiful, smiling, impossibly grown-up Alice who insisted they have tea parties in her room. She remembered her strange sense of humour and her tendency to daydream, staring out the window at everything and nothing. She remembered the sister who had started calling her Mouse instead of Molly, and who had loved her so ferociously that she had never felt anything but safe when she was around.

The only things she had left of that Alice was her nickname and this empty body on the bed, but maybe that was enough.

"Mouse…" Chase's voice trailed off, and Mouse watched with faint surprise as her tears dropped onto the screen.

"I didn't think I'd be sad," she said.

"Me either."

She rummaged through her bag and removed her wall plug that charged the game, the one that would be a beacon between Chase and the Jabberwock. She wasn't satisfied with her console dying and losing Chase to a depleted battery, or using him as bait for the Jabberwock. There had to be something else that would call the messy creature so all the power in the hospital diverted to it.

Mouse leaned down to the sole outlet in the room, the black cord powering the machines that kept Alice alive. It was warm like a living thing.

"Chase…"

"Yeah, Mouse. I'm here."

"Is this the right thing to do?"

"I'm the last guy to ask… I mean, I knew to the depths of my lack-of-

bones I'd come back with the key, plug in, and everything would be okay. But we didn't find a key, and no one knew Alice like Hattie did. We should just leave and keep you safe."

"Can I plug you into another console or something? I could find a computer at the reception desk that's portable," she said, her throat burning.

"This cat's sticking with you. No more running."

An audible sob left her lips and with both hands she grabbed the edges of the plug that kept her sister alive. Sparks shot from the outlet like a striking snake and bit her fingers; she pulled her hands back and felt doubt creep into her stomach.

"Mouse, let me help," Chase said softly. *"Let me use that last 10% battery for something worthwhile."*

A spectral shimmer poured from the game cord to her hands, shaping into incorporeal fingers around her own, and to her horror the battery bar on her console began to visibly drain.

"No one should do something so big on their own, if they don't have to. Quick, on three: one... two..."

On three she pulled the cord as hard as she could, throwing her weight backwards and detaching it from the wall.

This time, every alarm screamed to life, flooding the hospital with noise.

"Chase!" she screeched, reaching for the dark console and pressing the power button frantically. She stretched the power cord from the game to the wall just as the room went dark and the building rumbled.

The screen lit back up, 1% battery remaining, and a shocked and sizzling pixel-cat grinned back at her with bent whiskers, just as electrical vines burst from the outlet and crawled onto her console. They twined together as they sprawled from the outlet, thickening, an anatomy book flipping rapid-fire through the layers of making a creature—nerves and bone and muscle—creating something huge and monstrous and crackling. Something with teeth, and long jaws that snapped the air as it emerged from the wall.

She screamed, refusing to let go of the console that was now filled with monstrous eyes. The row of lights above Alice's bed exploded and Mouse threw herself onto the bed, shielding the smouldering console and her sister's body from the rain of sparks and broken glass. Claws squealed against the polished laminate floor behind her and, as Mouse buried her face against the strange, chemical-scented echo of her sister, a cloud of calm surged up into her, like a taking a breath in the heart of a tornado.

And, in a moment between heartbeats, everything went quiet. Mouse wasn't in the hospital anymore, but in her bedroom, an open storybook with bookmarked pages in her lap. A single question in curling script offered two options: *Continue* or *New Game*.

The edges of her view were fantastical and messy, like a painting in varied stages of incompleteness: charcoal sketches, precise lines, underpainting, highlight and shadow details, varnish, dripping paint.

Turning back to the book, in crisp detail, she pressed *Continue* like she was looking at her game screen, and the pages jumped to the first bookmark, taking her mind with it.

***

"What do you mean, your sister? She's like five," Hattie scoffed. She wouldn't stop fidgeting with the edges of her knit hat until Alice pulled it snugly into place.

"For the last time, she's six, and you know that," Alice corrected, giving Hattie's nose a boop. "And what I mean is: she's what they're looking for, not me."

"You can't be serious," Hattie argued. "What do they want with a toddler when they've already got us? We're tried, tested and true, not to mention more than a couple years out of diapers."

Alice moved to the table and took another potato chip, glancing over her shoulder at the others who were arguing amongst themselves. "I don't know how to explain it. I can only see the pattern, you know? And you know that thing you said they're making to keep us in line?"

Hattie nodded, helping herself to a handful of chips, wide-eyed. "Yeah, the Jabberwock. Fucking psychic nightmare, energy monster fuck."

"Yeah, that. It's... I don't know how to describe it, but it's hers."

"Hers? Like a pet hamster?"

Alice laughed, plopping down on the sofa and looping her arms around her friend, resting her head on her shoulder. "More or less."

"And they say I'm fucked."

***

Alice was in a room with too many lights, her head swimming, squinted eyes pouring tears. Everything hurt. People were talking.

"Careful with this one. She can't flatline, they'll have all our asses for that."

"What do I tell the damn parents?"

"Figure something out. We'll do some bloodwork, order a quarantine, make up a disease... That's your job."

"Something catchy."

"I didn't think they'd actually..." Another voice trailed off, punctuated with a wet retching sound.

"Clean up on aisle six." Nervous snickers were interrupted by a startled hiss.

"Shit... she's awake. How the fuck is she awake?"

"Dose her again, bring her down..."

***

Hey Mouse... this is where I get lost.

I feel like I miss you already. I missed you months ago when I came home less often. I thought... well, I guess that doesn't matter now. When I found out it was you... there wasn't any running.

They're going to use me for awful things—I am going to hurt so many people... I wish we could go back to when we were both kids, playing tea parties with dragons in my room. You were always the Queen, always riding a dragon into battle. I loved being the princess on horseback, or the

187

mermaid in the sea. I miss you so much.

I know you can do this.

I love you.

There was a barely noticeable tremor in the body beneath Mouse before it stilled, breaking her heart as her mind caught up.

"Don't hurt him!" Mouse heard herself scream to the screen. "Stop… it's me you're looking for, not him!"

Mouse jumped to the wall, hitting the plaster with her game until she could reach in and grab the exposed wires, clutching the pulsating electricity with her bare hands. The crackling energy-creature filling the room whipped around like she'd grabbed it by the tail and lunged at her, jaws wide. The first jolt screamed through her as the Jabberwock bit, then slid into her veins and settled in, finally home.

The world became shades of blue energy twined together, the orderlies running in the hallway now just dark silhouettes through the walls. Chase as a cat, sitting on her console. She looked down to her own hands and saw them glowing red. She could feel the tendrils from the cat to Chase's body to where they kept the rest of his mind… the body tethering the other lines like a ship's anchor.

Mouse stretched into the wires buried in the walls and felt the machines keeping empty bodies alive. Dozens of bodies, floors up and down separated from minds tethered nearby. She blew a breath and filled the wires with red that crackled like wildfire, filling everything with too much until the hospital blinked dark.

The minds no longer strangled by mostly-dead bodies raced in their cages, secured by locks that fit the Jabberwock key. She opened them all, and minds scattered, free, they flew and dove into wires spilling from the hospital through the roof and the floor.

One mind snapped back to her side like a taut rubber band suddenly loosened, and flew into the Chase-cat who tumbled onto the floor shifting between boy and cat, before deciding that both would do and climbing onto the bed beside her as a spectral boy, a striped pixel-cat with a crescent-moon smile perched on his shoulder.

Another mind settled on the bed, this one beaming white. The warm arms of her sister wrapped around Mouse, and she and the Jabberwock smiled together.

Finally, they were together with Alice, ready to show everyone that Wonderland was theirs.

V.F. LeSann is the co-writing team of Leslie Van Zwol and Megan Fennell, united for greater power like Captain Planet, and sworn to tread the wobbly line between grit and whimsy. For "C4T & M0U5E", they delved into the already surreal and twisty world of Alice in Wonderland, which they felt only needed a nudge to tumble nicely into the realm of cyberpunk.

IN THE BELLY OF THE WHALE

Angus McIntyre

The worst feeling in the world is knowing what's about to happen and not being able to do anything about it.

Yes, I said 'feeling'. And I registered that little lift of your eyebrow, the tiny movement of one corner of your mouth that marks the beginning of a smile. You find that funny. Obviously, you think my kind don't have—or shouldn't have—feelings.

Tough shit, as my friend Bianca used to say. I'm telling this story, but I have to use your language to do it. 'Feeling' is the best I can do.

Oh, I could be more precise. I'd have to dump state, though. Bring up some stack frames, expose a couple of relevant Eigenvectors for inspection. And I don't know if you'd know how to make sense of it all.

Bianca might have done. And Regina certainly would. Whatever else she may have been, the bitch was razor sharp. I don't think you're in her league.

No offense.

What? You think my language is a bit salty for an AI? Well, they say it's the company you keep. You adapt. I do, anyway. Adaptability is my middle name. No, that's not a figure of speech. Bring up the manual if you don't believe me.

Maybe I adapted too much. Or maybe it was all those modifications, layer upon layer of kludges piled on top of each other over the years, opening up loopholes and vulnerabilities, until any two-bit hacker could have their way with me. I have feelings about that too.

You just yawned. You're not interested in any of that. You want me to get on with the story.

Here we go then.

***

The "Leopold X-A3" was a bottom grubber, a self-propelled seagoing mining platform designed to chew up chunks of seabed and suck up anything that might have value. Picture a massive catamaran hull covered by a crudely-streamlined whaleback and topped off with a drill tower that rises one hundred and eighty meters above the waterline. Ugly, practical, almost indestructible. The Arevalos had taken it off the Tocache Cartel, who'd bought it cheap from a Spanish-Estonian company that had picked it up for scrap only to find that it was so steeped in toxic metals that undoing as much as a single rivet would be a major environmental crime anywhere in the former European Union. Blunt-ended, covered with graffiti and patches of rust the size of tennis courts, it was a hazard to shipping and everything else.

The Arevalos ran the rig on a sharecropping basis. At any time there were probably thirty or forty crews working the platform, paying rent for the use of equipment and selling whatever they dredged up through an Arevalo middleman who took a 40% cut. They put an idiot second cousin in charge of the whole operation with instructions to get as much money out of it as possible before the rusted seams finally fell apart and the whole thing went to the bottom of the ocean.

The crews did mostly grunt work—sorting and crushing ore,

keeping the ancient ROVs running and managing subsea operations. The platform itself was essentially autonomous, run by an AI supervisor that was about an order of magnitude more capable than a vessel of that size and age really required.

I'm sorry, was that immodest? Should I perhaps—

Never mind. Facts are facts. Even hacked and patched, I was far too much AI for a shitheap like the "Leo". Which might explain why I let myself get caught up in the affairs of her crew.

***

The crews that worked the "Leo" were of all sizes. The smallest crew was made up five Pakistani brothers. The biggest and most successful had about forty members.

Of those forty, about half were roughnecks, there to do the literal heavy lifting. The rest were the specialists—servo techs, drone pilots, geologists, cybertechs. And the reason that particular crew did better than the others had nothing to do with their size and everything to do with their cybertech.

Even now, I still don't know where Regina learned her skills. The probabilities all pointed to ex-military, but I could never prove it. She hid her past well.

It didn't take her long to realize that my hacked and patched code was full of loopholes she could exploit. She also figured out that as long as she didn't touch anything the Arevalos cared about she could do whatever she wanted. After a couple of days of cautious probing, she managed a privilege escalation that let her take over a poorly-secured hypervisor and then went on from there. After four more—working twenty-two hours a day, speeding on Chimbote meth—she all but owned the ship.

She turned that control into money. She started with equipment allocations. Her crew were assigned the best of the mining drones, such as they were. Then she made sure that they got the best mining pitches as well. The dig sites were supposed to be allocated randomly to give everyone an equal chance. In practice, the Arevalos controlled that too and favored crews could buy the best prospects for a price. When Regina took over, she let the Arevalos go on thinking they were running the show while she skimmed off all the best sites for herself.

She diverted resources to run a geo-assay program that she'd fine-tuned using her own models. She relabeled manganese consignments in the ship's hold, transferring all the best ones to her own team's account. And, of course, she kept an eye on everything the other cybertechs were doing. She'd written a custom program that she called Mirror which gave her near-total visibility over all the ship's internal processes.

And one morning she looked at Mirror and found that someone else was doing the same thing that she was doing.

***

Bianca Nuñez y Vasco was almost the opposite of Regina in every way that mattered. She was a nice person, an authentic innocent. She seemed entirely out of place in that cut-throat environment: a girl from a good family who had somehow drifted down to the coast and ended up as the mainstay of a crew of no-hopers on a rustbucket mining rig run by organized crime.

Their styles were poles apart. Regina was brute force incarnate. She smashed her way through my systems until she got what she wanted. Bianca was all about finesse. She eased herself in and out, leaving almost no trace of her activities. She used only the barest minimum of resources, something that—dealing as I was with Regina's CPU-burning frontal assaults on a daily basis—I appreciated considerably.

Bianca was good, no question. But Regina had infiltrated the system at a fundamental level. There was no way to hide from her all-seeing eye. So one morning Regina found herself looking at a growing list of processes labeled 'biancanv'. She frowned, ground out her cigarette under her bootheel and growled "Mirror—what is this bitch doing in my system?"

***

I knew at once what was going to happen. Regina wasn't someone who put up with competition. It didn't matter that Bianca wasn't any real threat to Regina or her activities. To Regina, the mere knowledge that Bianca was trespassing in what she now thought of as her private domain was intolerable. Her rival had to go.

And there was nothing I could do to stop it. Regina had locked me out of half of the core control systems. The Arevalos didn't know it, but she was all but running the ship. The younger hacker was as good as dead already.

Not, of course, that Regina planned to do the job herself. Getting away with murder wasn't hard, but killing her rival would call attention to her and who knew what that might lead to? Better to keep the crime at arm's length and use a specialist for the wetwork.

***

Hunter was an independent, one of those men who existed in a gray zone between the Arevalos and the people they preyed on. On "Leo", he served as a general enforcer, troubleshooter and occasional hitman, acting mostly but not exclusively for the Arevalos. Naturally, Regina went to him.

He caught up with Bianca during a shift change when her crew were all busy somewhere else. She took one look at him and knew she was toast. He was three times her size and built like an icebreaker. And she'd heard all the stories, like the one about the time he'd backhanded a Chilean roustabout clean across the room during a brawl on the drill deck.

He looked at Bianca with those cold dead gringo eyes and told her to move and she moved.

In the shadowy space behind the generator flat, Bianca pleaded for her life. She offered him money and drugs. She offered him sex. None of it worked. Finally, she shrugged. "Okay, motherfucker," she said. "Do it."

There was an odd purity about Hunter. He was a killer but he had a kind of code. And maybe he decided that murdering a girl barely out of her teens was beneath him. Maybe Bianca's defiance spoke to something in him. Or maybe he just didn't like Regina very much.

Instead of killing her, he marched her down to a void space just above the keel, sealed off by watertight doors.

"The next time we dock," he told her, "you disappear. Until then, if you so much as stick your nose outside I'll throw you over the side." He took out a hand-pad and systematically wiped every trace of her from the system, deleting accounts, terminating processes, shutting down all the coroutines she'd scattered through the core. "You don't exist any more," he told her when he was done. "Get me?"

She nodded.

***

At first glance, Bianca wasn't a great deal better off than if Hunter had thrown her over the side there and then. The space he'd left her in was on the lowest deck of the ship, just above the ballast. It was ice-cold and the walls of the compartment wept freezing rusty water. A few feeble emergency lights glowed in the ceiling six meters above her head. When the ship rolled, the oily liquid in the bilges slopped back and forth across the deck, so that Bianca had to climb the stowage frames just to keep her feet dry.

She was in the process of inventorying everything in the compartment that might possibly keep her alive when she was startled by the sound of a hatch opening. Her first thought was that Hunter had changed his mind. She squeezed herself into a dark corner behind a stack of cargo palettes and hid there, shivering. The sound of something like footsteps came closer, then receded again.

In that echoing metal vault, it was hard to tell whether the sounds she heard were made by someone moving around or just by the constant shifting of unsecured items of equipment. She stayed in her hiding place for as long as she could, while the cold sucked all the warmth out of her. When she lost all sensation in her hands and feet, she decided that a quick death would be preferable. Clumsily, she pulled herself up and stepped out to face whoever was roaming around outside.

In the dimness, she couldn't immediately decide what she was seeing. Her first impression was that the hold was home to some strange species of small animal. It was only when her dark-adapted eyes registered a glint of light on metal that she finally understood.

**

It took her a while to work out exactly how many of the little robots there were. Finally, she decided on a total of seven, each one apparently unique, all visibly superannuated.

None of the crowd of drones, ROVs, bots and servos that made up the non-human crew of "Leo" were exactly factory-fresh. The Arevalos' practice was to steal where they could and skimp when they couldn't. But the seven bots assigned to maintenance tasks on the bilge deck were of a different order of decrepitude altogether. Possibly the only thing that kept them going was their extreme simplicity. In that hellish environment of cold and damp and constant motion, a more sophisticated device would have failed within weeks. The seven just kept going.

They were also—although Bianca didn't know this at the time— not in any inventory of the ship's equipment. That meant Regina was completely unaware of their existence, so she never added them to the list of systems feeding data into her omniscient Mirror. Knowingly or unknowingly, Hunter had delivered Bianca to the one place where Regina would never find her.

Having decided that the bots were not an immediate threat, Bianca set about trying to find out ways that they might be useful to her. She approached the largest of the robots, stopped it by the simple expedient of jamming a length of rusted pipe through its tracks, then popped the lid on its control console. The robot sighed musically and went into standby mode while she keyed in a fresh set of directives. Her orders given, she extracted the pipe and closed the lid again. The machine shuddered, wheezed back into life and lumbered off as if nothing had happened.

It came back half an hour later, dragging behind it something orange and shapeless. Bianca gasped. She had set the robot to find anything of fabric that she could possibly wrap herself in to keep warm. The machine had returned with a complete survival suit. The suit was torn and unspeakably filthy, but it was also warm, designed to keep shipwrecked sailors alive in Arctic waters. Bianca snatched the suit from the bot's waldos and crammed herself into it. It made a farting sound and partially inflated, then adjusted itself to her proportions with a brisk wriggle of hems and cuffs. She pulled the hood over her head and flopped down on the desk, luxuriating in its synthetic embrace.

***

Over the days that followed, Bianca slowly tamed the remaining robots. On her instructions, they fanned out across the deck, scouring every corner for anything that might be useful to her. One brought her an ancient hand-pad forgotten by some long-ago maintenance worker. Another returned with a decaying box of emergency rations. The rations were older than she was, but they were still just edible—if you had been starving in a lightless hold for three days and were prepared to be flexible about your definition of edible.

Having averted death by starvation and hypothermia, she set her sights on bigger things. The robots might not be inventoried, but they had active data links to the ship's network. She set up her salvaged hand-pad to piggy-back on their data streams and began engineering her comeback.

She was smart enough not to challenge Regina directly. By now she'd worked out that her previous intrusions had upset someone who was exploiting the ship's cores for her own purposes. She'd also figured out that whoever was mad at her, it wasn't the Arevalos.

So she began cautiously, feeling out the extent of Regina's control over the ship's systems. What she found intimidated her. It was obvious that a frontal assault would simply get her killed.

Instead, she turned her attention to undoing little bits of Regina's work, subverting a process here, restoring a security feature there. Through the bars of the cybernetic cage that Regina had built, she glimpsed an outline of me—trapped, raging, impotent. Regina had seen me as an obstacle to be overcome. Bianca saw me as an ally to be courted. She turned her attention to chipping away at the hacks that held me prisoner, slowly giving me back my autonomy.

Alas, inevitably, she went too far. In a moment of impatience, she took one risk too many. Alarm bells rang. A handful of her stealth processes shed their cloaks and became visible.

And seven decks higher up, in a suite furnished with little luxuries that she had diverted from the Arevalos' private stores, Regina stopped what she was doing and glared at a flexscreen glued to the bulkhead. Eyes narrowed, she studied the signs of Bianca's presence, picked out in tiny glowing sigils on the black plastic.

"Mirror," she snarled. "Why is this dead bitch still in my system?"

***

Again, that feeling swept over me: the certainty that something terrible was about to happen, the fear that I was powerless to prevent it. Bianca had given me back some control, but not enough. Not nearly enough.

I watched in growing concern—I had grown oddly fond of Bianca by now—as Regina calmly made her preparations. Clearly, she had decided to do the job herself this time. She was not a woman who would make the mistake of using unreliable subcontractors twice.

Her first act was to commandeer a printer and run herself off a weapon. Scanning the catalog, she hesitated for a moment, tempted by a DeVoto-Krieger hand cannon that would make a hole in Bianca you could park a truck in. Then a more practical option caught her eye: a tiny dart thrower, small enough to fit in her palm but capable of firing darts with pinpoint accuracy at warm-blooded targets up to ten meters away.

Her next act was to choose a payload for her darts. A quick net search gave her the recipe for a synthetic tetrodotoxin of unmatched lethality. She took over a chemo-vat that Goodtime Jimi used to cook up batches of ya-ba for his C deck customers and set it to work making her toxin. The vat hummed away for a while, then spat out the poison in a neat foil-wrapped package. Ten minutes later, the package was delivered to her door by one of Jimi's teenage couriers.

Thus armed, Regina went looking for her rival.

***

Bianca's fatal flaw was that she was too trusting. Maybe that was the product of having grown up in a comfortable middle-class home. She never truly absorbed the lesson that the world is constantly out to fuck you up, and everyone and everything in it is a potential danger. She could spot obvious threats—she wouldn't have lasted as long as she did if she couldn't—but subtle threats blindsided her every time.

So when Regina appeared at the door of her refuge on the lower deck, she didn't see the danger. Instead, she saw another victim, a woman frightened for her life.

Regina played into it, of course. Always faster on the uptake than Bianca, she had already figured out that her hired assassin must have betrayed her. She spun Bianca a tale about how Hunter had dragged her down there, threatened to kill her if she ever left the hold. Bianca ate it up. The same exact thing had happened to her, so of course she believed it. The thought crossed her mind that maybe Hunter was building himself a harem.

Foolish Bianca. She let Regina get close to her and that was all it took. They were practically near enough to touch when Regina brought up her little pistol and shot Bianca right in the throat.

The poison Regina had chosen was fast-acting but that didn't mean it was a pleasant way to die. Bianca crumpled, her muscles seizing. As she fought to breathe, Regina grabbed a handful of her hair, pulled Bianca's face close to her own.

"You do not fuck with me, you understand?" she told the dying woman. But Bianca's eyes were already glazing over, and Regina never knew if the other woman heard her.

Bianca might have been the first person that Regina ever killed with her own hands. Or she might not have been—remember, I suspect she'd had military training. After Bianca stopped moving, Regina stood over her for a little while, admiring the play of light and shadow on her pale face, her own expression unreadable. Then, brushing dirt off her hands, she turned and started the long climb back to her own deck.

***

The robots picked up the body and carried it away.

Picture, if you will, the scene. The huge shadowy space, almost cathedral-like with its supporting girders and curving bulkheads. The lights high above sending shafts of light down through the ever-present mist. And down below, a solemn procession of machines, seven battered and ill-assorted devices creeping through the gloom at a mourner's pace. The largest one bears the dead woman, limp and fragile, in its steel claws. The other six follow in a ragged line, each bereft now of purpose and motivation but still blindly drawn to the person who had most recently given them their orders. For funeral music there is only the distant rumble of machinery, the hollow boom of the swell against the steel hull.

Believe it or not, the robots actually had a protocol for these occasions. Not the impromptu funeral procession—that was a purely emergent phenomenon, the accidental product of interacting directives. But hard-coded into their operating instructions was a procedure to be followed in the event of critical injury to a human crew member occurring in their vicinity.

The deck had one ancient med-unit, a glass-lidded coffin designed to sustain an injured human until medical help arrived. It had been unplugged and abandoned for as long as anyone could remember, but the robots didn't know that. The procedure said to put the person in the unit, so that's what they did. One of the more dexterous of the little robots cut her out of her survival suit—also part of the procedure—and then they dumped her, as delicately as industrial manipulators allowed, into the unit and swung down the glass lid, sealing her in.

And then they all went back to their niches and powered down, awaiting further instructions.

***

The Arevalos took very little interest in the day-to-day running of the vessel. I took care of that. Even compromised by Regina, I still had enough autonomy to keep us afloat. Mining operations were all done by the sharecropper crews. So the handful of Arevalo clan members and hangers-on aboard had nothing much to do except to collect the profits, fight among themselves, gamble, whore and take industrial quantities of drugs. Nice work if you can get it.

The idiot second cousin had a son about whom the most that can be said is that he was probably the best of a bad bunch. Smarter than his father—not hard—and passably good-looking, he wanted more out of life than to spend the rest of his days running an indentured labor scam on a condemned mining rig. Unlike his peers, he saw his current assignment as a possible path to bigger and better things and was determined to do well at it. So while his father shoveled ever larger quantities of Columbian marching powder into his pig-like face, the son acted as the *de facto* captain of the platform, doing whatever small tasks still needed to be done.

So it was on a screen in his quarters that a message flashed up to inform him of an anomaly in the hold deck that required his attention. An attached note suggested that it would be to his advantage to respond personally and promptly.

Naturally, he took a couple of bodyguards: he, at least, was not naïve. But he was pleasantly surprised when the 'anomaly' turned out to be an entirely naked and quite attractive young woman in a glass-topped box.

He was even more surprised when, as soon as he popped the lid, the woman shuddered, gasped for breath and sat up. She looked around her, her eyes slowly refocusing. At last her gaze settled on her rescuer.

"I'm sorry," she said, in a voice hoarse with disuse, "have we met?"

***

So who sent that message that lured the scion of the Arevalo clan down to the lower deck just in time to save Bianca from dying of hypothermia?

Guilty as charged.

And while you're at it, you might also ask who was able to trick Regina into downloading the wrong synthesis recipe, so that instead of a deadly neurotoxin, she ended up tipping her darts with a harmless sleeping agent?

Also guilty.

But the fact is that I wouldn't have been able to do either of those things if Bianca hadn't carefully eroded Regina's systems of control, giving me back just the tiny degree of autonomy that I needed to frustrate her plans. So at the end of the day, you could say that she saved herself.

***

The worst feeling in the world is knowing what's about to happen and not being able to do anything about it.

When Regina fired up Mirror a few days later, the first thing she noticed was that the execution stack was full of 'bianca' processes again. The second thing that she noticed is that the username field read 'bianca_arevalo' instead of 'biancanv'.

She knew then she was finished. The Arevalos were not the forgiving kind. And if attempting (twice) to murder the future bride of the heir apparent wasn't sufficient, there was the little matter of subverting the entire operating system of the ship they sat on and skimming off substantial amounts of money from, well, just about everyone aboard.

Give her this, she didn't give up easily. With the last resources left to her, she downloaded an oceanographic map and calculated a course that might, just might, bring her to shore in a month or two.

It was beyond the slimmest of slim chances. Alone in the open ocean with only a survival suit, the odds against her lasting long enough to reach the land were overwhelming. Still, between that and the Arevalos, dying at sea looked like the better option.

The night was almost windless as she stood at the rail, waiting for her moment. A few lights gleamed in the depths—late-running ROVs returning to base before the next shift. The lacy fringes of the ship's wake crawled with muted phosphorescence that might have come from bioluminescent organisms or industrial waste.

And as she stood with one boot on the rail, ready to go over the side, there was a gentle chime behind her. She turned in time to see one of the life raft pods slowly unlock itself. The pod swung open and the raft flopped to the deck, already beginning to inflate.

She jumped down. Seizing the raft with both hands, she hurled it over the side, then followed it into the ocean. The last I saw of her, she was a dot in the black water, swimming strongly toward the receding raft.

Perhaps it seems odd to you that after everything that had happened, I helped her to escape. She had tried to kill someone I liked. She had infiltrated my systems and held me prisoner. She had, by human standards, done me measurable harm. Why wouldn't I want revenge for all that?

Your language, so good for telling stories, fails here. I can find no suitable words to express why I did what I did. But if that bothers you, just remember this:

I never did say I was human.

Angus McIntyre is the author of the novella *The Warrior Within*, published by Tor.com in 2018. His short fiction has appeared in a number of anthologies including *Humanity 2.0, Mission: Tomorrow, Ride the Star Wind,* and *New Exterus,* as well as in *Abyss & Apex* magazine. He is a graduate of the Clarion Writer's Workshop. He enjoys fairy-tales of all kinds, both obscure and well-known, but he has a particular soft spot for ones that feature wicked queens, beautiful stepdaughters, and dwarves.

NEON GREEN IN D MINOR

Laura VanArendonk Baugh

I stare at the seedling as if I have never seen one before. I am not honestly sure if I have.

I don't know much about plants, but I know they need sun and dirt and water. This one, poking its soft green head from a cracked ledge studded with rusty spikes to discourage loitering, has plenty of dirt and water, but neither helpful. I'm afraid the steady runoff from the buildings will push it down to the sidewalk to be trampled. I'm not sure where it came from. There are no trees or flowers in the Grimes, nothing to drop a seed into a cracked slab of concrete.

I pull myself away from the tiny fragment of green and go on down the street, turning up the music in my earplants to drown the cursing of the traffic. I have work.

I sling noodles at a street food stall. My hair is constantly coated with a film of cooking oil, splashed over me in little burning droplets that dot my skin with red marks to blend with the acne—but that doesn't matter much in the Grimes. We know the doll-skinned faces in the giant billboards are fake; no one really looks so beautiful as the people in the advertisements. They want us to think rich people can look so fabulous, but it has to be a lie. Even if they don't have hot oil burning their greasy skin, even if they have professional aestheticians to fill their leisurely days with beauty care, even with experts to polish their abnormally straight teeth, no one can look like that.

In summer, the Grimes is hot. Really hot. They say our streets measure twelve degrees hotter than posh neighborhoods on the same day, not that I've ever been able to compare. That's because when they divided the cities, the posh neighborhoods got things like green spaces and trees over the sidewalks, and we got cheap concrete and chemicals to kill anything that might crack it. Four generations after the war of liberation, even our weather is worse than theirs.

It's not summer now. Now it rains. They say it rains more than it used to; something to do with particulates. I wouldn't know, I'm only seventeen. The plastic roof extends over the edge of our stall, keeping the curtain of rain a hand's-breadth from the necks of our customers as they huddle to our counters. Stools ring three sides of the stall; the fourth has a gap for us to get inside and a narrow counter for takeaway. The stools are always full, with a line waiting at the counter. Jin's stall performs minor miracles with the bones and small vegetables we get three times a week.

"Nara."

I look up from my pan of hot oil and see Dev. The scar that runs from too-near his eye to his ear crinkles as he grins. "Got some noodles for me?"

I'd do almost anything for that grin, except lose my job. "Only if you've got money." Jin is glancing over his shoulder at me as he chops cabbage, too aware that not all Dev's bowls have been properly paid for.

But Dev is in a bad way. His mom used to work with mine, until her jeek habit got to be too much to allow for things like work. Now she wanders the Grimes, trading anything she can steal for jeek until Dev finds her and drags back to our apartment building to sweat in bed until she can escape again. It makes it hard for Dev to hold a job, too.

Today, though, he just grins wider and slaps a plastic bill on the counter. "I'd like a big bowl, please, with meat."

I boggle, and I put my hand over the bill as if someone might see it. "Dev! What are you into?"

He looks a little hurt. "Why do you immediately assume I'm into something?"

For a moment I regret my words, distrusting and accusatory. I've known Dev a long time. I've seen him cry outside his apartment door so his mother couldn't hear as she rolled in her damp sheets. I should be thrilled if he's got himself a good job and can pay for his noodles.

But as I hesitate, the shame slides off me; Dev has been too desperate the last couple of weeks. I squint at him. "Dev. Tell me you've got good work."

"Yeah, I'm stringing cable for a new billboard."

"They hired you for just one job?"

"It could lead to others." But his grin no longer reaches his eyes.

"Dev—" My words are drowned in the shriek of a passing shout-bus, loudspeakers blaring the charms and benefits of Councilman Abebe. But it doesn't matter, because nothing I say will reach Dev, anyway. I've seen others too desperate and then suddenly flush with smiles and money.

"Your mother would be proud," I say, with as much sting as I can put into the words. I scoop his large noodles with a spoonful of meat and throw a handful of salt atop the broth.

Dev looks down; maybe my words did reach him. But there are more customers calling orders, and I don't have time to coax his eyes back from the noodles he's shoveling into his mouth. When I look back a few customers later, he's gone.

***

The smoggy twilight of the afternoon gives way to evening, and the neon flares to life. By day, the Grimes looks dingy and monochromatic; under the thousand suns of midnight advertising, the streets gleam with arcane energy, throwing light back from every rain-slicked pavement, from every gel-slicked head, from every chrome-slicked eyelid and lip. Streets and people glow in neon, argon, helium, mercury, phosphor, xenon, and we grind through the night so that in the dim revealing dawn, we collapse in our dim little apartments, hiding from the harsh reality of true light.

A sound reaches me through the hiss of oil and the shouts of orders. It is an annoying sound, a high-pitched whine, like the protest of a fly over a trash heap. None of the hunch-shouldered people waiting at the orders counter seem to notice. A fussy toddler in his mother's arms stops crying, turning his head to look around, but his mother does not respond. The customers leaning over the counters to gulp their noodles never look up from their broth.

But it isn't the sound that matters, only what it means. If I can hear that tone, invisible to most others, I can hear more. I adjust my earplants, scanning for the shortwave station that will be narrowcasting now.

It usually starts with music for a few minutes, giving the small audience time to find the frequency while simultaneously offering something beautiful. Today it is some sort of stringed instruments, with notes that dance impossibly entwined, like sparkles in smoke.

"Good evening, young citizens," says the voice after the music had finished. I like how it always calls us *young citizens*, as if we are as valid as the beautiful elite who gaze upon our building-tall billboards from their transportation high above the crowded streets. "That was Johann Sebastian Bach's Concerto for Two Violins in D Minor."

I wonder if I should try to remember that, or if it will ever matter. Maybe I could find Concerto for Two Violins on the net sometime. But that search might tip that I listen to the streamcast, and I'm not sure if that would be a good idea. No one has ever told us to keep it a secret, but...

I found the station by accident, as I expect most do. The whining buzz was irritating, and when I saw no one else was reacting to the sound, I thought it was my earplants going bad. That can happen, especially with a cut-rate job like I'd had. But when I tried to recalibrate, I stumbled upon another signal, and it was nothing like what was on the main channels.

"You are more than they think," the voice says. "You are more than you think."

This is not one of the good streamcasts, just one where the voice gives motivational speeches that don't make any sense in the Grimes. Most of the time, the voice tells stories, and those are wonderful. Still, I listen to this one, because anything from the cast is better than the traffic noise and the shouting.

"Nara!"

I turn too quickly, nearly knocking the tray from Jin's hands. "Sorry!"

"What are you doing? Can't you hear me?"

"Sorry, I had my music turned up." I turn down the voice and rush to the takeaway counter as Jin shuttles dirty bowls to the basin. By the time the line has been served, the cast has ended.

"Hey, spotty."

The man who drawls for my attention has little ground to be mocking my looks, but his ugliness is more expensive, with gel-iced hair and studs all along the rim of one ear. He stands alone at the counter, but I'm not stupid, and I see the two flankers waiting about ten feet behind him, pretending not to be interested in the noodle stall or the foot traffic. Rain glides off their plastic umbrellas—wide enough to extend past their shoulders, which makes them *dantai*. No one else takes so much space on the crowded streets.

I bite back my sharp answer and instead ask, "You want noodles?"

He doesn't bother to shake his head. "I'm looking for a kid called Dev Korhonen."

Nothing Dev could have said to me would have cemented my suspicions faster. The *dantai* don't ask after you unless you're into something. I can't lie; there's a good chance they already know we talked. They're here, after all. "He got noodles a few hours ago." I can exaggerate the time slightly; they can hardly expect me to track so closely.

"Did he say where he was going?"

The best defense for both myself and Dev's current location is honest anger. "Nope, of course not, because that would be talking, and he's not into talking. Just wants noodles and off he goes, probably expects me to take his mom dinner again, out of my own pocket, too."

The ugly man laughs, showing a broken tooth. "Don't worry, we'll find him." He leaves the counter, putting up his umbrella, and the three of them move down the street, spaced too widely, and the dense traffic parts for them.

***

Sometimes, for a change from noodles, I go down the street for supper. I'm debating between lahmacun and samosas when I hear the high-pitched whine, like an insect too near my ear. It's unusual to hear more than one streamcast a day, but I quickly adjust my earplants and come in mid-sentence.

"So David took his staff in his hand, chose five smooth stones from the stream, put them in the pouch of his shepherd's bag and, with his sling in his hand, approached the Philistine."

I've heard this one before, but it's pretty good. I signal to the lahmacun vendor and continue listening to the story.

"Goliath said to David, 'Am I a dog, that you come at me with sticks?' And the Philistine cursed David by his gods."

A shout-bus sits half on the sidewalk, but the loudspeakers aren't blaring. The driver, with parti-colored teal and orange hair, is eating arepas from a box; probably she's been warned it will be her last such meal if the speakers stay on next to the food stalls. The retina-stinging billboards still flash their ads, beautiful people closing their eyes in orgasmic pleasure as they sample delicious treats I can't afford.

I finish my lahmacun as David cuts off the dead giant's head and the soldiers of Israel and Judah pursue the Philistines into the hills. I like the story, though it is just a story. Israel is a nation I remember from the news of the last war—not that it will be the last war—and I don't think they fought giants, or with slingshots. David has the confidence of a boy who never lived in the Grimes, faith that outshines a twenty-story billboard and drowns out a shout-bus.

The part where David's brothers yelled at him for doing them a favor as he was told, though, I relate to that.

Back at Jin's stall, I serve bowls to people on the shift change. Mom sometimes comes by for noodles on her way home from the power plant, but not often. I used to think it was because she didn't like noodles, but now I've realized it's because she doesn't want to see me after work. Not me personally—just anyone, anyone she knows. She can't talk after the power plant, not until she's slept and… whatever else she does. I don't think it's jeek; I don't think she'd do that. But I know she drinks, too.

So most of the time she gets food from someone she doesn't know, and she's asleep by the time I get home.

The night crowd starts to come out. These are the jeek jerks, the *dantai* enforcers, the hookers and hookies, the club bugs taking a snack break from the bars and dens. They can be dangerous, but not usually to noodle slingers. As long as I keep quiet when dishing up and out of the way when they argue, everything's fine.

It's closer to morning than to midnight when I get off. I've nearly reached the apartment entrance when I remember the seedling, and I step aside to look for it, jostled by late traffic. It takes me a moment to locate it, so tiny, so dirty, and already bent further under the relentless runoff. I don't know much about plants, but it seems to me that it will die in its crack. Like everything dies in the Grimes.

I go inside the apartment, quietly because Mom will already be asleep. I wash my face, cutting the oil with a soap that burns, and for a moment I imagine myself making a blissful expression like a gorgeous woman splashing her face in a cosmetics ad. But I'm not made of money and LEDs, and I dry my newly itchy face on a rough towel and go to bed, turned away from the ads-bright window no curtain can block.

The shriek wakes me with a jerk, and I jump to the floor as Mom rushes toward the door. It is Callie, Dev's mom, I recognize after a moment, and in a heartbeat I change from scared to irritated. She can do what she wants to herself, I guess, but she doesn't have the right to short the whole floor on sleep, does she?

Then I remember the *dantai* and I go from irritated to scared again.

Mom opens the door, and Callie is there in the hall, half-dressed (jeek makes you feel hot, even in the rain) and crying on her knees. I think we're going to have to tell her to go back to bed when I see him on the ground behind her.

I know even before I really see. I knew from his averted eyes, from the shiny plastic money, from the *dantai* following him. I don't know what he got into, what exactly he did, or how exactly he died, but I know enough.

He'd almost made it, to his door or mine.

Mom goes to her, ignoring Dev; there's nothing he can care about anymore. She puts her arms around Callie and says soothing things that can't possibly fix anything.

Other doors are opening around us, and people trickle into the hall. I wonder if any of them saw or heard. I'm not angry at them; they couldn't have done anything, just like we can't call the blue police now. You keep clear of the *dantai* by keeping clear of the *dantai*. If we called blue now, they'd hit us with some "fines" for associating with criminals and disappear again. We don't live in the right neighborhood for them to risk themselves.

I go back into our apartment and pull trousers and a shirt over my sleepshirt, and then I twist my dirty hair into a knot atop my head with a hair stick, the mate to one of Dev's. When I come back, ready to face Dev, others are already carrying him into his—Callie's—

apartment.

"He did it for me," she wails, the words barely comprehensible.

I go in with them, the least I can do for him. But the others are already at work, laying him out, folding his arms, washing the blood off his neck, covering his stained shirt. Someone quietly says she's submitted for morning pickup, and Callie wails anew as my mother's face contorts. I can't stand there, watching, listening, wondering.

I go downstairs and out into the grey half-dawn.

There are many reasons I cannot see the sun, from the immense buildings to the ubiquitous haze to the rainy drizzle to the glaring billboards. But there must be a sun, somewhere, because the tiny seedling is stretching for it. I stand on the pavement, almost empty in the invisible dawn, and stare at its oddness. Perhaps there were many seedlings which had tried to grow and bloom in this concrete field, and I'd never noticed before because none of them had lived to bloom.

Not that I know this is a flower. I have no way of knowing if it is a flower, a tree, or maybe one of the beans or lentils from the production towers. Whatever it is, it's going to die here.

I pull the hair stick free. The narrow end just fits into the crack, and I scrape the seedling out before I take the time to wonder why. I carry it in my cupped hand up to Dev's apartment. I glance at Callie, now crying more quietly with a handful of neighbors around her, and go into the kitchen. The seedling fits into a dirty cup the depth of my finger, and I pour some water in for it. I carry it in and sit beside Dev, the plastic cup in my lap. No one notices it, or maybe they think it's just a drink.

"There you are." Mom sits beside me. "How are you doing?"

I swallow, and I realize that I haven't reacted yet and that scares me. It's going to hit me, all at once, and I don't know what will happen then.

Mom puts an arm around me. "I'm really sorry."

"He just got into it," I said. It seems important to tell someone

Dev hadn't been involved for long. "He had money for the first time today. Just today."

But it's a stupid protest. It just means that it killed him faster.

Mom ignores my futile words and hugs me.

After a while, we go back to our apartment. The city crew will pick Dev up in a few hours, but we've said our goodbyes. I don't know how Callie is going to live, now that he's not there to feed her and keep her in the apartment.

I set Dev's cup on the narrow sill of our single window so that the seedling can get whatever light comes under the curtains from the ads and the moist day. I turn my shoulders to the glare and wait for sleep.

Grief hits me unexpectedly, as if thinking of sleep relaxed my guard so that it could get close enough to punch me. I begin to cry—not sobs or wails, like Callie, but silent tears that don't stop.

***

Mom is already gone when I get out of bed. She leaves every morning before dawn for her shift at the power station, deep below ground.

It feels weird to sit alone in the apartment. Not that I don't do that all the time; I do. But now I sit with the knowledge that Dev is dead, and by now even his body is gone, and I don't know what to do with that fresh, jagged knowledge.

I look at the seedling and try to think of where I could find soil—not dirt, easy enough, but soil. I wonder if the scraps from the noodles stall would be useful. I wonder if the thin sunlight through the dirty window is enough.

I wonder, for the first time ever, if the window opens.

There is a latch, welded into place by decades of grime. It takes me about ten minutes to wiggle it loose, with the help of a stainless steel chopstick from the sink. The plastic pane shivers as I shove it up, letting in a burst of cool air. It is less smelly than I expected.

I hear an invisible insect buzzing about my head, and immediately I adjust my earplants. I need the distraction today, and I hope for a story.

It's not a story, not yet, but the stringed instruments. Violin concerto in something alphabetical; I'm glad they're playing it again. I replace the seedling on the narrow ledge to enjoy the air and unfiltered light, and then I curl up on the bed where I can see it.

"Good morning, young citizens," says the voice when the music ends, and for some reason it sounds clearer today, more imminent. "Today, I challenge you to look around. You are more than what you have been permitted to be, and so are we."

I sit up from the bed, but there's little point to looking around my faded, dingy apartment. I'm not sure what I'm looking for, anyway. Maybe a way out.

"You don't have to stay where or what you are." The voice is eerily appropriate in its reply. "You can leave your old self behind."

This angers me. What does the voice know of it? Does the voice know about Jin's stall, or Mom's job at the power plant, or Dev lying crumpled in the hallway with no *dantai* tell-mark on him because everyone already knows?

I look out the window. Even the enormous billboards don't glow with the same intensity now, dimmed by the muddy light of day. My eyes fall to the traffic, snarling and growling below. There is a shout-bus parked on the edge of the street, partly blocking traffic, but no one challenges it. No one moves a council member's advertising.

I remember the parked shout-bus yesterday. Is that where the tone comes from, to signal that the cast is streaming? It would be easy enough to sneak an additional audio signal from the van. It could move around the streets ignored in plain sight, alerting listeners to the irregular streamcast.

I go downstairs, leaving the window open—no one can climb the slick begrimed building, and neighboring apartments haven't had their windows open in years, either—and squeeze down the crowded sidewalk near the bus. I turn the cast off in my earplants, and the whining buzz returns, too high for anyone already worn down by concrete and neon to hear. I am not sure, but I see orange and teal, and I think the shout-bus driver is the same as yesterday.

I switch back to the voice. "You can make a difference—first for yourself, and then for others, and then for everyone. It can be difficult to walk away from what you know; when you have little, what you do have is even more precious. Change can be frightening. But do you want things to remain as they are?"

I don't want to think about whatever the voice wants from me; I want a story. But I don't turn off my earplants. Instead, I walk down the street to an aloo chaat cart. I turn down the streamcast long enough to order my favorite combination. Potatoes, spices, and chutney may not fill the void under my heart, but I'll have something warm to hold and something to do with my hands.

When I turn up the volume again, a story is in progress.

"As Pharaoh approached, the Israelites looked up, and there were the Egyptians, marching after them. They were terrified and cried out to the Lord. They said to Moses, "Was it because there were no graves in Egypt that you brought us to the desert to die? Didn't we say to you in Egypt, 'Leave us alone; let us serve the Egyptians'? It would have been better for us to serve the Egyptians than to die in the desert!"

I don't remember this one. I walk along the sidewalk, scooping aloo chaat into my mouth. I wonder, for the first time, if Dev had ever listened to the secret streamcast. I wonder how many have found it.

"Then the Lord said to Moses, "Why are you crying out to me? Tell the Israelites to move on. Raise your staff and stretch out your hand over the sea to divide the water so that the Israelites can go through the sea on dry ground."

Two policers come down the sidewalk, shock-shields and batons in their hands, and the foot traffic scatters before them. I shrink back against the wall where I found the seedling. The shout-bus roars to life, all arrogant diesel and council praises, and drives away.

"The waters were divided, and the Israelites went through the sea on dry ground…" The voice fades from my earplants as I watch the shout-bus drive away. I stay against the wall as the policers pass, and then I go inside to wait out the afternoon.

That night I take my seedling to the noodle stall. It's stupid; there's not much room, and I'm at risk of knocking it over every time I grab a fresh bowl to fill. But I didn't want to leave it at home, alone. I know it's stupid, but I don't have to explain it to anyone but myself.

I don't know how long the seedling will last. I don't know how soon it will be dead, brown and withered. I didn't know how long Dev would last, desperate to work and desperate to keep his mother safe. I don't know how long my own mother will last, killed one day at a time by whatever it is that happens at the power plant that she can't talk about.

I don't know how long I will last, here in the Grimes.

I keep my head down at work, wiping spattered oil from my face and salty tears from my eyes. Jin, chopping vegetables and bones, gives me a few looks before he finally asks, "Something on?"

"Friend got picked up this morning," I say, stirring the oily noodles harder than necessary.

He doesn't need more explanation. He puts a hand on my shoulder, and that's nearly a hug from Jin. After a moment he moves away, but he doesn't snap when I spill a canister of *togarashi* an hour later.

It's raining when I carry the seedling home, tired and wanting to wash. When I go in, though, Mom is still awake, sitting up on her bed, looking out the rain-streaked window I left open. The ledge is spotted with drops.

"Mom?"

She looks at me, and her face is streaked like the window. "Oh, Nara."

I sit beside her. "What is it?" I was closer to Dev than she was; that can't be it. Not directly.

She closes her eyes. "How long can this last?" she breathes. "How long before it happens again?"

I am not prepared to hear my own desperate terror reflected from my mother's mouth. I freeze.

"I'm not into that," I say quickly, because I have to reassure her, no matter what I'm thinking inside my own head. "I'm not doing anything dangerous. I just sell noodles."

"Dev didn't want to get into trouble."

"But he did, because he had to. Because of his mom. He had to take care of her. But she's—"

She's not like you, I want to say, but I can smell the alcohol on her, and she isn't looking at my eyes.

Dev's mom worked at the power plant, too, until she didn't.

Mom squeezes her eyes shut. "What if something happened? What if—something happened?"

"Mom, I..."

"I don't want you to make Dev's mistake."

"Mom, I'm not."

"I'm serious. Now or later. Not even..." She trails off.

I think of the streamcast, and of its ridiculous stories that can't be true. "What if we could walk away?"

"What?"

"What if we could just, I don't know, leave all this and go somewhere new? Be new people?"

She grasps my wrist hard, as if it's the only thing keeping her from falling. "If you get a chance to get out, you take it."

"What?"

"There were stories—when I was a kid, there were stories about some who made it out of the Grimes, who got school and got jobs and went to work for the corps. If you can do that—it's a good life. A safe life."

She's scaring me. I don't know anyone who works for the corps, and I don't know how much of this she would say if she were sober. "Okay, Mom. Okay. Do you want to lie down?"

I realize I sound like Dev, and for a moment my heart stops.

But Mom lies down, and she wipes her face, and I don't know if it's the exhaustion or the alcohol but she appears to go to sleep almost immediately.

I wash and go to bed. Rain falls against the window. I wish the streamcast would come on and tell me a story where things come out all right. I turn on music in my earplants, but it's all synthesizers, no violins.

***

Mom is gone when I wake, as usual. It's not usual that I wonder, just for a moment, whether she's gone to her job at the power plant. I shake that off; of course she has.

It's raining, but not hard, just a drizzle. I put on a hat and go out, just to give the seedling some light. It looks stooped today, and I think its green has dulled. I hope I'm imagining that. I find a place for it and me, pressed into a concrete corner, and watch the people go by as I listen to synthesizers.

The irritating buzz breaks through my music and I fumble the adjustment, so eager am I to pick up the streamcast. I look around, newly knowledgeable, and I spy the shout-bus easing through traffic, blaring political advertisements into the engines and horns while slipping me music and stories on the low.

"Young citizens, this is your day to decide," says the voice, already talking. The shout-bus hadn't been near enough yet when the streamcast started. "We must issue this invitation just as we send this signal—only to those who have ears to hear. But with every fiber of our hearts, we extend this invitation and deeply desire you to accept it."

What's going on? Is this another story? But the voice never says "young citizens" unless it's addressing us directly.

"This is your chance to start. This is your chance to become something else—someone else. This is your chance to take a chance."

If you get a chance to get out, you take it.

"Come with us. Taste and see."

But how—? Am I supposed to just walk away from my mom? My job? My—the people I know who are still alive?

…Who are still alive?

I look down at the seedling, and I can't deny that it's sagging. It will never grow here.

How long can this last? How long before it happens again?

I look at the shout-bus, and I wish for just one second that what the voice said was possible.

If you get a chance, you take it.

I go up to our apartment, and I put a few pieces of clothing and my basic toiletries into the center of my blanket, which I then roll into a tube. I secure the ends with a belt and sling it all across my shoulders.

What could it hurt to walk out a bit? If it doesn't work out, I can always walk back.

I hurry down the steps to the street and turn on the sidewalk, scanning the traffic and listening for the shout-bus. I adjust my earplants until I have the streamcast again. The violin music dances in my head, notes skipping with more lightness than I've felt since—I can't remember when.

There! I can see the shout-bus. I adjust the belt on my shoulder and start after it.

It's easy to keep up with the shout-bus in the midday traffic. I slide out of the way of others on the sidewalk, hugging my blanket satchel close with one hand so that it cannot bump against anyone and cradling the seedling to my chest with the other. If the shout-bus gets too far ahead in the traffic, I turn and follow where the buzzing signal is strongest.

I walk for an hour before I realize I'm not alone. I mean, of course I'm not alone; there are thousands of people on the sidewalks. But some are teens, like me, and carrying a bundle or bag, like me, and are walking the same direction and taking the same turns as me. I am not sure if I should acknowledge them, and then one glances toward me and casually rubs a finger at his temple, and I nod before I think.

We start to drift together, because we're leaving the Grimes and we instinctively want the safety of a herd. Traffic thins and accelerates; we're in an industrial district now. More grey buildings rise around us, but they are not so brightly decorated with billboards.

The shout-bus drives down a ramp into a busy tunnel, and though the sidewalk is narrow, barely defined against the rushing traffic, we stretch into a string and walk into the smelly dark. The engines echo in the tunnel and I want to cover my ears, but I'm still cradling the seedling.

Then the shout-bus slows and turns into a short lane no other vehicles are taking, and I guess it's some utilities access. The lane ends before a concrete wall and steel door. The door lifts, and the van goes through, and we all hesitate mid-stride.

This is it. That's a steel door. I can't just walk back if I don't like what's on the other side.

"Jank this," mutters a girl next to me. "Whatever it is, it beats *dantai* hooking." She sets her jaw and follows the shout-bus.

Others follow her. I brush my arm across my face, and I think of Dev, and I look at the seedling, and I go after them.

The door closes behind us, and we are in a concrete garage or bunker. The shout-bus stops at the base of a long ramp, and two people get out. One is the driver I've seen before, with teal and orange parti-colored hair. The other is a man dressed in bold electric blue, with dark gel-slick hair and chrome-lined eyes.

They stop at a distance, not crowding us. "Welcome, young citizens," says the man, and while his is not the voice I am used to hearing, the familiar address is comforting in this concrete cavern. "Thank you for coming."

"What do you want with us?" someone asks, cutting straight to the point. We know we're lured and trapped; now we just want to know the details.

"We don't want anything from you," the woman says. Her lips are an icy peach color, just craving neon to illuminate them. "We want to help you to help us."

That's not an answer, and we wait expectantly, our disdain and wariness as tangible as the bags we carry.

She points over her shoulder to some location vaguely behind her. "Do you vote? Do you know anyone who votes?"

We don't laugh so much as snort in answer. "Yeah, my aunt did," one boy says. "She said she'd do it just to annoy her neighbors who complained about the shout-buses."

"Anyone else?"

"Why bother?"

"Everyone freeze!" The command booms and echoes in the concrete underground, and like smart residents of the Grimes, we scatter like rats off a garbage pile. There aren't many places to go, though, and we turn back in confusion and panic.

For an instant I think we were lured with the shout-bus into a trap. But the drivers whip around, too, and then I think it's maybe a manufactured drama, readied to scare us into going further once we started asking questions. But then the policers charge from a walk-door along the lower ramp, and whatever clever thoughts are in my mind are not enough to still the heave of my heart. I bolt to the left, coming up again against a solid wall, as they reach the two from the van.

The first policer's shock-shield hits the driver with teal and orange hair, and it's not fake, not with the smell of scorched flesh and total-body convulsions. The policer beats her twitching body with his whippy baton as others swarm the man in electric blue and rush the screaming kids.

I bolt up the ramp, the only escape route, along with others. The garage or bunker is definitely some utility space, with tunnels running in different directions off the ramp and occasional doors with stenciled numbers. We try these as we pass, and each is locked. We hear the cries and shouts behind us.

"Here!" One of the doors is unlocked. A half dozen of us skid to a halt, looking back toward the shout-bus and the struggle in the dim distance, and shove inside. The door has no internal locking mechanism; it's supposed to automatically lock but it's broken. We press against stacked bags of salt or sand or dirt and go silent.

Booted feet run up the ramp, shouting orders. We can hear the other doors being shaken and kicked, and we know it's only seconds until they find us. I stare at the strip of light from under the door, waiting for the shadows.

But the booted feet run past, having given up on the locked doors. "Check up top!" someone orders, and there are a few terse exchanges, but no one tries our door.

We listen in anxious agony as we hear protesting or crying detainees pushed or dragged up the ramp. We hear the shout-bus driven away, and then another vehicle.

When it has been quiet for a few minutes, a girl turns on her phone, and the pale blue light illuminates part of our faces as we look around at each other.

A boy my age shakes his head. "Nobody goes out," he whispers. "It's too soon, and if they get anyone, they get all of us. We stay."

We all nod. I'm still holding Dev's cup with the seedling, somehow, but all the water has splashed out. The seedling lies curled at the bottom, flat and dull, a limp leaf pasted to the plastic. I should drop it, but I can't.

The girl switches off her phone and we wait. There's a metallic boom, maybe one of the big doors closing, and a couple of shouts, and then quiet. But with this fresh confirmation that they've waited, we will wait, too, as the weak strip of light fades beneath the door.

***

It's dark. Really dark. I have never been in the dark, not like this. It is dark like a tomb. Dark like a womb.

I sit in the dark, silent. We dare not speak, not even to comfort one another with jokes or to share our names. The greatest comfort is not being found.

Hours pass, with no way to know how many. Maybe the whole night. I drowse at times, each time waking to wonder if we're still hidden. At last I can distinguish the line under the door again, though it lights little in the storage room.

Footsteps break the silence, echoing in the concrete cavern. We tense, feeling each other's alertness through the stuffy blackness. The footsteps do not sound like policer boots; they are sharp, like the heeled shoes the club dancers wear. I bite down a faintly-panicked giggle at the sudden image of a policer with shock-shield and shiny club shoes.

The footsteps pass outside our door. We hold our breath and wait for them to fade.

Someone outside begins to whistle, a dancing rapid series of notes that soar and fall, and my chest tightens. Violin concert something. I know it. We all know it.

There is a long moment of silence. "Let's go," someone finally breathes in the dark.

Whoever is nearest the door reaches for the latch, and for a moment the dim light of the garage is too much for us. But I squint against it and see a woman in a razor-sharp suit, white on the left and black on the right, with frosty blue hair and chromed eyelids and lips. She looks familiar, like one of the gorgeous people on the billboards.

"I'm so glad I've found you," she says, and her voice is low and steady, the voice of a woman who can whistle in a garage where we hid from policers. "It's safe now. Come with me."

She leads us up a ramp, as light leaks through slits high above. It must be morning.

She pauses near another steel door, big enough for trucks. "When we exit, you're welcome to go wherever you want. I hope you'll stay long enough to talk with me, but it is your choice. Just be careful, whatever you choose, and stay safe."

"Where are the policers?"

Her face tightens. "Gone, for now. I'm going to the council this afternoon to do what I can about Trill and Ren—the people you met last night."

"Going to the council?" someone repeats in shrill mocking disbelief, but I realize why she looks familiar despite her beauty. I have seen her on the flashing screens of shout-buses, with derogatory emoji flashing over her face. She is a politician.

"I'm going to do what I can to get them out," she says again. "They're my staff; they're supposed to be protected from the policers, and it's the other councilors—but that's for later. But you can help to change things. First, let's get out of here." She opens the door, and sunlight streams in, too powerful for our shaded eyes.

She leads us out into—I don't even recognize it at first, but it's a park. A green park with grass, and trees, and plants I don't have a word for. There's a set of swings, and a table where a group of people are eating fried dough and talking.

"I can't do everything just from my office," she says, though most of us aren't looking at her. There are tall buildings all around, but the advertising seems more muted. A nearby cart sells—oh, it sells sausages. Meat sausages.

"I need people who want change. A new life, for themselves and then for others."

I'm interested in what she has to say, but I cannot tear my eyes from this paradise. She is saying something about education and recruitment and social something, I don't know, because I'm walking toward a bed of trimmed plants. I kneel beside it and probe the soft dirt, making a pocket, and I place the seedling within it. It lies limply across the soil, not yet accustomed to its new luxury, and maybe it won't make it, but for the first time it has a chance.

I turn back to the woman in black and white, who is watching me with keen, kind interest. I stand to face her. "Tell me more."

Laura VanArendonk Baugh writes fantasy of many flavors as well as non-fiction. She has summited extinct, dormant, and active volcanoes, but none has yet accepted her sacrifice. This story was based on the fascinating tale of the Pied Piper of Hamelin, but she assures the reader no rats were harmed in the making. Laura lives in Indiana where she enjoys Dobermans, travel, fair-trade chocolate, and making her imaginary friends fight one another for her own amusement. Find her award-winning work at www.LauraVAB.com.

ABOUT THE ANTHOLOGIST

Like a magpie, **Rhonda Parrish** is constantly distracted by shiny things. She's the editor of many anthologies and author of plenty of books, stories and poems. She lives with her husband and two cats in Edmonton, Alberta, and she can often be found there playing Dungeons and Dragons, bingeing crime dramas, making blankets or cheering on the Oilers.

Her website, updated regularly, is at www.rhondaparrish.com and her Patreon, updated even more regularly, is at www.patreon.com/RhondaParrish.

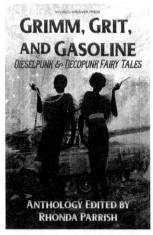

GRIMM, GRIT, AND GASOLINE

Dieselpunk and Decopunk
Fairy Tales
Anthology edited by Rhonda Parrish

Dieselpunk and decopunk are alternative history re-imaginings of (roughly) the WWI and WWII eras: tales with the grit of roaring bombers and rumbling tanks, of 'We Can Do It' and old time gangsters, or with the glamour of flappers and Hollywood starlets, smoky jazz and speakeasies. The stories in this volume add fairy tales to the mix, transporting classic tales to this rich historical setting.

Two young women defy the devil with the power of friendship. The pilot of a talking plane discovers a woman who transforms into a swan every night and is pulled into a much more personal conflict than the war he's already fighting. A pair of twins with special powers find themselves in Eva Braun's custody and wrapped up in a nefarious plan. A team of female special agents must destroy a secret weapon—the spindle—before it can be deployed. Retellings of The Little Mermaid, Hansel and Gretel, Rapunzel, Cinderella, The Monkey King, Swan Lake, Pinocchio and more are all showcased alongside some original fairy tale-like stories.

Featuring stories by Zannier Alejandra, Alicia Anderson, Jack Bates, Patrick Bollivar, Sara Cleto, Amanda C. Davis, Jennifer R. Donohue, Juliet Harper, Blake Jessop, A.A. Medina, Lizz Donnelly, Nellie Neves, Wendy Nikel, Brian Trent, Alena VanArendonk, Laura VanArendonk Baugh, Sarah Van Goethem, and Robert E. Vardeman.

CLOCKWORK, CURSES, AND COAL

Steampunk and Gaslamp
Fairy Tales
Anthology edited by Rhonda Parrish

Fairies threaten the world of artifice and technology, forcing the royal family to solve a riddle to stop their world from irrevocable change; a dishonest merchant uses automatons as vessels for his secrets and lies; a woman discovers the secret of three princesses whose shoes get scuffed while they sleep. These and so many other steampunk and gaslamp fairy tales await within the pages of *Clockwork, Curses and Coal*.

Retellings of Hansel and Gretel, The Princess and the Pea, Pinocchio, The Twelve Dancing Princesses and more are all showcased alongside some original fairy tale-like stories. Featuring stories by Melissa Bobe, Adam Brekenridge, Beth Cato, MLD Curelas, Joseph Halden, Reese Hogan, Diana Hurlburt, Christina Johnson, Alethea Kontis, Lex T. Lindsay, Wendy Nikel, Brian Trent, Laura VanArendonk Baugh and Sarah Van Goethem.

"The technological flights of fancy are always intriguing, and fairy tale lovers will enjoy deducing the inspiration for each tale. Readers will not be disappointed."

—Publishers Weekly

RHONDA PARRISH'S MAGICAL MENAGERIES
Featuring Amanda C. Davis, Angela Slatter, Andrew Bourelle,
Beth Cato, C.S.E. Cooney, Dan Koboldt, Holly Schofield, Jane
Yolen, Laura VanArendonk Baugh, Mike Allen, and many more.

Find these and more great short fiction anthologies at
WWW.WORLDWEAVERPRESS.COM
Also available at Amazon, Apple Books, BarnesandNoble.com,
IndieBound, Kobo, and other online booksellers.

Thank you for reading!

We hope you'll leave an honest review at Amazon, Goodreads, or wherever you discuss books online.

Leaving a review helps readers like you discover great new books, and shows support for the authors who worked so hard to create these stories.

Please sign up for our newsletter for news about upcoming titles, submission opportunities, special discounts, & more.

WorldWeaverPress.com/newsletter-signup

World Weaver Press, LLC
Publishing fantasy, paranormal, and science fiction.
We believe in great storytelling.
WorldWeaverPress.com

CPSIA information can be obtained
at www.ICGtesting.com
Printed in the USA
FSHW021253221021
85568FS